Praise for *Oath o...*

"This heart-racing, fast-action romantic suspense has it all. . . . Lynette Eason knows how to entice her fans and keeps them interested throughout the book. This is sure to become a beloved keeper."

RT Book Reviews

"Although concerned and delicate with both grief and romance, Eason's well-rounded story doesn't spend too much time bogged down in either as the harrowing plot unfolds. Eason's fans will enjoy this first installment of a promising new series."

Publishers Weekly

"A great read with broad appeal, to even experienced cops and firefighters. Lynette Eason's blend of realistic, fast-paced action, suspense, twists and turns, and dynamic characters make this a real page-turner."

Wayne Smith, FBI (retired)

"Lynette Eason once again pens a gripping thriller with her latest book, *Oath of Honor*. I can't wait for her next installment of the Blue Justice series!"

Carrie Stuart Parks, award-winning author of *A Cry from the Dust*

"Lynette Eason's *Oath of Honor* promises to be the beginning of another roller-coaster ride series. Readers are going to love Isabelle and Ryan's story while getting to know the entire St. John family. This engrossing novel will have them hooked from page one."

Lisa Harris, bestselling and Christy Award–winning author of *The Nikki Boyd Files*

CALLED TO PROTECT

Books by Lynette Eason

WOMEN OF JUSTICE

Too Close to Home
Don't Look Back
A Killer Among Us

DEADLY REUNIONS

When the Smoke Clears
When a Heart Stops
When a Secret Kills

HIDDEN IDENTITY

No One to Trust
Nowhere to Turn
Nothing to Lose

ELITE GUARDIANS

Always Watching
Without Warning
Moving Target
Chasing Secrets

BLUE JUSTICE

Oath of Honor
Called to Protect

CALLED TO PROTECT

LYNETTE EASON

Revell

a division of Baker Publishing Group
Grand Rapids, Michigan

Published by Revell
a division of Baker Publishing Group
PO Box 6287, Grand Rapids, MI 49516-6287
www.revellbooks.com

Printed in the United States of America

Library of Congress Cataloging-in-Publication Data
Names: Eason, Lynette, author.
Title: Called to protect / Lynette Eason.
Description: Grand Rapids, MI : Revell, a division of Baker Publishing group, [2018]
  | Series: Blue justice ; 2
Identifiers: LCCN 2018007094 | ISBN 9780800727031 (softcover : acid-free paper)
Subjects: LCSH: Policewomen—Fiction. | Missing persons—Investigation—Fiction.
  | GSAFD: Christian fiction. | Mystery fiction.
Classification: LCC PS3605.A79 C35 2018 | DDC 813/.6—dc23
LC record available at https://lccn.loc.gov/2018007094

Published in association with Tamela Hancock Murray, The Steve Laube Agency, 5025
N. Central Ave., #635, Phoenix, AZ 85012.

18   19   20   21   22   23   24   7   6   5   4   3   2   1

Dedicated to those who put their lives
on the line day in and day out.
Thank you for all you do.

LAW ENFORCEMENT
Oath of Honor

★ ★

On my honor,
I will never betray my badge, my integrity,
my character, or the public trust.
I will always have the courage
to hold myself and others
accountable for our actions.
I will always uphold the constitution,
my community, and the agency I serve.

★ ★

Prologue

Sixteen-year-old Penny St. John smoothed the shirt over her slim waist and turned to admire herself in the mirror. He'd like the look. Just thinking about Carson Langston made her smile. She'd never had a real boyfriend before. She'd been more interested in gymnastics and running track, but Carson had caught her eye at the mall when he'd struck up a conversation with her in line at the pizza place.

That had been three weeks ago. Tonight, he said he had a surprise for her. Anticipation swirled. She didn't fancy herself in love. She was too practical for that, but she did like him a lot. Just yesterday he'd given her the gold bracelet she now wore on her left wrist.

Penny pulled her phone from the back pocket of her shorts and tapped the Instagram app. Posing with pouty lip, she snapped a picture and posted it. Next, she grinned and posted that one. Wow. She looked good.

With a giggle, she made her way downstairs and found her cousin, Linc St. John, in the kitchen with her brother, Damien. "Hey, you two, don't you have anything better to do on a Friday night than sit around and talk cop stuff?"

9

Damien frowned at her. "What do you think you're doing?"

"Going out with a friend, why?"

"Because you need to put on something besides that pajama top. And don't you have a pair of jeans or something? Those shorts are too short."

She stuck her tongue out at him. "They are not. They come to mid-thigh. And this top is fine. It's loose and comfortable."

"It shows too much skin."

"My shoulder, Damien. My bathing suit is more revealing and you know it. Seriously. You need to get a life."

"I have one. It's my mission in life to watch out for you."

Penny rolled her eyes. "You mean harass me to death."

"Has Mom seen that shirt?"

"Yes." She walked over and kissed his forehead. "She helped me pick it out. I'll be back before midnight. See ya. Bye, Linc."

"Bye, Pen. Be careful," he said.

He was more than twice her age, but he was one of her favorite cousins. She almost turned around and went to change, but truly, Damien knew as well as she did that the shirt was fine. He was just having a hard time coming to terms with the fact that she was growing up. And, honestly, she was grateful for his protective instincts even as she strained against them.

The shirt was fine and Carson was waiting.

"Who are you going out with?" Damien asked.

"A friend," she said again with a glance out the window. "And there he is. Talk to you later. Love you."

"His name, Penny."

"Carson Langston." She stuck her tongue out and bolted out the door.

She heard him yell her name as she dashed down the walkway, but she wasn't about to let him have an opportunity to give Carson the third degree. How embarrassing.

Just because Damien was twenty-four years old, he thought

that made him her keeper. She was determined to prove it didn't and that she could take care of herself.

She shot a quick glance over her shoulder as she opened the door and her eyes locked on Damien's. For a moment, she regretted the way she left and sighed. She'd apologize to him tomorrow. For now, she was going to enjoy the night. She slid into the car, turning toward Carson. "Thanks for picking me up."

"Of course." He reached over and squeezed her hand. "Anything for you." He pressed the gas and pulled from the curb.

"So, what's my surprise?" she asked.

"I'm taking you to meet a friend of mine."

She frowned. "Okay."

He laughed. "What? You don't want to meet my friends?"

"Of course, I just thought it was going to be the two of us."

"Don't worry, we'll have a blast. My friend is going to love you. Now relax."

Penny's worries eased at his friendly smile and twinkling blue eyes. "Fine, we'll meet your friend, but then we're going to go do something. Just you and me, okay?"

Without taking his eyes from the road, he reached over and stroked her cheek. "Okay."

Ten minutes later, Carson wound through one of the nicest neighborhoods in Columbia. "Your friend lives here?"

"Yep."

"Wow. What does he do?"

"He's in sales."

One mansion after the next passed her window. "What does he sell?"

"Whatever will make him money."

"Hmm." That sounded . . . weird. What did he mean by that?

A kernel of unease curled in her belly. Carson took her hand and squeezed it, then lifted it and pressed his lips to her fingers. She sighed and smiled at him. He was so good to her.

Then he was turning into a driveway that curved around to the front of a four-story home. "Do you want me to wait here? I'm not exactly dressed for anything fancy."

"You look awesome."

"How do you know this guy?"

"I work for him. I just need to drop something off."

"Oh."

But he got out of the car without anything. Maybe it was a flash drive or something in his pocket. Or money. But why wouldn't he just say so?

He opened her door and held out his hand. She reached for it and he laced his fingers through hers as she followed him up the stone walkway to the front steps. The door opened before they reached the top and he released her hand.

A man in his midthirties stood there with a wide smile on his face. "Come on in. So glad you're here."

With Carson's warm hand against the small of her back, Penny stepped inside the massive foyer. Marble beneath her feet and a bazillion-dollar chandelier above her head. Wow.

The door shut behind them and the man's smile faded. His eyes roamed over her and he shot a look at Carson. "Good, good. Nice."

Alarms instantly jangled. "Um . . . I don't mean to be rude, but could I use your restroom?"

The man lifted a brow, and at first she thought he was going to refuse, but then the smile returned. "Of course. Carson can show you the way."

"Thank you."

Carson gripped her hand, harder than he'd ever done before, and pulled her with him.

"What are you doing?" She jerked out of his grasp. "That hurts."

Anger flashed in his eyes for a split second then disappeared. "Sorry."

"Did I do something wrong?" she asked. "I mean, I can wait on the bathroom if I have to." But she didn't plan on it.

Her willingness to please him did the trick and his features smoothed out. "No. Of course not. It's fine, but don't take forever." He opened the door for her. "I'll be waiting for you."

"Okay. Thanks."

Once inside the bathroom with the door shut, she pulled out her cell phone and tapped Damien's name. The phone rang twice. "Penny?"

"Damien, I think I need your help," she whispered.

"Where are you?"

"At a house in—"

The call dropped. With a frustrated groan, she glanced at the battery. It was full. She'd had it plugged in the entire time she was getting ready. She dialed her brother's number again. And got nothing. The signal on her phone was gone. Had they done something to make it so she couldn't call out? "No. Come on, come on, please."

She tapped a text to him even as she knew something was terribly wrong. Fear like she'd never felt before twisted inside her. She was so stupid. Every warning Damien had ever lectured on about human trafficking rang through her mind.

But no. Carson wouldn't do that, would he?

Flashes of his behavior tonight confirmed her fear. She pressed send on the text and got the little message that it was unable to be delivered. Tears sprang to her eyes and she drew in a breath. She would not panic. She'd keep her cool.

A knock on the door caused her to jerk. "I'll be there in a minute." She flushed the toilet and eyed the cabinet under the sink.

"Come on, Penny."

"I'm washing my hands." She turned the water on, reached under the cabinet, and pressed her hand against the base of the sink. She did the same near the back of the toilet bowl. Then she snagged a few hairs from her head and dropped them behind the picture on the wall. Her last act was to shut the sink off, take her cell phone, and type as much as she could before the next knock.

"Penny! Come on! Do I need to come in there?" The knob rattled.

It would have to be enough. He was going to kick the door in if she didn't hurry up. She slid the phone under the large armoire-like corner cabinet, then stood.

With a prayer on her lips, she opened the door. "What's the rush, silly? I—"

A liquid spray hit her in the face and she gasped. Exactly the wrong thing to do. Whatever he'd sprayed her with burned her lungs. Carson's face blurred. "What—"

She went to her knees before Carson caught her. "It's okay, Penny, don't fight it."

1

Officer Chloe St. John pulled her SUV to a stop on the Gervais Street Bridge behind the teeming chaos just ahead. A cargo van had crossed the double yellow line and gone headlight to headlight with an eighteen-wheeler, causing a minivan to slam into the rear left corner of the trailer. All in all, the fifteen-car pileup had caused multiple injuries and fatalities.

She climbed out and the rain hit her in the face. Chloe shuddered. The torrential downpours that had hit Columbia over the last seventy-two hours had caused the water under the bridge to turn into a raging, turbulent force to be reckoned with. At least today only a light drizzle fell from the still-swollen gray clouds.

And then the victims' terror reached her. As did an explosive splash.

"A second car just went over!"

"Help me!"

"Over here!"

Sirens screamed. Rescuers shouted orders. Chloe raced to the edge of the bridge and looked over. Divers were already in the water. One of them was probably her brother, Brady. She sent up a silent prayer for his safety and the others'.

She returned to her vehicle and released Hank, her Dutch shepherd K-9, from his special area, and he hopped down beside her, quivering with energy and ready to work. She scratched his silky ears. "Hold tight, boy. Let's get our bearings."

EMS was already on the scene as well as multiple fire trucks and police cars. A helicopter hovered overhead. Chloe spotted a familiar face. Right where she said she'd be. "Izzy!"

Her sister turned, tension lining her features. "Chloe, glad you're here. Bring Hank."

Chloe and Hank trotted over to Izzy, who stood next to a woman holding an infant wrapped in a blue blanket. A paramedic rummaged through the bag on the ground. Chloe recognized the medic. Alice Johnson. The EMT looked at Izzy. "Can you bandage this?" A gash over the victim's left eye looked like it needed stitches.

"Yes. Go." She took the bandage.

Alice paused, then headed for her ambulance. "She needs a blanket. Hang on."

"Is your baby hurt?" Chloe asked the woman.

"No." The victim's jaw trembled and shivers wracked her. "She's fine, I think." Shock. Alice passed Izzy a blanket and she wrapped it around the woman, who hunched under it, checking to make sure her baby was covered as well.

"I've got to go." She spun.

"Hey, I need tape," Izzy called.

The woman tossed her a roll. "I'll be back."

Priorities.

"What's going on besides the obvious?" Chloe asked.

"We found drugs," Izzy said. She held the white bandage to the woman's head. "This thing is way too big. I need some scissors, and of course, she didn't leave me any."

"Hold on." Chloe reached behind her service weapon into a small pocket on her holster and pulled out a Swiss army knife.

Izzy took it and used the scissors to cut the bandage to size. She handed the knife back to Chloe, then taped the bandage to the woman's head. With a soft pat to the bowed shoulder, she said, "Sit tight, okay? They'll get you to the hospital as soon as they can."

Izzy stood and directed Chloe to the side of the road. "The drugs came from one of the vehicles and we need you and Hank to figure out which one. We suspect it's the eighteen-wheeler sitting over there, but a cursory search hasn't turned up any more and we're too busy trying to help keep people alive to do a more thorough search." Izzy was a detective, but she was also trained as a first responder. "The critical ones are being transported to the hospital immediately, of course, but we're matching patients with cars, so we need Hank to do his thing. When we know which vehicle the drugs came from, we'll know who to arrest. If the person's still alive. So far we've got four DOAs and a couple of others who looked close to joining them."

"Where did you find the drugs?"

"This way."

Chloe followed Izzy through the ruckus. She sidestepped two paramedics rushing past her and pushing a stretcher. Izzy stopped beside the vehicle that had slammed into the back of the eighteen-wheeler. White powder from a couple plastic bags lay in the middle of the lane. Which meant there was probably more where that had come from. Question was, where had it come from? The truck or the van or the SUV that had T-boned the van? Or had someone thrown it out when they realized cops were going to be covering the area?

"You're sure it's drugs?"

Izzy shrugged. "Figured Hank would tell us."

He took one whiff and sat. "There's your answer."

"I'm stunned." Izzy rolled her eyes. "Want to see if he can find any more?"

"We're on it." Chloe led Hank to the damaged vehicle behind the tractor trailer. "Hank, find the dope." Most commands were given in Dutch, but not this one. Hank went to work, sniffing the seats, the tires, the trunk.

And got nothing.

"This one's clean," Chloe said.

She led him toward the cab of the eighteen-wheeler to have the trailer doors opened. Officers Josiah Henry and Olivia Nash had the driver out of the cab and were questioning him. The man looked to be unhurt, but it was obvious he wasn't happy. "I'm going to be late making my delivery and I'm going to get fired. I need to get out of here now!"

"Where do you think you're going to go? You're trapped right now."

"I can push through with the truck if you'll just get everyone out of the way."

Chloe shook her head. What an idiot.

He spotted Hank and Chloe heading his way and his eyes went wide. He shoved Olivia into Josiah, climbed back into the seat of the cab, quick as a monkey up a tree.

Olivia grabbed the door handle and yanked. It was locked. She jumped up onto the step board and yelled that the passenger had scrambled out of the other side.

Chloe crouched to see the man's legs underneath the trailer, then she and Hank sprinted back toward the minivan to cut him off.

"Hank, *apport*!" The command to get him. Chloe pulled her weapon.

Hank shot away from her, his sleek brown-and-black body a blur as he easily caught up with the fleeing man, who held a pistol in one hand. The dog lunged and latched onto the arm with the weapon, and the two of them went to the ground, with the man screaming his agony. "Get him off me! Get him off!" And yet he still clutched the gun. Victims screamed and ducked.

"Drop the weapon!" Chloe raced toward them. She was joined by two other cops, Greg and Sharon. All three of their voices blended as one. "Let go of the weapon and I'll call him off! Drop it! Now!"

Their perp stilled and Chloe slammed her foot down on the hand that held the gun. Sharon dropped a knee into his upper back and grabbed his left arm.

He let out another howl as Chloe leaned over and yanked the weapon from his now slack fingers. "You broke my hand!"

"Hank, *los, laat los*!" The order to let go.

Hank released his bite and moved back to sit, tongue lolling as he watched the action.

Greg shook his head. "We've got a genius on our hands. Thought he was going to outrun Hank. Who really thinks that's possible? What a dumb . . ." He continued to mutter his poor opinion of the idiot on the ground while he held him there.

Sharon removed her knee and jerked the man's wounded arm behind him.

He screamed again. "I need a doctor! That dog nearly killed me! I'm going to sue you. I'm going to sue the whole department! I'll have your badges. I'll . . ."

Chloe turned a deaf ear to the threats and the stream of curses that spilled from him while she and Greg held him down. Sharon fastened her cuffs around his wrists.

And then a gunshot rang out.

Chloe ducked and spun. More screams rang out around her.

"Go," Chloe told them. "I'll hold on to this joker until you can put him in the back of your car." She didn't have room to transport a prisoner.

They took off. She pulled her charge to the back of the trailer and shoved him next to the large tire. Pulling her cuffs from the case on her belt, she attached one cuff to the pair around his wrists and the other cuff to a metal rail running along the bottom of the trailer. "Stay there unless you want to get shot." She glanced at Hank, who hadn't taken his gaze from the prisoner. "Or bit."

The man planted his back up against the rubber and glared at her as he yanked on the cuffs. "Where do you think I'm going to go?"

She ignored him when she caught movement in the passenger side mirror and her heart thudded. He hadn't been there only moments before when her prisoner had scrambled out of that very door. So, a third one had been somewhere inside the cab? Chloe grabbed her radio.

Pop. Another shot. Then two more. Chloe flinched, even though none of the bullets came near her. But she couldn't help wondering whom they might have hit. Saying a prayer for her fellow officers, she kept watch, her senses on hyperalert and her gaze never resting.

Another loud crack.

The bullets were fired from the truck. Chloe glared at her prisoner. "You know who's shooting?"

"No." He scowled, his expression conveying his disgust for her and anyone who wore the same uniform she did. "This is ridiculous. I need a doctor. Take me over to that ambulance." He jerked his chin toward the vehicle sitting ten yards away on the side of the highway. The paramedics were bent over a patient and still working in spite of the gunfire, and using the ambulance as a shield.

Chloe kept her weapon ready and her head down. "We've got a live shooter and you want to cross that wide-open expanse? How stupid are you?" Big-time stupid. She mentally dubbed him Stupid Man.

He winced. "At least put my hands in front of me. My arm is killing me. That beast about took it off. I need stitches. Probably gonna bleed to death."

"I'm really worried about that," she muttered as she scanned the area. She kept up the running dialogue absently, while most of her attention was focused on the action going on around her.

He called her a name she didn't consider flattering, and she flicked a glance at him. Still secure and not trying to get away, in spite of his mouthiness. Good. Maybe he was slightly less stupid than she originally thought.

Chloe peered around the edge of the truck again, letting her gaze take in the scene before pulling back. People hiding, cops planted with guns aimed at the cab of the truck. Her radio crackled with rapid-fire calls and codes. She kept one ear on it while she kept an eye on the man attached to the truck. "Who else is in there?"

His nostrils flared. "No one."

"Of course not." Liar.

As if to prove her right, the truck's engine rumbled to life. Where did they think they were going? With the front tucked into the headlights of a cargo van and a minivan slammed into the rear left corner, they couldn't go anywhere.

However, Chloe released Stupid Man from the truck and hauled him to his feet by his non-wounded arm. She led him around to the back of the trailer, away from the side mirror, wondering if the occupants of the truck's cab realized she and their accomplice were right there. If they did, they didn't care. If they didn't, she'd feel much better out of sight of that side mirror.

Once at the back of the trailer near the two large doors, her prisoner tried to run. Chloe tackled him, and she didn't even have to give the order for Hank to jump at the man's face, snapping and snarling.

Stupid Man curled into a fetal position. "Get him away! Don't let him bite me again!"

"Hank, *stil*." The dog backed away, his eyes still on the quivering man. "Get up and try to engage your brain," she ordered.

He complied and she refastened the cuffs to the handle of the trailer's door while she listened for more shots. And although she still heard screams and cries and harsh orders from law enforcement, she hadn't heard any more pops of gunfire.

The truck inched forward. Chloe stayed with the truck, using it as cover. Screams sounded. More shots rang out. None in danger of hitting her or Stupid Man, though, since the bullets came from the truck's cab.

The truck surged and rolled forward a good three feet.

With horror, Chloe knew the cab had to be pushing the vehicle in front of it. Along with any victims in its path. "Stop!"

Another lurch and the trailer separated from the minivan crunched into its rear. Chloe ordered Hank to guard Stupid Man, then raced to the front of the cab on the passenger side, away from any bullets that had been flying on the other side. "Police! Stop!"

The passenger looked at her and yelled something to the driver. And then she heard, "Shoot her!"

The man in the passenger seat turned and met her gaze. She held her gun on him. "Tell him to stop right now!"

In one fluid motion, he lifted his weapon, aimed it at her . . .

. . . and pulled the trigger.

———————

Through the high-powered scope on his Colt M4 carbine, Derek St. John saw the passenger in the cab fire his weapon right at his sister's head.

And Chloe had dropped like a rock. Or had she dropped before the crack? He couldn't be sure.

Terror beat at him, his finger hovering over the trigger. Just before Chloe had appeared in his line of sight behind his target, a cop trying to get into position had run across his line of fire, causing Derek to miss his chance to pull the trigger. He wanted to punch something. Instead, he ordered his heart to slow and his mind to focus.

He'd been given the green light. The call had gone out over the radios and no one was supposed to move. And now Chloe might be dead because an officer had blown the shot for Derek. Had the man not heard the order?

At the moment, it didn't matter.

What mattered was Chloe.

Derek wasn't exactly in the most ideal position to make the shots, but it was the only one he had.

He drew in a steadying breath. He had to focus, to be cool, be steady, and return to the zone.

Looking through the scope once more, he saw the driver raise his weapon and aim it at an innocent victim. A woman not quite hidden behind her car.

Derek pulled his trigger and a nanosecond later the bullet hit its mark. The driver's body went slack. The passenger next to him jerked and turned, aiming his weapon at the cop now hovering at the edge of the driver's door, hand on the handle, ready to yank the door open in a heroic, if dangerous, possibly stupid, move. Derek could see the cop's plan as clearly as if he'd written it out with full illustrations. He was going to open the door, pull out the dead driver, and shoot the remaining passenger.

Fortunately, the passenger moved and Derek had a clear shot. A second pull on the trigger and the threat was over. The officer dove out of sight, hopefully appreciating how stupid it was to get into the line of fire from a sniper. Idiot.

Derek lowered his rifle and swiped a hand across his eyes. Two lives. He'd ended two lives. Two more faces he'd see in his dreams. But they'd made their choices, and if Derek hadn't made his, innocents would be dead instead of the two men bent on destruction.

And now . . .

"Chloe," he whispered.

2

Chloe rolled to her feet, her weapon still clutched in her hand. The bullet had missed her, but not by much. As soon as she'd seen the weapon turn her way, she nose-dived into the concrete onto the walkway that bordered the road.

Two cracks later and the truck came to a grinding stop.

"Shooter's down! Shooter's down!" She heard something about SWAT and figured one of them had ended the situation. Probably Derek—or one of his unit members.

Officers descended on the truck and Chloe went back to her prisoner who'd been dragged a couple more feet but hadn't suffered any damage other than a possible coronary from his fear.

Hank whined, then shifted at her side. "What is it, boy?"

He paced, sniffed, paced some more. Then he sat and looked at her. He smelled drugs in the trailer.

"Good boy," she said. "We'll take care of that in a few minutes." She shifted her attention to the man cuffed to the truck and lasered him with a look. "Stay put. If you try to get loose or get away, Hank will stop you again, you understand?"

His eyes shifted to the animal.

"Hank, *bewaken*." She pointed to Stupid Man. At the Dutch

command to stand guard, Hank's ears went up and his eyes locked on the man.

Stupid Man jerked and Hank growled.

Panic blossomed on his face and Chloe figured he wouldn't be going anywhere. She tried the door to the trailer and found it locked.

Losing patience, she grabbed the prisoner by his shirt and hauled him closer. "Where's the key?"

He snarled.

"Hank, attack!"

The handcuffed man's snarl turned to terror. "No, no, no, no, no."

"The key!"

"In-in my front left pocket."

Chloe glanced at Hank as she dug the key from the man's pocket. He sat, watchful, but definitely not in attack mode. "He only understands the word 'attack' if I say it in Dutch."

His face flushed and his eyes hardened with hate and pure rage. It was a good thing his hands were out of commission.

Chloe opened the door. "Hank, find the dope!"

"There's no dope in there," he said.

"Hank says there is." She turned to the officer approaching. "Get him out of here, please."

"With pleasure."

"Chloe!"

She turned. Derek. "Hey."

"Are you okay?"

"Yeah."

He hugged her. "I could see the guy pointing the gun at you through the window. I saw him pull the trigger and then you dropped."

"I ducked when I realized he had a gun and I didn't have time to aim and fire. The bullet missed."

"Good. Good job."

Hank barked. Once. Twice.

"Derek?"

"Yeah?"

"I need you to let me go," she mumbled into his chest. "I need to breathe and let Hank work. He's getting restless."

Derek gave her another bone-crunching squeeze. "I thought he shot you, Chloe." His hoarse voice resonated within her. He'd had a scare.

Frankly, so had she. The bullet had whizzed past her cheek, coming as close as it could possibly come without touching her. Her adrenaline still gushed. "I'm fine. I promise." She'd keep the details to herself of how close to death she'd come. She didn't want to think about it or talk about it. It was over and she was alive, she'd focus on that—at least for now.

"I know."

He finally released her, and she realized the others were waiting for her to take the lead. Chloe cleared her throat and let Derek help her into the back of the trailer. Hank hopped up beside her. It was packed floor to ceiling with furniture. Only a small path led down its center.

Hank twitched and shifted, anxious to get to work.

"Waiting on me, huh, boy? All right, then, find the dope."

He nosed the floor, from back to front, came back, circled, then sat. "Hank's got a hit."

"What's he got?" Derek asked.

"There are drugs in here, just not sure—" She tapped the floor. "Wait a minute." She rapped again. "Hear that?"

"It's hollow."

"We've got a fake floor here."

"Let's get this furniture unloaded."

"What about the guys in the cab?" she asked.

Derek scowled. "Not a problem any longer."

"Did they hurt anyone?"

26

"Winged a kid who'll be fine with a cool scar later and got Ralph in the leg. But they didn't kill anyone." Ralph Jamison was due to retire in less than a month and was one of Chloe's favorite people.

"Will Ralph be okay?" she asked.

"Yes. The bullet was through and through and didn't hit anything too vital. Paramedics are working on him now."

Chloe blew out a breath. "And Izzy?"

"Back here waiting on you two to tell us what we're doing," her sister called.

"Waiting on the rest of OCN to get here," Derek said. Organized Crime and Narcotics.

"They're here," a new voice said. "Had trouble navigating the chaos out there."

Chloe recognized Vincent Adler, a detective on his way up. At six feet four with the build of a linebacker, his presence shouted authority. As far as Chloe was concerned, he was tailor-made for the job. He stepped up into the trailer and Chloe backed off, although Hank kept trying to get to the front of the trailer. "Hank, *zit*." He sat, but she could tell he didn't like it.

"We've got to get this furniture out of here to get access to the floor," Derek told Vince.

"Where are we going to put it?"

"Any place you can find a spot," Derek said and heaved a chair to his shoulder to carry out the back.

Vincent gave the orders to his team and they went to work. Chloe called to Hank and waited outside, still aware of the accident scene. Ambulances leaving, loved ones arriving, paramedics still working. The coroner weaving his way to the truck's cab to the men Derek had shot.

Chaos, yes. But it was organized chaos at this point.

Izzy stepped up to her. "You okay?"

"Yeah."

Her sister, dressed in black pants and a white T-shirt with the city's CPD emblem on her left shoulder, placed her hands on her hips. "That was a close one."

"Close enough. But I'll take the miss."

"Absolutely."

"How's being a detective treating you?" she asked like she did every time she saw her sister at a scene.

Izzy gave her the same tight smile she always gave her at the question. "It's everything I thought it would be. And more. And less."

"Thanks for clearing that up for me."

"Any time. How are you and Crestwood?"

Chloe scowled. "We're not." Jordan Crestwood had been her boyfriend for the past six months, and she'd thought they might be heading toward a lifetime commitment. Apparently, Jordan was just a good actor and had decided dating the chief of police's daughter would be good for his career. She'd figured that out when she caught him in a lip-lock with another woman. She hadn't shared the details of their breakup with her family and didn't feel inclined to do so at this moment.

"Oh. Sorry?"

"I'm not." Time for a subject change. "Ryan around?" Ryan Marshall, Izzy's husband and Chloe's brother-in-law, also a detective with the city of Columbia.

"No, he got called away to a homicide over on Academy."

"Lucky him."

"Yeah."

"Have you seen Brady?" Chloe asked, looking around. "I caught a glimpse of him earlier, I think. In the water." Brady, their brother and a former Navy SEAL, now worked with the Underwater Criminal Investigation division and was on the dive team when they needed him.

"Saw him just a few minutes before the shooting started. He's already pulled two children and a mama from one of the cars."

"Alive?"

"Yep."

"Good," she whispered. "Good." *Thank you, God.*

Within minutes, the trailer was empty, the furniture now sitting on the side of the road in the emergency lane—and anywhere else they could find a spot. Hank was itching to get back inside. "Guys," Chloe said, "Hank's not finished in there."

"Let him back in," Vincent said. "The furniture could have been covering more up."

Chloe released the agitated dog, and he darted back inside and raced all the way to the front area just behind the cab. She climbed in after him.

Vincent looked up. "We'll work this while you see what Hank's got to say."

Derek and Vincent examined the floor. Now assigned to OCN, Derek deployed as SWAT when needed. He'd been needed today. A scraping sound followed by a grunt of discovery had her turning.

"Well, well," Vincent said. "Look what we found."

He held up several bags similar to the ones that had been found on the road. "There's a hole in the bottom of the trailer—storage. Someone altered it so they could stuff the bags into this compartment from below. Must have hit something that jarred the latch loose and a couple of the bags slid out."

Hank whined and continued his restless behavior.

"What is it, boy?"

He pawed at the plywood on the front wall, then raced the width of the trailer, back and forth, nose in the air.

"Guys? Hank's on to something else. Might be more drugs back there."

"We'll get back there in a minute," Derek said.

And then the pounding started—a frantic beating on the other side of the wood.

"Hey! Derek, Vincent, come here, now!"

They joined her. Vincent turned. "Somebody get me a crowbar!" Seconds later, an officer slapped one into his hand.

"Let's get this wood off," Chloe said.

One hard jerk pulled the first piece off and it clattered to the floor.

Weeping and cries for help reached her. Together, she and Derek and Vincent pulled the rest of the plywood down. In stunned disbelief, Chloe found herself staring into at least a dozen pairs of terrified eyes.

Deputy US Marshal Blake MacCallum ran a shaky hand through his hair as he read the text for the millionth time.

> You have 24 hours to kill the judge. Make it look like an accident. If you fail, she dies.

Thirty minutes before his shift started, while he was still munching a bagel and cream cheese, the text had shown up on his phone. That had been five hours ago and had contained a picture.

A picture of his daughter, seventeen-year-old Rachel, holding a newspaper with today's date, her pretty green eyes filled with terror. The gun against her temple broke his heart—and sent a fear beyond anything he'd ever known shafting through him. As well as relief because the picture was proof she was alive.

> Does she have her insulin? She's a type 1 diabetic.

That was the second time he'd sent that text. And the second time he didn't get an answer. But the date on the newspaper reassured him. She was getting her insulin from somewhere.

Rachel had disappeared a little over a week ago, along with her

30

best friend, Lindsey Edgars. The day of the girls' disappearance—before he'd even realized something was wrong—he'd received the first text with a picture of her that demanded he tell no one she was missing. That if he informed his "cop buddies" or the media got hold of it, she was dead.

And they would be in touch.

So, he'd sent the text informing them of her diabetes and waited, breathless, terrified. Desperate to know what they wanted while trying to offer his comfort to her friend's mother without letting on that Rachel was missing too. Lindsey had a missing persons report filed and was on the evening news. Mrs. Edgars wondered why Rachel wasn't.

"Why can't you find her?" she'd cried just last night. "You find fugitives for a living. Why can't you find a seventeen-year-old girl!"

Her questions haunted him. Because part of him wondered the same thing. Instead of letting his guilt and fear get the best of him, he'd worked feverishly behind the scenes. Eating occasionally, snagging a nap here and there while he continued to fulfill his duties with his job so no one would suspect anything was wrong.

He'd finally exhausted every idea on how to find his daughter by himself and came to the conclusion that he simply couldn't do it. After three days of continued silence from Rachel's kidnappers, he'd told his best friend, FBI Special Agent Linc St. John, what was going on and asked for his help. Linc had promised to utilize his resources and do everything he could to find Rachel—without letting anyone know he was looking.

And now this.

Kill the judge.

So that's why they'd taken her. Leverage.

Twenty-four hours. Minus the five that had passed since the text.

When he'd first received the message, he'd immediately contacted Linc with the new information.

I have 24 hours to kill the judge I'm protecting.
If I don't, Rachel dies.

Linc
WHAT?

Need to meet with you.

When and where?

He'd set up the meeting and met with Linc, who'd ordered him to continue as though nothing was wrong while Linc utilized his bureau resources to trace the text. That had been five hours ago.

Blake was still waiting while he guarded the man he was supposed to kill.

His phone buzzed again and he glanced at it with a mixture of irritation and fear. When he saw who it was, the irritation won out.

Frank
Are you coming to visit?

His brother just wouldn't give up, badgering Blake to visit their father.

No. I'm in the middle of something and couldn't get away even if I wanted to.

Okay. Might do you good to say goodbye.

I said goodbye years ago. You should have, too.

He's our father.

He was our abuser. He was no father and we don't owe him anything.

32

The texts stopped.

Blake swept away the bitterness that memories of his childhood always brought with them and focused on his priorities.

This shouldn't have to be a priority because it shouldn't be happening. Rachel was *supposed* to be at swim practice. She was *supposed* to be hanging out with her best friend. She was *supposed* to be safe, not being used as a pawn to manipulate her father into committing murder.

Blake watched the man who was sitting on the sofa in his luxury home, reading through a stack of files. US District Court Judge Benjamin Worthington. A stern man, known for his harsh rulings for those who appeared before him in court and his rabid stance against human trafficking, he, nevertheless, had been perfectly hospitable to Blake and his partner, JoAnn Talmadge.

The death threats had started three weeks ago when the judge went before the Senate. The same Senate who had confirmed his presidential appointment. He'd presented his support for a bill that, if passed into a law, would make prison terms much more strict for those convicted of human trafficking—even offering up the possibility of the death penalty. Blake and Jo were just one pair of marshals assigned to protect the man after the vicious threats began.

But someone had found a weak link.

Blake was the only one with a teenage daughter.

Who was now in the hands of the people who wanted Ben Worthington dead.

The judge stood. "I'm going to change and work out. By the way, Stan, Paula, and Miles are coming to dinner later."

The home gym on the lower floor was as well-equipped as any club and the man used it regularly.

And his grown children often stopped by. The daughter and her fiancé, Miles Childs, more so than the son. Their meals were often simply heat and serve, thanks to the cook who prepared them weekly for the family.

Blake nodded. "Let me know when you're ready to go down and I'll sweep it for you. I'll also let the marshals coming in for the next shift know to expect Paula and Miles tonight." Paula Worthington was a prosecutor with a reputation that rivaled her father's when it came to putting criminals behind bars. Her brother, Stan, worked as a parole officer while taking night classes toward his PhD in criminal justice.

"I'll be about ten minutes, thanks." Ben disappeared down the hall to the master bedroom. His wife, Lucy, had yet to make an appearance today. She often chose to stay squirreled away in her home office, working on her latest novel.

"You okay?" JoAnn asked. She stood in the doorway of the kitchen, having just completed her perimeter check of the grounds. JoAnn's short blonde hair curled around her cheeks in an attractive wind-swept style. With blue eyes and high cheekbones, she could have graced the cover of any magazine, yet had chosen to go into law enforcement. And while she'd made it clear she'd be fine with taking their partnership to a more intimate level, Blake found himself not interested. Right now, his only concern lay in finding his daughter without having to commit murder to do so.

He cleared his throat. "Yeah. Why?"

"You had a look on your face that I've never seen before."

He nodded. "Just got a disturbing text. It's nothing, though."

She frowned. "Want to share?"

"No, but thanks."

She blinked. "Okay." And dropped it.

Guilt pierced him. JoAnn was a good woman and an excellent partner. And it was quite possible, the longer he kept his mouth shut, the more danger Rachel was in.

"Sorry, Jo. I just need to think for now. I may want to talk about it a little later."

"No problem. All's clear outside." She walked into the den and crossed her arms. "There have been no more threats since the third

34

one." The judge had received three specific threats to his life over a period of seven days. It had scared him bad enough that he'd called in the marshals. "Everything's been quiet for two weeks," Jo said. "You think we're still necessary?"

He met her gaze. "Yeah. I do."

She frowned. "All right, then."

Judge Worthington, who'd insisted they call him Ben, came from his room, decked out in his pricey workout attire. "I'm ready, but I'll need to head to the courthouse in about an hour and a half."

"That's fine." Blake stood, his mind still on his daughter.

JoAnn touched his arm. "Stay here. I'll clear it."

His partner had read him like a book. He was distracted, and while he could hide it from most of the world, JoAnn had learned to pick up on his moods. He nodded. "I'll stay with Mrs. Worthington."

And he'd stay alert although there'd been no attempt to harm the judge at home—or anywhere else. But they couldn't ignore the threats. Especially now.

His phone buzzed and he wasn't sure if he wanted to look at it or not. With a sigh, he turned the screen toward him and relief zipped through him.

Relief it wasn't a text with a picture of Rachel dead or another threat. The name still brought a grimace. Another text from Rachel's swim coach.

> I don't know what's going on, but Rachel's missed four practices. If she misses another one, she's off the team.

Blake curled his fingers into a fist, then relaxed them and pressed them to eyes that burned from lack of sleep. *It's not his fault. He doesn't know.* Rachel getting kicked off the swim team was the least of his worries right now.

The judge and Jo had disappeared into the basement and Blake drew in a steadying breath.His phone buzzed again.

Linc

No way to trace the texts or the number. All texts were sent from different locations. Some miles apart. Still pulling on resources. Hang tight.

Blake rose. He checked the doors and windows, looked in on Mrs. Worthington who didn't even notice him peeking in the door of her office, then dropped onto the couch. Lowering his head into his hands, his mind spun.

He couldn't allow anything to happen to an innocent person because of his lack of focus. And yet his thoughts went to "what if . . ."

It wouldn't be hard to kill the man. A simple attack while he slept and he could break his neck before he knew what hit him.

The fact that he played out the scene in his mind from start to finish horrified him.

No, he couldn't do it.

But Rachel—

Not even for Rachel.

But—

He looked at his phone again. Her eyes pleaded with him, her sheer terror jumped from the screen to wrap around his throat.

Blake didn't have murder in him.

But he might have to if he wanted to see Rachel alive again.

3

One by one, they'd coaxed the girls from the back of the trailer and passed them off to social workers, counselors, and paramedics. "Seventeen girls," Chloe said. She leaned against her Chevy Tahoe while Hank lay at her feet chewing on the end of his toy rope—his favorite reward for a job well done. "One can't be older than twelve."

Derek stood beside her while the young women were given bottles of water and reassured that they were safe. They were also encouraged to talk to the victim advocates who would be arriving at the hospital to offer additional support.

Some of the girls would cooperate. Others wouldn't. Those who told their stories would heal faster than those who stuffed their emotions down. Chloe took the rope from a happy Hank and tucked it into her belt.

"Sometimes I hate people," Derek said. "Are there any good ones left?"

She raised a brow at him. "Yes. Us. And we're not supposed to hate anyone—even the bad ones. We're just supposed to catch them and put them out of business. Leave your emotions out of it."

"You sound like Mom."

"Thanks. She's pretty smart."

He huffed a short laugh. "Because that's what you do, right? Leave your emotions out of it?"

She shot him a sideways glower and he smirked, knowing full well her emotions sometimes got entangled in a case. They fell silent. She finally sighed. "That was good shooting, Derek. Stop questioning yourself."

His troubled gaze met hers. "It's scary how you can read me." He swiped a hand across his face. "I didn't have a choice. It was either them or innocents."

"I know that and you know that. The question is, why do you feel guilty about it?" Every single time he had to make the choice to take a life, he grieved the loss until he finally accepted he'd done what he had to do to save lives.

He gave a subtle shrug. "I don't. Not really. I just regret the abrupt ending for those two. There are no more opportunities for them to do the right thing."

"True. But you saved many who now have that option. One of them shot Ralph. And a kid. No one died—at least because of a shooter—and that's thanks to you."

He relaxed a fraction. "Yeah, I know." He hugged her one-armed. "Thanks, Sis. You can always make me feel better."

"That's what sisters are for. Especially favorite ones, right?" They both knew Izzy was his favorite. And rightly so as his twin. Chloe didn't hold it against him.

"Exactly." He rolled his eyes, then his shoulders. "Guess I'll have a couple of days off. Come see me so I don't get too bored."

"Right."

It was standard procedure after a shooting to be on leave while the incident was investigated. It was a clean shoot. Derek would be fine.

One lane of the bridge had been reopened and traffic crawled at a snail's pace. The two men Derek had killed had already been removed from the scene. The screens that had been put up to prevent gawkers from seeing the gruesome sight had also been taken away.

Chloe found her attention drawn back to one of the girls. She'd been the last one off the truck and she'd looked familiar for some reason.

They'd be transported back to the police station, their identities sorted out, and then reunited with their families. As long as everything went according to plan.

But Chloe couldn't take her eyes off the one girl with the pink-and-black off-the-shoulder shirt. Why did she look so familiar?

Chloe moved closer so she could study her. She was pretty, with strawberry-blonde hair, blue eyes, and a spattering of freckles across her nose and cheeks. Cute. Young. Victimized.

And then it hit her. It wasn't the girl, it was the *shirt*.

She grabbed Derek's arm. "That's Penny's shirt."

"What?"

"The one she was wearing when she disappeared." Chloe pulled up her cousin's Instagram account and found the last picture posted. "Here, look."

He studied the picture, then lifted his gaze to look at the girl with the shirt Chloe was so interested in. "Whoa. That's freaky. But Penny disappeared six months ago. There's no way that's hers."

"Stranger things have happened. I want to talk to her."

She started toward the group of girls huddling together on the side of the road. A bus had been called to transport them to the hospital.

Derek's hand fell on her upper arm, halting her. "Let's wait and follow them to the hospital," he said. "They're going to be there for a while."

Chloe stayed still, but chafed at the restraint. However, he was right. They needed to get the girls off the road and away from the scene. Help them feel safe.

The bus arrived and the officers helped the girls onto it. They shuffled along, heads down, eyes averted. All but two. The girl with the shirt like Penny's and another dark-headed young woman who looked to be about sixteen or seventeen. The two of them huddled together, whispering words Chloe would give her right arm to be able to hear. One of the girls stumbled and pressed a hand to her side. The girl wearing Penny's shirt held her upright.

Chloe frowned and made her way over to the one who appeared hurt. "Are you all right?"

Without looking up, she nodded. "I'm fine."

"I don't think so. Let's get you taken care of."

"No, I—"

"Hey, Stephanie," Chloe called to the nearest female paramedic, "come here, will you?"

"No! I'm fine!" She backed away from Chloe. Hank stepped forward with a whine and the girl froze.

Chloe placed a hand on Hank's head. "Don't be scared of him. He won't hurt you, he's just concerned like I am."

Stephanie hurried over. "What's up?"

"Can you make sure this young lady is okay? She seems to be in pain and I don't like the way she's breathing."

The girl's frantic eyes met hers. She did not want to be examined. Chloe held her gaze. "It's okay, really. You're safe."

The other girl wrapped an arm around her friend's shoulder. "Let them check you, Skye," she said softly.

"What if they're watching? They're always watching. They'll know. Remember the consequences. There are always consequences." The last word came out on a gasp as a sob slipped from her. Pain contorted her face and she went to her knees while she continued to babble about secret cameras and eyes everywhere.

Chloe, Stephanie, and Skye's friend acted as one. The friend grabbed Skye's upper arm while Chloe and Stephanie lowered her to the hard concrete. Her words stopped and her breathing grew shallow and labored. Wheezing. Her eyelids fluttered.

Chloe looked at Skye's friend. "What happened to her?"

"He tossed her down the stairs," she muttered. "Then kicked her."

Anger burned bright and hot in Chloe's midsection. She pressed a fist to her stomach and drew in a breath to get her emotions under control. "What's your name?"

The girl hesitated. "Beth."

Stephanie looked up and met Chloe's gaze. "We need to get her to the hospital now. I think she's got a couple of broken ribs and a possible punctured lung. Jeff!"

Her partner looked up from the woman he'd just finished bandaging, saw the expression on her face and rushed over. "What is it?"

"Broken ribs, a pneumothorax, trouble breathing, and a fever. She needs to be transported immediately."

Within seconds, they had Skye loaded into the back of the ambulance.

Beth climbed in beside her.

"Hey, you can't go," Stephanie said.

The young girl met the paramedic's gaze. "Then she's not going."

Chloe looked at Stephanie. "Let her ride, Steph, she's going there anyway."

After a brief hesitation, Stephanie nodded. "Fine. We'll be at Providence Health Hospital."

The doors shut and they were gone. Chloe rushed to let Hank into his area in the back of the SUV, then climbed behind the wheel.

From his vehicle, Derek saluted her with two fingers and motioned for her to go first. She pulled away from the edge of the bridge and made her way as fast as she dared to follow the path the ambulance had taken.

She arrived and parked in the police parking spot near the door.

41

Derek pulled in behind her. The other girls would be arriving soon. They'd bring them to the hospital first to have them checked out. Then they'd assign them victim advocates and question them. It was going to be a long day for them. But at least they would get to go home at the end of it.

Chloe left Hank locked in his temperature-controlled area for now and hurried through the emergency room doors. Derek stayed on her heels. She stopped at triage and showed her badge. The woman at the desk buzzed the doors and she headed for the back. She stopped one of the nurses she'd met a few weeks ago. "Eve, hey."

"Hey, Chloe, I've got a busload coming in."

"I know. Two are already here. Skye and Beth. That's all I know to call them."

She walked behind the counter and clicked her keyboard. "Ah . . . yes. Room 2. But the girl, Skye, she's headed for surgery."

"Okay, what about her friend, Beth? She okay?"

"At first glance. I left her in the room to be checked out."

"Is it all right if I talk to her for a minute?"

"Sure."

Chloe made her away into room 2. Beth looked up and leapt to her feet, only to drop back into the chair when she saw Chloe. "Oh. It's you."

"Waiting for news on your friend?"

"Yes." She rubbed her hands together. "She's not strong. She wouldn't get on the trailer without me."

"What do you mean?"

She shook her head. "When they were loading the girls on, Skye was crying and screaming and they told me to go with her. But she still fought and he threw her down the stairs. I managed to get her back up and in the trailer so they wouldn't hurt her anymore. So, where is she?"

"In surgery. They took her right back because of the broken

ribs and lung issue." Chloe processed the load of information the girl had just dumped in her lap while trying to decide on the best line of questioning.

Beth glanced at the clock on the wall and stood, pacing from one end of the room to the other. Every so often, she would shove a strand of blonde hair behind her ear. A fine tremor ran through her hand. Before Chloe could speak, Beth had turned the waistband of her pants down. "I need to switch out my pod."

"What do you mean?"

"I've got type 1 diabetes. My pod—my insulin—is almost empty. And I need a PDM. They didn't give it to me to take when they put me on the truck."

"PDM?"

"Personal Diabetes Manager. The thing that allows me to control the dosage amount and provides other information."

"Ah. Okay. We'll make sure you get exactly what you need." Chloe sighed. "Look, I can't begin to understand what you and the other girls have been through—"

"No, you can't."

"But could you please tell me where you got that shirt?"

Beth stilled. "What?" She looked down at the top. "This?"

"Yes."

"Why?"

"Because my seventeen-year-old cousin was wearing it—or one like it—the night she disappeared and now you're wearing the same shirt. I need to know if the two things are connected."

The air around them stood still. Cold. Frozen. Carson said nothing as his friend paced the wooden front porch, then turned and unloaded on him. "Where are they? More importantly, where is *she*? How'd you lose her? I thought you had her under control."

"I don't know where she is!" Carson was tempted to pull the

weapon he had strapped to his ankle, but that wouldn't help the situation. Besides, this was a friend, the only guy who'd ever made Carson feel like he could be someone. Feel like he was important. He'd given him his identity and he could take it away.

Carson drew in a calming breath. "Come on, man, I thought she was at the hospital, but no one could tell me where she was. There was no Rachel MacCallum brought in. The other girls were there, but I couldn't get to them to ask if they knew what happened to Rachel. They had people all over them. Family, cops, just too many. I'm not worried about them talking, though. We're too careful. There's no way they can provide any information that would lead the cops to us."

"I'm not worried about the others. They can be replaced. Rachel can't. She's the means to the end goal—and she has to stay alive until we reach that goal."

"I know," Carson said, subdued. His friend was right. Without Rachel, their bargaining power was gone. "I'll find her."

His partner raked a hand through his hair. "This could be a disaster."

Carson wracked his brain trying to put a positive spin on the situation. Desperate, he blurted, "Okay, so, the lost income hurts. We'll have to build up the inventory again, but the auction can go on as planned with the remaining girls. No one knows anything. Everything is under control."

"She knows what you look like."

"Yes, but that doesn't matter since she knows me as someone else. She doesn't know my real name."

The man in front of him calmed slightly. "Right. That's true."

"So chill."

"I won't chill until he's dead. And that girl was our ticket to make sure that would happen."

"Hey, I didn't put her on the truck," Carson said. "Manny did."

"So, Manny's calling the shots now?"

"Look, the other girl—Skye—wouldn't shut up. I thought about drugging her but didn't want to do that since the auction was so close. Rachel was able to keep her calm and quiet. Stillman and the others were supposed to bring her back as soon as they delivered the rest of 'em."

"Stupid. Unbelievably stupid," he muttered.

"Take it up with Manny."

"Oh, I plan to." The quiet words sent a chill up Carson's spine. His friend had always had a reputation for ruthlessness, but lately, he'd taken that to a new level. But Carson owed him and that was that. Not to mention the fact that he was also the means to an end—making as much money as possible. So, as loyal as he was to this guy, he was even more loyal to his own bank account. Just the thought stiffened his resolve.

"How much insulin is left?" his friend asked.

"Not much. One pod, I think. And her PDM is in the office."

"Hmm. Well, we don't need much. If her father doesn't do as ordered, it's a moot point. It's not like we need her alive for the auction. No one would buy her with the high-maintenance medical issues she has."

"Maybe," Carson said. "You never know. She's one of the prettiest ones we've ever had."

"Right." His eyes narrowed as he thought. "That's actually true. And we don't have to tell anyone she's got the issues. I'll think about it."

"So, what do I need to do now?"

"Find the girl."

"I can do that."

"You might want to start at the hospital again. That's the first place they'll take them. She's got to be there. Maybe she just wasn't processed when you were asking about her."

"All right, I'll try again."

"And this time, make sure you don't fail." A pause. "You know

I love you like a brother, but I can't have any weak links. Make sure you cover your tracks."

Carson shivered at the unspoken threat. He knew the man would make good on it. He'd watched him kill before. One minute he'd been sharing a drink with the man at the bar. Ten minutes later, in the alley out back, he'd put a bullet in the same man's head.

Maybe it was time to get out while he could.

4

Before Beth could explain about the shirt, the doctor had come in to examine her. After prescribing her more insulin and praising her that her sugar levels were only slightly elevated, he left the room.

Beth let out a breath. "Your cousin disappeared?" she asked.

"Yes. Wearing that shirt. So, please. Tell me?"

"It was in a box at the house," she said slowly. "He told me to find something. This was scrunched up at the bottom, but it was the most decent thing in there." She shuddered. Tears flooded her eyes and she looked away. After several long silent moments, the tears disappeared and a blank, fixed look covered her features.

A coping mechanism, Chloe thought. Survival mode.

When Beth recovered her composure, she remained quiet, her eyes staring at the wall.

"Who told you to get something to wear? And where's the house?" Chloe asked.

Beth shook her head. "It doesn't matter about the house. They change locations every few weeks—and you can be sure as soon as they heard about the wreck and us being found, they cleared out. And I don't know where to tell you to begin looking anyway. It could be anywhere." She tilted her head. "Although, it's probably within an hour's drive from here."

"Yeah. Okay. So . . . what about the 'who'?"

"I . . . um . . . don't know his real name. One of them went by Manny." She looked away, then at her watch again.

"Do you know a girl named Penny St. John?"

Beth hesitated. "Is she your cousin? The one the shirt belongs to?"

"Yes. Do you know her?" Hope sprouted.

"No, I don't think so. I don't remember her name anyway. What does she look like?"

Chloe pulled up the last picture of Penny on her cell phone. Wearing the same shirt Beth had on.

She held the screen so Beth could see it.

"Wow. I see what you mean. It *is* the same shirt."

"Penny disappeared six months ago. She left to go on a date and never came home. How did they get you?"

Beth's laugh held no humor. "There was this really cute guy. Nice. I'd known him for a couple of weeks, but wasn't interested in dating him. I already had someone I had my eye on." A hint of a smile curved her lips, then disappeared. "My friend thought I was crazy not to return his interest. Anyway, she texted and told me to meet her at 'our place.'" She wiggled her fingers around the two words. "That she had a surprise for my birthday."

"Where exactly is your place?"

"On the steps near the big fountain in Finlay Park."

"I'm familiar with it. What happened when you got there?"

"Linds had a blanket on one of the steps with some special sugar-free cupcakes and balloons. She yelled, 'Surprise!' when I walked up. And at first, I thought it was cool and sweet. But then Carson and another guy came over to us."

A chill swept Chloe. She knew that name. "Carson who?"

"Langston."

"Whoa." The room spun for a moment and Chloe blinked to steady her gaze.

The girl frowned at her. "What is it?"

"Carson Langston was the name of the guy my cousin was last seen with. We've looked everywhere for him, but it's like he dropped off the face of the planet."

"It probably isn't his real name."

"Yeah. We figured that, but didn't have a face or any other name to go by. He was a definite dead end."

"The other guy's name was Manny, but I didn't catch a last name. Anyway, their appearance kind of ruined the moment, but I was like, whatever. So, we actually ended up having a pretty good time. I could tell Linds was proud of herself, and while I wasn't crazy about the guys being there, I didn't want to sound ungrateful. When we were ready to leave, they insisted on walking us to our cars and after that it's all pretty fuzzy."

The cars. Had they been found? She made a mental note to ask.

"How did he knock you out?"

"I'm not sure. I remember something wet hit me in the face. When I woke up, I was in a cage." Her eyes narrowed and her nostrils flared. "Like an animal. Lindsey was next to me."

She glanced at the clock on the wall once more. Her face crumpled and Chloe moved to take the girl into her arms. Beth leaned against her and sobbed.

"Tell me who to call, honey. Your mom?"

She shook her head and the tears continued to flow. "She's dead."

"Your dad, then."

"I can't. They'll hurt him."

"No, they won't. We won't give them a chance to."

Through her tears, the look Beth gave her could only be described as one of pity. "You have no idea how powerful these people are or how far their reach goes."

"And you do?"

"I have an idea—probably just an inkling." A pause. "They were going to sell them," Beth said, her voice so low Chloe almost couldn't hear it.

"Them?"

"The girls in the cages. The ones who were in the back of the trailer." Her eyes widened. "There are others still at the house."

"Where were they going to sell them and when?"

"At the auction. I'm not sure when it was supposed to take place. In the next couple of days, I think. That's where we were going when the wreck happened."

All senses on alert, Chloe took note. "Do you know where the auction was to take place?"

"Um . . . I don't know. I just overheard them talking about it. Somewhere here in Columbia, though, I think. They said the trip wouldn't take long, but they could have been lying." Her eyes welled again. She dabbed them with a tissue. "I heard them mention a senator and making sure they had a girl that fit his tastes."

Chloe grimaced.

"They take precautions with masks," Beth said, "but they're pretty much unconcerned about being stopped." Tears squeezed from under her lids. "My dad's a cop. If anyone can protect himself, it's him, and I still don't want to tell you who he is because if I do, they'll know and they'll kill him."

A cop? Chloe mentally reviewed the news. She hadn't heard of an officer's daughter being reported missing.

Chloe passed Beth several tissues. "What else can you tell me, hon?"

"They held a gun to my head and took my picture," Beth said. She swiped the moisture from her cheeks.

"Did they say why?"

"No. Sometimes they talked freely, other times they just did what they needed to do and left without saying a word. But this time,

Carson came and got me. He shoved me into a room and Manny was there. Carson put the gun to my head while Manny snapped a picture with his phone." Her frown deepened. "He didn't do that to the other girls. I asked."

"I don't know. I'd say that's not typical. Unless it was an intimidation tactic to convince you that they're serious." Or to post on the internet so potential buyers could take a look. But the gun nixed that idea. They might make her pose, but why hold a gun to her head?

She huffed. "Well, it worked. Scared me to death." A pause. "Something else that's weird. They gave me my insulin. The prescription was correct and everything. And they made sure I checked my sugar levels whenever I needed to with the PDM. And I ate well. They had healthy foods ready for me." Her fingers curled into fists and Chloe watched her consciously relax them. "They were prepared. They planned this way ahead of time."

"It sure sounds like it." She squeezed the girl's fingers.

"They had a doctor there. He examined each girl and then gave certificates to the man who was going to sell them. Certificates for the, uh, untouched ones, if you know what I mean."

Chloe kept her grip from tightening on Beth's fingers through sheer will. "I know what you mean." Untouched, pure. Virgins. Ones who would bring more money than the more experienced girls.

Beth's brows dipped. "They treated them like prize cows or something—complete with that stupid certificate. They weren't human to them. They were . . . inventory. How can people *do* that?"

They? Chloe wondered. She didn't include herself in the group? Was there some psychological reason for that? Denial? Her way of processing and coping?

Beth finally looked up and met Chloe's gaze. "I know about human trafficking. I've heard the warnings, I've seen the ads on television." A harsh laugh escaped her. "But . . ."

Called to Protect

"Yeah." Nothing could prepare someone for what she'd just gone through. Chloe swallowed against the nausea that threatened. "Did they drug you? Get you hooked?" Beth showed no signs of it, but some traffickers were known to get their victims addicted to drugs to keep them in line. And coming back for more.

"No, not me. They threatened to. Said if we gave them any trouble, they'd shoot us up. Carson carried a syringe full of heroin and he flashed it a lot. Almost no one gave them any trouble except one girl. Katherine. She fought back." She swallowed. "Actually, I think she just mentally snapped or something. She was completely hysterical and screaming at the top of her lungs."

"What happened?"

"They stuck a needle in her arm and she passed out. When she woke up, they did it again. And again. It was definitely heroin."

"She was a lesson to the rest of you."

"A very effective one. Pretty soon, she was begging them for it." Beth's eyes flooded with tears again and she sniffed. "No one else misbehaved. Including me." The girl dabbed her eyes and drew in a deep breath before letting it out slowly. "I didn't fight. I just did what they said."

Now, she was including herself. There was something odd about the phrasing of her story, but Chloe couldn't put her finger on it.

"You did the right thing."

Beth shrugged.

"They wanted you—the girls—clean," Chloe murmured.

"They said their buyers were picky."

Picky. That was one way to put it, she supposed.

Another wave of nausea swept over Chloe and she shut her eyes for a moment. *Keep your emotions out of it, remember?*

The nurse came in and Beth fell silent. Once she checked Beth's blood sugar with the new PDM, she gave Beth supplies to change her pod, tossed the old one, and turned to leave.

"Could I have an extra one?" Beth asked.

52

The nurse raised a brow. "Why?"

"I just . . . I don't know. I just want one. Please? I ran out one time and it's not an experience I care to repeat. Now, I always carry a spare. Or two."

Chloe met the nurse's eyes and nodded, doing her best to encourage the woman to agree. Compassion darkened her gaze. "Sure. I'll get the doctor to order you an extra one." She winked. "Or two."

Beth relaxed a fraction. "Thanks."

Once the nurse was gone, Beth turned back to Chloe. "They had cameras everywhere and they were always listening. At least it seemed that way. We managed a few whispers here and there, but conversations didn't happen often."

"Was Katherine in the truck with you? Is she here at the hospital?"

"No. They kept her with Lindsey and some others back at the house. I don't know why. I think it was because there wasn't enough room in the truck—or they were saving them for the next auction."

Chloe touched her hand. "You're very brave."

She grimaced. "No, I'm very scared. And I want to know about Skye. Why won't anyone come tell me anything?" Agitated, she started to pace the small area.

"Want me to see what I can find out?"

Beth's eyes met hers. Gratitude filled them. "Thanks. That would be great."

Chloe stepped out of the room and found Eve at the nurses' station. "Eve, could we get an update on the girl who came in with the pneumothorax and high fever? Her first name is Skye. That's all I know."

"I can't tell you much, you know that."

Chloe sighed. "These girls came in together. Rescued from a human trafficking ring. She's desperate to know about her friend."

Eve flinched. "Poor thing. All right." She consulted her computer. "I'll just say that she's out of surgery and in recovery."

"So, she'll be all right?"

"Looks like it."

"I'll pass this bit of encouragement on. Thanks." She ducked back into the room to find Beth pacing from one end to the other. "It looks like Skye's going to be all right."

The girl's shoulders dropped, her relief palpable. "Really?"

"Yeah." Chloe held out her phone. "Now, call your dad, okay?"

Beth didn't respond.

"Beth?"

She looked up. "She trusted me," she said. "The only time she didn't cry was when I was holding her hand. For some reason she thought I could keep her safe."

Unsure that Beth realized she was speaking the words out loud, Chloe grasped her fingers and gave them a light squeeze. "And you did."

A shudder ripped through the teen and her eyes focused back on Chloe, who held the phone out once more. "Not really." But she took the phone and dialed a number. Hesitated. Then hung up. "No. I can't."

"Why?"

"Because he doesn't want me—" her chin quivered and she bit her lip—"and I don't want him. And if I call him, I might get him killed." She gave a shaky laugh. "I don't know why I even care, but I do."

Blake was at his desk at home staring at the screen on his phone when the call came in for the second time. It was the same number that had called thirty seconds earlier, rang once, then disconnected. He'd just gotten the trace equipment set up and was about to dial the number back when it rang again.

He answered the call then hit the button for the trace. "Hello?"

"Hi, who is this?"

"This is Blake MacCallum. Who's this?"

"Blake? This is Chloe."

"Chloe?" Linc's sister? "Why are you calling?"

"I have a teenager here. I told her to call her dad and she dialed this number, then hung up. I dialed it back and you answered."

His heart skipped a beat. "Rachel? Is it Rachel?"

How could it be? Had they let her go? Had she escaped?

"Is your name Rachel?" he heard her asking.

"Put her on the phone," Blake said.

Sounds of the phone transfer, then Rachel's voice reached him. "Hey."

"Rachel, are you all right? Who had you? Where were you?" A pause. Anxiety twisted tighter in his belly. "Rachel? Where are you? Tell me where you are and I'll come get you right this second."

"I'm . . . I . . . I'm going to hurl."

"Rachel, wait," Chloe called.

"I'm going to the bathroom!" His daughter's voice faded and he pictured her heading for the door.

"Blake?" Chloe's soft voice came through the line.

"Yeah."

"She went to the bathroom."

"I heard." But it was Rachel. Sounding completely normal. *Acting* completely normal in her desperate desire to avoid conversation with him. Even in this circumstance. But, somehow, she'd escaped her captors. *Thank you, God.* "Where are you, Chloe?"

"We're at Providence Health. I thought she looked familiar, but then thought it was just the shirt?"

"The shirt?"

"Never mind that for now. She's not cooperating, Blake. She gave me a fake name. I don't know what's going on with her."

Her confusion echoed in his head. He closed his eyes. "It's okay. Our relationship is complicated. Tell me the truth, is she okay? Why the hospital?"

"Physically, she appears to be fine."

Physically. That sounded a bit ominous. "But she's at the hospital. Why? Is it her blood sugar?"

"No, her blood sugars are slightly high, but nothing to cause any alarm. It's a long story. We'll explain when you get here."

He was already opening the door to his truck. "I'm on the way."

"We're in the ER, room 2."

5

Rachel washed her hands and splashed water on her face. Patting it dry with a paper towel, she noticed the fine tremor that ran through her fingers. Her dad was coming. No, not her dad. Blake. He'd fix everything. They may not get along, but he was a problem solver. He would help her, right?

But no, why would he? After all, he didn't want her. And honestly, who could blame him?

But he'd sounded so worried on the phone. Like he really cared.

But she knew he didn't.

Tears pricked behind her lids once again as the volley of doubts waged war within her. What would it take to make him love her?

He admired strength. She'd tried to be strong.

He admired integrity. She'd tried to act in such a way that would make him see she had that.

He respected authority. She did well in school and had never had the first behavior issue.

"Why?" she whispered to the face in the mirror.

Obviously. Because he'd never wanted her.

Only now he was stuck with her because her mother was dead. She tossed the paper towel in the trash and drew in a steadying breath.

She could do this. She had to get Lindsey help.

And her father had the resources to do that. He might not want her, but he was a cop. He would help. Period.

Decision made, she opened the door to step back out.

"Are you sure?"

She froze.

She knew that voice. It belonged to Carson.

But no, it couldn't be him. Could it?

"Thanks, I appreciate it," he said. "I'm heading home, but I'll check in with you soon. I have your number."

She stared. It was definitely him. And he was grinning down at the nurse, who looked like she might melt all over the floor at his feet. He flashed twin dimples and the nurse simpered.

Rachel closed the door just enough to see out and held still, motionless, breathless, her palm slick on the doorknob. Should she scream? Bring attention to him? Would they lock her up if she shouted her accusations? He'd deny it, come up with some excuse, say she was crazy and had him confused with someone else.

But she wasn't. It was him.

And he was leaving.

She opened the door farther and started to call out, then stopped. *If you get away. If you call anyone. If you bring attention to yourself in any way while we're en route to the destination, I'll kill everyone you love. And I'll make you watch.*

Rachel shuddered and snapped her mouth shut. He'd kill Lindsey if she said anything. They might lock him up to question him, but he'd get a phone call. And that call would bring death to people she loved.

Starting with Lindsey.

His footsteps carried him toward the exit. *I'm heading home.*

Did he mean he was going back to the house where Lindsey was? Or to his actual home? But she'd heard his voice at all hours of the day and night. Maybe he lived at the house.

Rachel had no idea where she'd been held captive, she just knew that it was a house—and dark. Even if she talked to the investigators or her father, she couldn't give them the first clue as to the location of the place.

But this guy could. He was almost at the door that would take him out of the Emergency Department.

She swung the door open, deciding to go get Chloe, but paused . . . *I'll kill everyone you love. And I'll make you watch.* She stood in the doorway, wrestling with the decision.

"Are you all right?"

It was the nurse Carson had been talking to at the nurses' station. Rachel licked her lips. "Yes. No. Tell them—"

"Eve?" Another nurse leaned out of a nearby room. "Need you in here STAT!"

Eve took off, and Rachel swallowed, never taking her eyes from Carson's retreating figure.

. . . *I'll kill everyone you love. And I'll make you watch.* If she went to get help, he'd get away.

And if he got away, Lindsey might never be found.

She couldn't chance it.

Rachel slipped out of the restroom and let the door shut behind her. With a quick glance around her, she ducked her head and hurried in the direction Carson had gone, stopping only when she saw the insulin pods on the cart next to room 4, labeled with her name. Another quick glance around showed no one watching. Hand hovering over the pods, she hesitated. What good were the pods without her PDM. But next to the pods was an insulin pen. With that, she could at least give herself more insulin. She grabbed it and shoved it into her back pocket, then hurried after Carson, bursting through the outer door into the hall.

A spurt of panic shot through her when she didn't see him, but in another ten steps, she caught a glimpse of him in the revolving door that would take him out of the hospital.

Goosebumps pebbled her skin at the blast of chilly air he let in. Then he was outside and she had no more time to worry about her physical discomfort and no way to leave a note or signal someone. She hurried after him.

Just ahead, he pulled keys from his pocket and she thought it odd that he never looked back over his shoulder, never acted suspicious in any way.

He was totally unconcerned about being caught. It never crossed his mind that he would be stopped.

Heat crept up into her neck, then her cheeks, and her fingers curled into fists. Oh, he'd be caught all right. If it was the last thing she did, she'd make sure he was caught. Or dead. But how?

Rachel waited until he vanished inside the parking garage before picking up her pace. As she strained to go fast enough to keep him in sight, but slow enough not to call attention to herself, she faltered. What was she *doing*?

She couldn't follow him, she didn't have a car. But she might be able to get the license plate of whatever car he got into.

Yes. Then she'd turn it over to Chloe and she could send a team in to rescue Lindsey.

A plan firmly in mind, she stayed on his tail, trying to blend in and look as though she knew where she was going. If he looked back, he'd see her.

Just the thought turned her stomach. No, she didn't want to do this. She was just a seventeen-year-old kid. Even if she got the plate, there was no guarantee they would be able to trace it. These guys stole cars all the time. Or at least the plates off cars.

She stopped walking and turned to run back toward the safety of the hospital. People passed her, walking around her while giving her irritated looks for her abrupt halt in the middle of the walkway.

And then Lindsey's terrified face and pitiful cries echoed through her mind. No, she couldn't leave her friend.

But what else could she do?

Keep going, get the plate. It was the *only* thing she could do. She did another one-eighty and hurried toward the garage.

As she crossed the street, her heart thundered in her chest. Should she stop someone? Tell them to call her father? No, that would take too long as well. Ignoring the pounding, she stepped into the cool interior of the parking garage and stopped. Listened. Looked toward the elevator.

She caught a glimpse of him just as he stepped into the stairwell. Rachel pressed a hand to her stomach as though that would help settle it, then hurried to follow. At the door, she paused, giving him time to climb, not wanting him to hear her footfalls. She counted to five, then opened the door and started up. His footsteps on the next level echoed back to her. And the sound of a door opening.

So, he was parked on level 2.

Rachel continued up the stairs to the landing and opened level 2's door with caution. Part of her expected him to yank it open and snatch her. She shuddered at the mental image even as she scanned the area. A car alarm chirped.

Three people passed her from the stairwell and she ignored them, her eyes landing on the person she sought. He stopped at a red Suburban. Not too old, not too new, it blended with every other vehicle in the garage.

A sedan pulled to a stop and the driver called to Carson, who walked over to him.

It was now or never.

Rachel darted to the back of the SUV and noted the license plate. Or the lack thereof.

Panic sliced through her.

The plate had been coated with mud and all she could make out were the first two letters. GN.

What now? Slipping forward, with one eye on the men, she swiped a hand across the mud.

It wouldn't budge. What?

Chills danced down her arms once again. Paint. Great.

The two men continued their conversation and she thought she heard the word "auction." Shivering, she debated. Then with her heart in her throat, she climbed in the open rear window.

The odor of paint hit her hard. That must have been why he had his window open in the middle of November. She hunched down amongst all the equipment. Paints and art supplies littered the back while a rack of paintings and empty frames took up most of the rest of the space. One large tarp lay crumpled to the side. She pulled it over her and prayed he wouldn't need anything out of the back before she could escape.

Chloe stood still, phone in her hand, as she tried to wrap her mind around the fact that the girl with Penny's shirt was Rachel MacCallum, Blake's daughter.

Blake. She'd had a crush on him since she was twelve and had started noticing cute guys. She'd thought Blake was the cutest.

He and Linc were the same age, three years older than she, and had gone through high school together. And then Blake's girlfriend, Aimee, had gotten pregnant with Rachel. He'd immediately married her at the age of seventeen, and that had been the end of Chloe's childish dreams of happily ever after with him.

Fortunately, Rachel's maternal grandparents had been loaded and they'd had nannies and babysitters so Blake and Aimee could finish college.

Blake and Linc had both majored in criminal justice, just at different schools. In spite of the marriage, in spite of the child, Blake had still found his way to the St. John table at least once a week. Sometimes he brought Rachel and sometimes he came alone. As far as Chloe could remember, Aimee had never come.

Slowly, Blake's visits had tapered off until they ceased. Linc hadn't said much, but Chloe figured something had happened. Something bad.

Then bits and pieces had filtered down to her and she'd filed the information away. Now she pulled it from the dusty mental file cabinet and thought about her teenage crush.

She hadn't seen him in forever, even though she knew he and Linc got together on a regular basis now that both of them had returned to Columbia. She also knew they worked together occasionally, because her ears perked up each time Linc mentioned him.

At some point about four years ago, Blake's wife had left him and had taken their daughter with her. It had been a nasty separation, and after an intense custody battle, Aimee was awarded primary custody of Rachel and Blake had thrown himself into his job with a vengeance.

And then Aimee had died in a car wreck and Blake had finally gotten custody of his then fourteen-year-old daughter.

Chloe glanced at the clock on the wall and frowned. Rachel had been gone a good fifteen minutes. She stepped outside and looked for a familiar face. And her eyes landed on one. Not the one she wanted to see. What was *he* doing here? His back was to her, but she recognized him instantly.

Jordan Crestwood. SWAT member, friend to Derek and Brady. Ex-boyfriend to Chloe. She grimaced and almost ducked back inside, but she needed to ask about Rachel.

"Hey, Eve," she called to the nurse behind the desk.

"Yes?"

Jordan turned too.

"Have you seen the girl that walked out of here twenty minutes ago?"

"I saw her at the restroom door, but I got called away. It's been a bit crazy around here, sorry."

"I know." Chloe walked down to the bathroom and knocked. "Rachel?"

No answer.

She tried again. "Rachel? You okay?"

More silence. With a bad feeling growing in her midsection, she tried the door and the knob turned easily. Chloe pushed the door open and stared into the empty bathroom.

"Hey, Chloe," Jordan said from behind her. "It's been a while."

The bad feeling grew into a massive ball of dreaded certainty.

"What's wrong?" he asked.

"She's gone."

Blake pushed through the emergency room doors, absently noting the smell of antiseptic and cleaning product. All hospitals smelled the same, but only one held his daughter. He hurried to flash his badge at the woman who controlled the button that would let him in.

"It's a regular law enforcement convention around here tonight," she said.

Nodding his thanks, he headed to the back. Room 2, Chloe had said. He turned the corner and found her standing in the hall talking to Linc, two police officers, and hospital security. Linc straightened from his position against the wall.

"Where's Rachel?" Blake asked.

Chloe turned, tension in every line of her body. "We don't know."

"What do you mean you don't know!" All eyes turned on him. He took a deep breath. "Sorry. Sorry."

Chloe took his arm and directed him toward the room. Linc followed.

"Chloe?" a male voice called.

Blake stopped as she turned, annoyance tightening her face. "Jordan, I don't have time right now, okay?"

"Sure, I get it. Later?"

"Probably not." She shut the door and turned to Blake and Linc. "Rachel said she needed to go to the restroom. She went and that's the last I saw of her. I asked hospital security if they would pull footage so we can see what happened. That should be here at any moment."

"Is she hurt? Is it her blood sugar? Why is she here?" All he wanted was to see for himself that she was safe.

Chloe shot a look at Linc, and Blake appreciated the man's blank expression. But he could see Chloe wasn't fooled. She crossed her arms. "Blake, how long has Rachel been missing?"

He flinched. "What do you mean?"

"She was found on a tractor trailer with sixteen other human trafficking victims. How long has she been missing, and why hasn't there been a missing persons report filed on her? Why doesn't anyone know she's been gone?"

For the first time in his life, Blake thought he might actually pass out. Spots danced before his eyes and his head spun. Chloe placed her hands on his chest and gave him a gentle push. He sank into the chair behind him and turned to the one person he'd trusted with Rachel's life. "Human trafficking, Linc? I don't understand. That's not possible. How does that fit with the text? With everything?"

Linc frowned. "I have no idea. Let's see what the security cameras show."

"What text?" Chloe asked.

A knock on the door brought Blake's head up. He avoided Chloe's question for now. Monique Pascal, with hospital security, walked in carrying a laptop. "I've got your footage here if you want to take a look."

"Absolutely."

She already had it ready to play. A tap of one key set the video in motion.

Blake saw his daughter come out of the room where he now

sat and walk to the restroom. She paused at the door, looked both ways, then slipped inside. When she opened the door a minute and fifty-three seconds later, she looked left, and paused. She stood there for a good two minutes, had a quick exchange with a nurse at the station, who then looked away and rushed off. Rachel hurried down the hall with a brief stop in front of room 4. A nurse came out of the room a few seconds later, looked at her cart, shook her head and pinched the bridge of her nose.

"What's that about?" Blake asked.

"An insulin pen went missing with Rachel," Chloe said. "The nurse was bringing it, along with meds for a couple of other patients, and got called by an occupant as she passed by room 4. The nurse popped her head in to tell her she'd be right back. When she turned around, the pen was gone."

"What about her PDM device?"

"She doesn't have it."

He groaned. "Okay, but at least she has the pen for extra insulin. So, where's she going?"

"Here." Monique tapped another key. "She went out the front door." Rachel stepped into the revolving door and disappeared. "Then," Monique said. "Here. I caught up with her on the parking garage camera."

The computer screen blipped, then another video appeared. Rachel went to the stairwell and the door shut behind her.

His heart thudded and he broke into a cold sweat. She'd left under her own power, but why?

And the human trafficking thing? She'd been found in a trailer with other girls? Why would they do that when they needed her as leverage?

Because they thought they had him? That he would kill the judge and they never intended to let her go because she could identify them?

Maybe.

"But—" Blake said.

Monique raised a hand, cutting him off. "I've got one more shot." She clicked the keyboard, then pressed play once again.

Rachel exiting the stairwell door. She walked across the parking lot, dodging cars. And then she wasn't there.

"Where'd she go now?" Chloe asked.

Monique shook her head. "I don't know for sure, but watch this." She zoomed in on a red Suburban. Movement. The back window opening? No, it was already open. Rachel's face appeared for a blip of a second before disappearing once more. "I think she got in the back of that Suburban. And before you ask, I tried getting a plate, but it was mostly obscured by mud or something. I did get two letters. GN."

"I'm on that," Linc said. He got on his phone while the others processed what they'd just seen Rachel do.

Chloe cleared her throat. "So, do we consider her a runaway now?"

"No," Linc said with a glance at Blake.

Blake pinched the bridge of his nose. "I'm . . . I don't know what to think about this." He looked up. "She's a smart girl. Street smart in addition to brainy smart, but I have no idea why she'd leave." His lips tightened. "Unless it was to avoid me."

"What was her demeanor when she was here in the room with you?" Linc asked Chloe.

"Scared. Angry. Secretive." She frowned. "She told me her name was Beth."

"What?" Blake asked.

"Yes."

"But why?"

"I don't know. But, uh . . . at first she didn't want to call you."

"Of course she didn't." He swallowed and shoved his hands into his front pockets. "She hates me."

"Actually, she seemed to be more worried about you than anything else. She said she was afraid to tell me who she was because they would kill you. From what I understand, some of the other girls have the same concerns for their family members. Although, most have been convinced to tell who they are. But Rachel was really scared to do so."

Blake shook his head and raked a hand through his hair. So, Rachel did care about him. Then why was she so angry with him? What had changed in the last year to cause her to turn against him so vehemently?

"Blake?"

He blinked. He'd been so lost in thought he'd missed her question. "What?"

"Why do you think she hates you?"

"I'm not sure, because she won't give me the full story. Her attitude is like, 'If you're too stupid to figure it out, you don't deserve to know'—but about a year ago, she started calling me Blake. As far as I can tell, her mother convinced her that I'm pretty much worthless and the reason I wasn't around the last few years was because I didn't care enough to be there. And while it's not true, I can't seem to make her believe otherwise." That was probably part of it, but there was more. He just didn't know what, and Rachel wouldn't tell him. "So . . . right now, we don't talk much. She spends all of her time either hanging out with Lindsey, her best friend, or at the pool, swimming. She's on the long-distance swim team. Wants to go to the Olympics . . ." He shook his head. "That's pretty much the only thing that hasn't changed since her mother died. Bottom line is, Rachel hates me and I don't know why or what to do about it."

"And yet . . . ," Chloe said.

"And yet what?" Blake asked.

Chloe gave a slight shrug. "She punched your number in my phone."

"It only rang once. She hung up, didn't she?"

"Yes, but—"

"She knew Chloe would call the number back," Linc said. "Or that you would call the number that showed up on your screen."

Blake pursed his lips. "You think she was reaching out?"

"I think she wanted to," Chloe said. "I think she's trying to ask for help without actually asking for it."

He rubbed a hand down his face and turned to Linc. "We have to find her."

"We won't stop until we do," Linc said.

Exactly what they'd all said about the St. Johns' niece, Penny. And they were still looking.

"Linc?" Chloe waited until her brother looked up and met her gaze. "Rachel had on Penny's shirt. The one she was wearing when she disappeared."

He blinked. "You asked her about it?"

"Of course. It was the main reason I sought her out. She said it was in a box in the house where she and the other girls were kept."

"Could she tell you where the house was?"

"No."

He sighed. "Maybe one of the other girls will be more help."

"How are they?"

"Getting checked out and questioned. We've pried parents' names from a few more of them. We've got three holdouts still terrified to tell us who to call. We'll run fingerprints and see what we can turn up. When the girls disappeared, crime scene techs probably processed their rooms and put the information into NCIC, so we'll see if we can get a match that way. It's going to be a long night for them. For all of us."

"Lindsey," Blake said. "Where's Lindsey?"

Chloe frowned. "Who?"

"I was so focused on Rachel, I didn't think to ask if you'd found

Lindsey as well. She and Rachel are best friends and disappeared the same day. I'm sure they were together. Lindsey's been all over the news. Her mother has been calling me every day, trying to talk to Rachel. I've had a beast of a time putting her off."

"Wait a minute," Chloe said. "She doesn't know Rachel's missing too? I'm confused."

Blake fell silent and Linc shoved his hands into his front pockets. Chloe's eyes darted back and forth between the two men. "What's going on? Why are you being so mysterious?"

"Rachel's disappearance is more than what it looks like on the surface," Blake finally said.

"Okay." She crossed her arms, ready to listen.

"I . . ." He shot a look at Linc, who shrugged. Blake seemed to come to a decision. He straightened and pulled his phone from his pocket. "Shortly after Rachel and Lindsey were taken, I got this text." He tapped his screen and handed her the phone.

She looked at it and lifted her gaze to meet his. "Whoa."

"Yes."

"But, why?"

"I'm one of the marshals assigned to Ben Worthington. Before I even knew something was wrong, I received a text that they'd taken Rachel and more instructions would be forthcoming, but in the meantime, I was to wait. So I did—and then brought Linc in to help when I couldn't wait any longer. I found out about Lindsey later that night. Then nothing for a week. I got the most recent text this morning. The gist of it is that they want me to kill the judge."

She gasped. "Or they kill Rachel?"

"Yes."

"Whoa." As lethal as he looked at this moment, Chloe figured if he got his hands on whoever had taken Rachel, that person would sorely regret doing so. "So, what's our next move?"

"Our?" Linc asked.

"I'm in this now." She let a grim smile curve her lips. "And I have a dog that can track more than just drugs as long as I have a scent item."

"True." He crossed his arms and frowned. "All right, Chloe, you talk to Skye once she's awake and see if she can add any details to Rachel's account. And see if she knows why Rachel would disappear like she has."

"On it. What are you guys going to do?"

"Talk to our supervisors and figure out a plan to nail some human traffickers."

Rachel's breath left her lungs when Carson finally pulled the Suburban to a stop. She curled tighter into herself. He'd been on the phone with someone most of the way, discussing the fact that she was missing and how he promised to find her. She shuddered and swallowed back the nausea that had lodged itself in her throat.

Please don't come back here, please don't come back here.

With her eyes squeezed shut, she waited. If he was going to find her, she didn't want to see it coming.

His door slammed and she flinched. This was it. If he came to the back, she was done.

But nothing happened.

The back didn't open.

No rough hands grabbed at her.

No harsh shouts filled the air.

A slow breath left her. Tremors shook her, and for a good five minutes, she simply stayed put trying to gather the nerve to climb out of the back of the vehicle.

Or maybe she should wait until dark.

No. There was always the chance he'd come back to get something. Slowly she slid out from underneath the tarp and edged to the tailgate. She shoved aside paint supplies and another tarp, along with several flyers advertising an art auction, and a box of protein bars. Hesitating for a brief second, she finally slid two of the bars into her pocket and slipped out the window.

Once her feet were on the ground, she stayed low behind the Suburban, shivering as a gust of wind blew her hair across her face. Pushing it aside, she drew in a deep breath and peered around the edge of the vehicle. All looked quiet. But what if someone was looking out a window? She shivered and looked across the distance to the ramshackle barn. A haven. Her escape.

But the open expanse between the vehicle and the building terrified her. No, she couldn't chance it. Not in the light of day. If she got caught . . .

No, getting caught wasn't an option. She needed to get out while the getting was good and find a place to hide. Unfortunately, there wasn't one nearby. She'd have to risk being discovered by hiding in the only place available.

Without another thought, she scrambled under the Suburban and tucked her arms beneath her. It would be cold, but she'd wait until dark when no one would see her running across the field to the barn. Cold was better than trapped in a cage again.

Once in the barn, she'd see if she could figure out where she was, find a phone, and call Blake.

7

Blake shoved back from the conference table located in the FBI's office on Westpark Boulevard and crossed his arms. This day had gone from worse to circling the drain. JoAnn sat to his left, and Chloe, who had just walked in with Hank, sat across from him. She raised a brow.

Linc tilted his head at Blake. "You okay?"

"No. It'll be dark in less than thirty minutes and we're no closer to finding Rachel than we were six hours ago." He raked a hand through his already mussed hair for probably the thousandth time and stood to pace the office. "It's supposed to snow, you know."

"It's Columbia, it's not going to snow," JoAnn said. She twirled a pen in her right hand.

"We'll watch the weather, but I'm inclined to agree with JoAnn." Linc sighed. "All right. We've all acquired a bit of information in the last few hours, let's go over what we've got. Rachel was taken, along with her best friend, Lindsey, a little more than a week ago. You received a text the day of her disappearance, then nothing until today when they told you to kill the judge."

"Right." Blake rubbed a hand down his face. "And then today, Rachel shows up in a truckload of human trafficking victims." He glanced at Chloe. "You spoke with Skye Harper, the girl Rachel was so concerned about?"

"Yes. I had to wait for her to wake up from the anesthesia, but she was able to talk a bit."

"And she knew nothing?"

"Not much. Some little things that might add up to something. I asked her about anything she saw, overheard, et cetera. She said they could hear the men talking sometimes, but mostly, she said she just tried to keep her head down. She did mention the upcoming auction the girls were being taken to. Apparently, their kidnappers made no secret about that."

"But she had no idea where they were kept before transporting them?"

"No," she said. "I asked her all the questions I could think of that would trigger memories. The one thing she did mention was that she never heard traffic. She said they could hear when someone left or pulled up outside, but there wasn't a busy road nearby."

"So, they were held in a rural area," Blake said.

"Most likely. If they were held in a neighborhood, seems like they would have heard the occasional car, but she said no. Never. She did say she heard an airplane occasionally."

"Could they have been near an airport?" Jo asked.

"I didn't get that impression. She said it wasn't regular, just every so often and it sounded like a smaller engine. She said once they arrived at the house, everything was routine. Like the people who'd taken them had done this with so many girls, it was just a process and no one deviated from it. They were told up front that if they caused any trouble or tried to escape, they would be harshly dealt with."

"I'm guessing Skye gave them trouble," Blake said.

"Yes, but only when they were loading to leave the house. She panicked and freaked out at the thought of never seeing her family again. When she tried to run, she was pushed down a flight of stairs and kicked at the bottom. Hence the broken ribs." Her gaze flicked to Blake. "She also said that Rachel was the one who was able to calm her down."

Blake nodded. "What else did she say about Rachel?"

"Just that she wasn't supposed to be on the truck and was only there because one of the men—Carson, I believe—said they'd already promised a certain number of girls to the buyers and Rachel had to get Skye there."

"So Rachel went too," Blake murmured.

"Yes."

"Skye did say that the guy who pushed her down the stairs was beaten by one of the other guys, and she didn't know if he was dead or alive when they left the house. The guy who told Rachel to go with Skye also told her not to try anything or think she was going anywhere because she was special and she'd be back at the house before dark."

Blake frowned. "Because of me. They needed to keep her nearby."

"So," Linc said, "they had to deliver the girls—including the wounded Skye. Everything was planned."

Chloe shook her head. "Skye would have died before they got there. She barely made it as it is."

"We know they were heading from West Columbia into downtown," Linc said.

Blake grunted. "Which tells us exactly nothing."

"Not necessarily," Jo said. "The fact that Rachel would be back before dark tells us they weren't going too far. Could be several hours away, but they'd be back that night. At least our radius isn't the whole country."

"True," Chloe said with a nod, "but I think right now our biggest leads are the tractor trailer, the girls we rescued, and the vehicle carrying Rachel."

"And the two guys Derek took care of."

Linc checked his iPad. "Right. The truck was registered in the names of Wilson Bowles and Clyde Harrison. They were identified as guns for hire and both had rap sheets as long as the Mississippi River. But nothing that tells us who hired them."

"And the guy you collared?" Blake asked Chloe.

"Stupid Man? David sent me some information on him." David Unger, an information specialist with the department who could find just about anything on anyone. Chloe checked her phone. "His real name is Van Stillman. Also a long rap sheet. Also very good at keeping his mouth shut. So far, not even the offer of a deal has unsealed his lips. However, something interesting did come back."

"What's that?"

"It took some digging, but David managed to find out that Stillman's got an association with Alessandro Russo."

Blake sucked in a breath. "Alessandro Russo?"

"I take it you're familiar with him," Chloe said.

"He's a bandit we've been looking for. JoAnn and I trailed him all over South Carolina, then down into Georgia and Florida." Bandit, the most common name used for a fugitive. "One of the biggest organized crime heads in the state. He's into all kinds of stuff. Mostly extortion, murder, and gun running. While it's rare for the Italian mafia to be involved in drug running, it looks like Russo brought them into it too. It's not surprising that he's linked to human trafficking now. It was only a matter of time. Last I heard, he was still in Florida, but his trail went completely cold and we turned his case over to the Miami Marshals' Office. They haven't been able to track him down yet, either."

"That's because there's evidence he's returned to South Carolina," Chloe said. She raised a brow at her brother. "You want to continue?"

"Sure." Linc pulled up a video and it began to play on the screen on the far wall. "We've got him on security footage leaving the Hyatt in downtown Greenville." A man in a suit and tie walked out of the hotel, followed by his bodyguards. They climbed into a waiting limousine and it drove off. "When agents arrived, he was gone, his trail lost. I ran him by Derek, who said OCN was real interested in having him behind bars as well, due to his drug affiliations. He's got every branch in law enforcement after him for one reason or another. They suspect he's behind some bomb activity as well."

Blake waved a hand. "We'll come back to him in a minute," he said. "I want to focus back on the vehicle in the parking garage. Why would Rachel climb in the back of that guy's car? Did she know him?"

"We couldn't really get a good angle but ran him through the facial recognition software with what we had. Unfortunately, we got nothing. He could have just been a stranger and she was using him as a way out of the garage quickly," Linc said.

"But that makes no sense," Chloe said. "And besides, she seemed so deliberate in her actions. Like she was following him."

Linc nodded. "I agree with Chloe. I think we need a task force set up ASAP to go after this human trafficking ring." He looked at Blake. "And if this Alessandro Russo is involved, then we'll want the US Marshals on this force too."

"Marshals, DEA, Homeland Security, FBI, Batman, and the Power Rangers too," Blake said. "Whatever. I don't care what it takes, I just want this guy found and my daughter—and the other girls—home safe. Jo and I can keep looking for Russo when we're not on judge duty. And the more minions we capture, the closer we'll get to him. So, every time there's a call related to this case, Jo and I need to be there as well—or if we can't be there, we need to be brought up to speed ASAP."

"Agreed," Linc said. "Anything technology related goes to us. We've got a new girl in the tech department who's a genius. Her name's Annie. So, if you're all right with that, we can use our resources and add everything to our database as it comes in, which will enable us to keep all the information in one place."

"Hey, Columbia PD technology is state of the art," Chloe said.

"Maybe better than yours. And David can find information as fast as your bureau flunky."

Linc smirked and rolled his eyes. Blake now understood Linc's exasperation with his sister. Chloe knew as well as he did that the bureau's resources far surpassed anyone else's, but apparently that wouldn't stop her from razzing him about it. If he hadn't been so worried about Rachel, he would have enjoyed the ringside seat to their sibling antics. Something he missed terribly with his own brother.

"We'll get David and Annie on it, working together so they can compare notes," Linc said. "I'll fill them in."

"That's a good idea," Chloe said. "OCN is already involved due to the drugs found at the scene, so you've already got them aware of what's going on. When you set up the task force, can you make sure I'm in on it?"

"I think I can arrange it, sure," Linc nodded. "You may have to work on other things as well for your department, but yeah."

"Good. Make sure they know that anything related to drugs that could be connected to human trafficking, Hank and I get the call." She'd be sleeping with her cell phone on her pillow.

Blake was gratified to see a plan coming together. It would be the best way to handle it. Chloe would see each scene and be able to recognize anything that looked different . . . or the same. If there was a different K-9 team called, something might get overlooked. "Chloe, I'll see if we can swear you and Hank in as Deputy US Marshals. That way you'll have federal arrest powers should you come across something—or someone like Alessandro Russo or human traffickers crossing state lines. If we have to chase them, those federal arrest powers will come in handy."

"Good. That would work."

"I want Russo," Blake said softly. "Want him behind bars so bad I can taste it." And he had for a very long time.

"Yeah." Linc ran a hand over his jaw. "Okay, I'll get this taken care of right now."

Chloe looked at Blake. "I'm just curious as to how your judge connects to this whole thing and why someone wants him dead so bad."

"I was just thinking the same thing." He nodded to Jo. "Our next shift is tomorrow. I think it's time to have a chat with the man."

———

The sun had gone down three hours ago, taking the slightly warmer temperatures with it. Rachel huddled against the wall of the barn, knees drawn to her chin, and shivered in her thin blouse. She thought she'd overheard someone say something about snow a couple of days ago, but dismissed it as ridiculous. It didn't snow in Columbia. At least not more than a few flakes.

However, she had to admit, she was cold. Very cold. And hungry—and an idiot. Had she really thought she could save Lindsey?

She pulled one of the protein bars from her jeans pocket and ate it slowly. With no way to check her blood sugar, she was just going to have to pray it didn't drop too low. Or go too high. High was better than low, but neither were good. With little food, she was in more danger of it going low. She thought about removing the pod, but couldn't bring herself to do it.

Once again, she'd made a stupid, possibly life-threatening, choice. She should have stayed at the hospital. Should have told someone her story. But it hadn't taken her long to figure out that these people had been doing this for a very long time. And no one had discovered it or caught them. So maybe, somehow, Rachel could help by gathering as much information as possible and making sure she lived to give it to the right people.

She shivered again. Yeah. She was an idiot. Stupid, stupid, stupid. Just like her mother had yelled at her when she'd failed algebra and had to take summer school classes.

Stupid, worthless girl, do you see now why your father doesn't want you? She'd tossed the report card onto the table and stalked off, her disgust with Rachel plain.

But at least Rachel hadn't gotten caught yet. And she had a roof over her head. Such that it was. Maybe she wasn't quite as stupid as her mother thought she was.

Then again, she was still stuck, with no way to get help for herself or any of the others. She fingered the insulin pen in her pocket. But she would be okay on insulin for at least seven days.

Seven days. Where would she be in seven days? Would she even be alive?

Panic welled and she stuffed it down.

A sound to her left jerked her attention around and her pulse skyrocketed. Had someone from the house seen her? Or just come to get something from the barn. She clasped her arms around her knees and stayed still, willing herself to be invisible even while knowing the childish wish wouldn't happen.

Another sound as soft as a brush of wings stirring the air. But she heard it.

Meow.

Heart thudding, relief snagging the breath from her lungs, Rachel stretched her legs and pressed a hand to her stomach. "Come here, kitty, come here." The cat sauntered over and climbed on Rachel's leg. After kneading her thigh, the animal curled in her lap. She was probably cold too. Rachel relished the slight warmth the cat brought with her. It wasn't much, but she'd take it.

Tilting her head, Rachel studied the ceiling while she thought. Her fingers stroked the silky gray-and-white fur as prayers tumbled through her mind.

A plan. She definitely needed a plan. Her gaze roamed the building. The barn was filled with old, broken-down farm and horse equipment. No telephone, of course.

But if she'd calculated right, Carson had driven for about thirty minutes—maybe forty—before pulling to a stop in the drive of the house. The same place she'd been when she'd awakened after being drugged. She recognized the barn from when they'd walked them up out of the basement and loaded them into the trailer early that morning.

And then the sun had fallen and now Rachel had to figure out her next move. Start walking and hope she went in the right direction? Or ran into someone willing to let her use a cell phone? What if no one believed her? What if no one would help her?

Oh God, what do I do? Help me!

The tears came and this time she let them out, sobbing into the fur of the sweet cat.

When she finally fell silent, her crying under control, Rachel forced her mind to work. She'd had her cry. It was time to figure out what to do next that wouldn't lead to her capture and wouldn't get Lindsey or her father killed.

She buried her protein bar wrapper in the dirt floor while her mind went back to that first awful day after the drugs had worn off, the pounding in her head had eased, and she'd been given food and water. She, Lindsey, and four other girls had appeared to be the newbies in the group.

Carson had walked the length of the cages holding up pictures, his nauseating mask something out of a horror movie. Briefly, she'd wondered why he bothered, then realized he wasn't the only one luring girls into the ring. Some of them had no idea what he looked like. "If you decide not to cooperate," he said, "if you try to escape, if you cause us any trouble, it's not only you that will suffer—" his dramatic pause had only heightened her terror—"but your families as well." He held out one of the photos to the girl in the cage next to Rachel. "You have a little sister, Melly, right? She's ten, right? Well, guess what? She's next."

"No," the girl whispered before bursting into tears.

"Then don't do anything stupid." To Lindsey. "You seem to be real close to your mother. She's easy to get to."

Lindsey's sobs echoed through the cavernous area.

He turned to Rachel. "You have a father." He passed her the picture and Rachel simply stared at it, mixed emotions coursing through her. She loved her father. And she hated him. Keeping her features expressionless, she passed the picture back, turned her back on the boy—man—she hadn't trusted, but hadn't feared, stretched out on the floor, and closed her eyes.

The room was silent except for Lindsey's crying and the whimpers coming from the other girls. Rachel had no idea why her own emotions had been frozen that day. She'd been incapable of responding. With tears, anger—even fear. It seemed to confuse Carson and he stared at her, his dark eyes glittering through the holes in the mask. Then he'd marched on to the next girl. And the next.

And while that numbness had quickly worn off, she was determined to get that back. Because right now, she couldn't afford to feel.

She sat up.

As soon as the sun started to rise, she was going to act.

Chloe rubbed her eyes and blinked. The clock on the wall pushed midnight and her adrenaline was crashing in spite of the gallons of coffee she'd consumed.

They'd made their way back to the hospital where, as an official task force—thanks to Linc's influential pushing and the quick action of the powers that be—they'd finished questioning the victims.

Unfortunately, they still didn't know much more than what they'd started with.

A house with an underground area, darkness, cages, threats, men with masks and guns. And terror. That had pretty much summed up their stories.

Krista, one of the victims, had tilted her head, a thoughtful expression momentarily replacing the fear. "But they fed us well and they didn't touch us."

"What do you mean?"

"I've heard of human trafficking, of course, and I figured the next step would be the . . . rape. You know?" She shuddered and shook her head. "But they didn't. The only time they put their hands on us was when they transported us—or when the guy they said was a doctor examined us." She grimaced. "They were rough, but it was almost like they were careful not to leave bruises too."

Because they already had buyers. And buyers didn't want their property damaged. Chloe had barely managed to hold back her own shudder.

"Except for Skye," Krista said. "When she started crying and fighting, trying to run away, the guy who was loading us in the truck just . . . snapped. He grabbed her and shoved her down a flight of stairs. He went after her, and she later said he kicked her when she was lying on the floor." Krista's eyes filled. "He treated her like she was nobody." Another shiver wracked her and she drew in a deep breath. "Anyway, that's why her ribs were hurting so bad."

Which supported Rachel's story.

"And then someone started beating on him," Krista said. Another eyewitness to the beating, corroborating Rachel's account.

"What was his name? The one who hurt Skye."

"They called him Manny."

"And what happened to Manny?"

"I don't know. This was while they were loading us all in the truck. I couldn't see what was happening, I just heard it." Her eyes met Chloe's. "Is it wrong to hope he's dead?" she whispered. Then sobs ripped through her.

Chloe had hugged her and held her until her mother had walked in and taken Chloe's place. Chloe had slipped out when she saw Krista wrapped in her mother's arms.

Her throat tightened at the memory.

Now in a borrowed conference room at the hospital where they'd agreed to meet after questioning the victims, they worked on the plan.

Linc had the lead FBI position. Tabitha St. John, the city's chief of police and Linc and Chloe's mother, had agreed to leave Chloe and Hank on the team. She'd also requested two DEA agents and two OCN agents, one of whom was Derek. Blake's partner, JoAnn, had been approved, and would work on tracking Alessandro Russo in between shifts of guarding the judge. And, as a courtesy, Blake would also be kept in the loop on any updates concerning Rachel.

For now, they were gathering as much information as they could to get started. Then they'd split up and get this thing taken care of. Hopefully.

"These people are careful," Blake said. "More careful than anyone I've ever run across before. They've gotten this down to a science. They have one, possibly two guys, who woo the girls into trusting them. Then once they're at the house, they keep the girls in the dark. Literally. The abductors wear masks so should one—or a truckful—of the girls manage to escape, she can't identify any of them."

"Which none of these girls could," JoAnn said, all caught up on the information they'd already gathered. "Except for the two known as Carson Langston and Manny with no last name."

Linc nodded. "And let's see if we can access their cloud accounts. I want to see what pictures they have on their phones and their text history."

The girls were scared. Their families had been threatened. They were potential witnesses for anyone caught and brought to trial. And then there was Alessandro Russo. A fugitive on the run, but with ties to a human trafficking organization based in their city.

It was a good enough argument to assign officers who would

work in shifts to protect each family. For now. Those resources wouldn't be available for long, so Chloe and the task force would have to work fast.

Blake steepled his fingers and rested his chin on them. "Jo and I are on judge protection duty in the morning. I was going to request someone else take my place, but now I plan on going to the judge's home and questioning him. Now that Rachel is free of them, I don't have to keep my mouth shut anymore. We can go after these guys full speed ahead."

"First things first," Linc said. "Let's see what Judge Worthington has to say about all this. He's agreed to meet us in the morning while Blake and Jo are there."

Nods of agreement around the table.

Chloe blew out a short breath and stood. "I'll see you all in the morning. I'm heading home."

When she stepped out of the room, she nearly ran into the woman standing outside the door. "Ruthie?"

"Chloe. Hey, I've been waiting on you." Dr. Ruthie St. John, skilled surgeon and another sibling.

"What's up?" Chloe asked her.

"Dad said Sunday lunch is on. Does that work for you?"

"Yes. Maybe. I don't know." Chloe frowned. "What's today anyway?"

"Thursday. Well, I guess it's Friday now." Ruthie touched Chloe's forehead. "Are you all right?"

"Yes. Fine. Just overworked and getting ready to be *over* overworked. Sunday may be just what I need by the time it gets here. If I can make it, I will. If not, I'll let you know."

"Great. I've left messages with the others."

"Is there some occasion I've forgotten?"

"Nope."

She nodded. "Good. Now I'm going home to get a couple hours' sleep before we dig in again."

Rachel didn't know what time it was, she just knew she was exhausted. And it was dark. And she was scared. So far, no one had bothered to come into the barn and she'd been alone for hours. Well, she and her new friend, Smoky Hope. Because the cat reminded her of a billow of gray smoke and Hope because, right now, she needed some hope in her life.

Thankfully, she'd found an old horse blanket that stunk and had who knows what kind of creatures crawling in it, but she'd pulled it over her and welcomed the warmth it had offered.

Goose bumps still pebbled her arms, but she no longer felt like a block of ice. Smoky Hope huddled next to her, curled against her belly. Loath to move, but deciding it might be a better idea to sneak out under cover of darkness rather than wait for morning, she held the cat to her lips and kissed its soft head. "Bye, sweet kitty. Take care of yourself. I'd try to take you with me, but that's probably not a good idea. At least you don't have to worry about starving, there are plenty of mice around here." Ick. She set the cat aside and stood, keeping the blanket pulled around her shoulders.

She opened the door, wincing at the shriek of the rusty hinges. Heart pounding, blood racing, she paused and listened while she peered out toward the house. A lone porch light burned and that was it. No lights in the rooms upstairs or down. She already knew the basement would be pitch black.

Nausea swirled at the memory. At the thought of going back down there.

When nothing happened, no more lights flicked on and no doors opened to investigate the sound coming from the barn, Rachel slipped out into the night. A quarter moon hung in the sky offering a bit of light, but not much.

Eyes scanning the area for any movement, she hurried across the open expanse of land, thankful she'd chosen the black converse tennis shoes instead of the clunky high heels someone had shoved at her. She'd tossed the heels and kept digging in the box until she'd found the tennis shoes.

Rachel reached the side of the house and stepped between the shrubs to peer in the window. The room was dark, and while she couldn't see it from her position near the barn, there was a faint light inside. Probably a night-light. The blinds blocked her view for the most part, but she could make out a bed and someone in it. Probably one of the men taking his break from guard duty.

Slowly, she made her way around the house, looking in each window, careful to make as little noise as possible. Her pulse hammering beneath her skin, she reached the opposite side and stopped.

Cigarette smoke and low voices reached her.

Sweat pooled beneath her arms and her palms grew slick in spite of the chill in the air.

What were they saying?

Should she try to listen?

If they were out here, did that mean there wasn't anyone watching the girls? Could she get inside and let them out of the cages?

Rachel bit her lip and shivered even as her stomach rumbled. Hunger hit her hard. The protein bar had lasted only so long. Pressing a hand against her stomach, she moved forward on silent feet. The voices became clearer. Carson and one she didn't recognize. She peered around the corner.

". . . get her back."

"I know." Carson held a cigarette to his lips and drew on it. As though he had all the time in the world, he blew the smoke out. It curled in the night air, aiming for the clouds she couldn't see but knew were there. How many times had she wished she could simply evaporate and disappear from the cage that had held her?

Too many to count.

But she couldn't focus on that right now.

"This is your fault, you know."

"My fault? I didn't have a wreck and then get myself killed and allow the girls to be discovered. You can't put this on me."

"Your face is on the security cameras now at the hospital."

"You told me to go looking for her! And so what? Even if they run me through some system, nothing will show up. That's why you hired me, remember?"

The other man snorted, took Carson's cigarette, inhaled, then tossed the remains to the ground. He stomped it out and crossed his arms. "He's still alive."

"No kidding."

"Then do something about it."

"It's in the works," Carson said.

A sigh slipped from the stranger and he raked a hand through his hair. With his back to her, she couldn't see his face, but she knew for sure she'd never heard his voice before. In that dungeon where she'd been kept, all she—and the others—could do was listen when their captors talked. This was a new voice.

And who was the "he" they were referring to? Who was it they wanted dead so bad?

"I'm going to bed," Carson said. "I've been up since yesterday morning."

"I'll keep watch."

"We've got three new girls coming tomorrow."

"Good. Losing that truckload of inventory cost us big-time. We've got a lot of money to make up."

"Roger that."

Rachel closed her eyes at the thought of the poor girls, the *inventory*, but she couldn't worry about them for now. Right now, she had to find help for Lindsey. Maybe if she was able to save Linds, her father would—

No. Don't go there.

She took a step back, her foot landed on something hard, and a loud crack echoed around her.

Carson stopped walking. "What was that? Hey! Is someone out here?" He turned to the other man. "You go that way. I'll check over here."

Rachel sucked in a silent breath and ducked down behind a bush, curling into the tightest ball she could, huddled up against the side of the house. Footsteps came her way. Seconds ticked. A flash of light passed over her head. Probably the light on his phone. She didn't dare move.

They were going to find her and she would never see her father or the rest of her family again. Lindsey and the other girls were going to be sold off and Rachel was going to die. Because she'd kill herself before she let herself be used like that.

Bottom line was she was a loser, a failure. Her throat grew tight, sobs wanted to burst through. Biting her lip, she refused to allow a sound to escape.

The footsteps passed by. "It's nothing, man. I'm going to bed," Carson finally said.

"Go," the unidentified man said, "we've got a busy day tomorrow."

Rachel kept her eyes closed and slowly let out a silent breath. They hadn't found her. She was still free. She still had a chance to help Lindsey and the others.

So, now what should she do?

8

Blake gripped a handful of his hair and walked the length of the den. He had a much better understanding of people who stated they were frustrated to the point of pulling their hair out. Yep. He got that now.

He'd arrived at the Worthington house for his shift, and neither the judge nor his wife had yet to put in an appearance. Linc seemed to be biting his tongue and hanging on to his patience by a thread.

JoAnn placed a hand on Blake's arm and raised a brow. "Chill."

"I'm chill."

"You're anything but."

He grimaced. "Where are they?"

"They're here," Deputy US Marshal Parker Hunt said. "She's still in bed and he's working in his home office. He said he had two phone calls to make and then he'd be happy to talk to you."

"You're going to have to have some patience," JoAnn told him under her breath.

"I don't have any left."

His partner rolled her eyes, but the concern for him was there. He knew she cared and he appreciated it.

It didn't do anything to help his raging desire to go find the judge and haul him bodily out of his office and question him, but he really did appreciate it.

Parker sat at the kitchen table and his partner, Justin Bolton, poured himself a cup of coffee. They would stay with Mrs. Worthington while Blake and Jo covered the judge.

They looked like quadruplets in their matching clothing. Navy blazers with their plastic pocket IDs and khaki pants. Justin had on his baseball cap with the USM emblem on the front. For this assignment, Blake and Jo both wore body armor as a protective measure. The judge would wear one too.

"He's got a ten o'clock court time," Blake said.

"That's an hour from now," Linc said. "But I'm going to have to run if he's not out here in the next fifteen minutes."

Ten minutes ticked slowly past.

The front door opened and Blake recognized Paula, the judge's daughter. Miles, the fiancé, followed her. "But you have to tell me this stuff, Miles," Paula was saying over her shoulder. "Seriously. How can you keep—" She broke off when she spotted Blake and the others. "Oh. You're here."

"Did you think we wouldn't be?"

"No, of course not."

Both carried fresh bagels if the odor emanating from the bags was any indication. His stomach rumbled as he stepped forward to take them from her. "Let me help."

"Thank you."

Miles was already in the kitchen pulling small plates from the cupboard.

Blake set the bags on the counter. "I didn't realize you two were coming for breakfast."

"I decided we needed an intervention," Paula said. "Dad needs to drop this crazy human trafficking issue and get out of the sights of whoever has a bead on him. This whole thing is ridiculous."

Blake raised a brow. "So, you just let them win?"

"Yes," she snapped, "if it means staying alive."

"If it wasn't your father, how would you counsel him?" Blake asked. "To run or fight?"

Her mouth opened, then snapped shut. She turned on her heel and left him standing there.

"Never seen anyone shut her up like that before," Miles said. "Wow. That was actually kind of impressive."

"I don't mean to discount her feelings for her father, but if he gives in to these people, it'll set a precedent."

"You think?"

"Don't you?"

Miles nodded, eyes thoughtful. He snitched a bagel from the bag and wrapped it in a napkin. "Well, I can't stay. I'm just playing delivery boy for Paula. There's enough for everyone. Dig in." He turned. "Honey?"

"In here," she called from the den.

Miles headed to tell his fiancée goodbye while Linc and Jo helped themselves to a bagel each. "Oh yum," Jo said. "Hey, Blake, there's blueberry."

"Save me one." He had a question for Paula. In the den, she and her fiancé were deep in conversation—the one they'd been having as they walked in the door?—and he almost turned around, but stopped when he heard her gasp. "Murdered? That's awful. I'm so sorry."

"Who was murdered?" Blake asked. He knew it was nosey, but he couldn't help it.

"Miles's brother," Paula said without taking her eyes from her fiancé.

"Half brother," Miles said. "And it was two years ago."

"Is that his picture?" Blake asked.

She held it out to him. "I was sorting his clothes for his next trip and this fell out."

Blake took a look. A younger version of Miles stood next to

a boy who looked to be in his teens. "Good-looking couple of kids," he said.

Miles's lips thinned. "Yeah. I miss him." He plucked the photo from Paula's fingers and stuffed it into his shirt pocket. "Let's move on to happier topics."

"But why haven't you ever told me about him?" Paula persisted.

"I don't know. I don't talk about him much," Miles said, obviously resigned to answering his fiancée's questions. Blake almost smirked. What else could one expect from a lawyer but a grilling?

"We were very close growing up," Miles said, "and then we kind of went our separate ways when we graduated from high school. I later learned he was murdered." He gave a short laugh that held no humor. "Sometimes when I'm having a hard day and I'm missing him, I pull his picture out and think about him. It's stupid."

"It's not stupid," Blake said. "I'm sorry for your loss."

"Thank you." He turned back to Paula. "But it's in the past. I want it to stay there, okay? Now, please." He lifted Paula's fingers to his lips and kissed them. "Change the subject." He glanced at his watch. "Ouch. Actually, it doesn't matter about the subject. I have to go." This time he kissed her lips. "I'll talk to you later tonight."

Paula bit her lip and frowned, then nodded. "Fine, but we're not finished discussing this."

"Somehow that doesn't surprise me."

With an aggrieved look at Blake, he left and she gave an exasperated sigh. "Where are my parents? I told them I was coming over and we needed to talk." She disappeared into the back of the house and Blake now had an inkling of why the Worthingtons hadn't put in an appearance yet. Nothing like good old-fashioned avoidance.

Linc stepped into the room, wiping his mouth with a napkin. "What was that all about?"

"Nothing." Well, it was something, but it wasn't on his priority list for the moment. "We'll have to leave in the next thirty minutes to get him there," Blake told him.

"It's a twenty-minute ride," Jo said. "We'll talk to him on the way, so quit grumbling."

Blake sighed. He knew he was being a bear, but worry for Rachel wouldn't let up the stranglehold it had on his throat. Why had she left the hospital without asking for help? He'd watched the security footage over and over and Chloe was right. Rachel had definitely been following the guy. But why? And why hadn't anyone been able to figure out who he was?

Linc shook his head. "I can't wait any longer. I've got an appointment at ten o'clock myself. I'll call you in a couple of hours to get an update."

He left with a wave, after Blake and Jo promised to keep him updated.

Ten minutes later, Judge Worthington's appearance shut off Blake's mental questions, only to bring different ones to the surface. Like, had the man lied about knowing who wanted him dead?

Blake turned to the judge. "We're ready when you are, sir."

"I'm ready. Sorry for making you wait. I had to deal with a daughter who wants me to cower behind closed doors and not go in to work."

"Understandable. She's worried."

"I get that, but I refuse to let these people win."

"Good for you, sir."

It didn't take long to get the judge loaded into the black SUV. Paula climbed into her BMW and peeled away, her scowl saying more than any words she might have uttered.

Chloe tipped the water bottle and downed half of it. From the bowl on the ground, Hank lapped up his water too. They'd worked hard for the past two hours training and keeping their skills razor sharp. She'd chosen Finlay Park for their morning exercise and couldn't help visiting the steps Rachel had told her about. Or the parking area where the girls' cars had been found. Sweatpants and the long-sleeved hoodie kept her warm along with the workout, and sweat dripped down her temple.

Clapping hands caught her attention and she turned to find Brady walking toward her, applauding hers and Hank's performance. "Nice job."

"Thanks."

"You always did have a special love in your heart for animals."

"Yep. Probably why I love all my brothers so much."

He grinned. "Ahh, a little witty this morning, are we?"

"It's the fresh air. Trying to clear my head and think this case through."

Brady sobered. "How's the investigation going?"

"Slow." She shook her head. "A lot of things just don't make sense. And the things that make sense individually, don't come together as a whole."

"That's sort of clear."

"I know."

"I've heard of Alessandro Russo. He's a bad dude."

"I looked him up before Hank and I came out here for our workout. He's got a lot in common with Tony Bianchi." Just saying the man's name sent shudders through Chloe. Tony Bianchi had been a powerful organized crime figure in their city. Fortunately, he'd been brought down by her mother and Columbia's finest that had included Izzy and her brother, Derek, especially.

Hank walked over to Brady and dropped his rope. Brady threw it and Hank gleefully bolted after it. "Guess Russo decided to stake his claim after Bianchi was killed."

"I guess. The door was kind of left open." Chloe sighed. "Now we've got to shut it again."

"Right."

"How are the people you fished out of the river?"

"Doing well. I checked on them yesterday. The mom had a

96

concussion and a broken collarbone. Kids were in their car seats when they hit the water. They had a bad scare but are recovering."

Hank returned the rope and Brady gave it another throw.

"That's good to hear," Chloe said.

"The job has its good moments."

"Are you glad to be diving again?" He'd resigned from the dive team to work as a detective full-time, but a shortage of experienced divers had sent him back to filling in when necessary.

"I love it. It's tough doing both, but until they hire a couple more divers, I don't mind."

Brady continued the game with Hank while they talked. "Does it seem to you that human trafficking around here is on the rise?" she asked.

He shrugged. "I think it's always been rampant, but yeah, we're just more aware and actively looking for the victims now."

"And sometimes they just fall in your lap," she said, thinking about the girls in the trailer.

"Rachel didn't know anything about Penny, huh?"

Chloe frowned. "No." Hank loped back and sprawled on the grass at her feet, panting and happy with the extra time playing his favorite game. "I think about her every day," she said. "Even more so now. I really believe if we find Russo, we'll find what happened to Penny."

"You think she's still alive?"

"I pray she is, but honestly, for her sake, it might be better if she's not. Is it awful to think, much less say, that?"

"I've thought it."

"I feel like we've failed her. A whole family of cops and we can't find her or the people who took her? That's unacceptable."

Brady didn't answer with anything other than a nod. So. She wasn't the only one who felt that way. As far as she knew, she was the first one to voice it, though. He slid an arm around her shoulders and pulled her into a hug. "We won't give up."

"I know." She stepped back. "Have you talked to Damien?" Penny's brother had her very worried about his mental state.

"No. He's still blaming himself for not stopping her that night, for not moving fast enough to get the license plate of the guy driving."

"Who we know was Carson Langston, which probably isn't his real name."

"I know and Damien knows. And he's still out walking the streets looking for her every minute he's not working."

"I've been checking websites. As many as I can find. So many girls," she whispered. "I want to rescue them all."

"You know as well as I do that we've got undercover officers on those websites day in and day out. We're making busts and putting these scumbags behind bars, but I'll admit, some days it feels like we're swimming against the tide."

"I keep telling myself that it makes a difference to the ones we do manage to rescue."

He smiled. "Absolutely. Gotta look at it that way or we'll go nuts." He glanced at his phone. "Linc said Blake and Jo were heading to the courthouse with the judge. I've got to run and tackle some paperwork. Catch up with you later?"

"Sure. I'll be at Mom's on Sunday." She paused. "Unless I'm not."

"Same here."

Chloe watched him leave, then woke her snoring dog. "Come on, Hank, time to go."

Hank rolled his eyes at her as though to make sure she was serious.

"Come on, you lazy mutt."

He bounded to his feet and nudged her hand. She scratched his head while she watched Brady climb into his truck. Her brothers were good men. Much like Blake MacCallum. Now there was a guy who'd gotten a raw deal early in life, but had risen above it. One had to respect that.

And she did. A lot. In fact, she felt a bit more than respect for the man. Old crushes apparently died hard. She knew Blake was all business right now. Romance wasn't on his radar and rightly so. But she couldn't help wishing that once Rachel was found—and they *would* find her—Blake would be willing to explore the possibility.

She tucked the water bottle into her pack. Until then, though, she and Hank had work to do.

JoAnn drove while Blake rode in the back with the judge. The man set his briefcase on the floor at his feet and checked his phone one more time before looking up. "All right, you've got my undivided attention. What is it you wanted to talk to me about?"

"We need you to think a little harder about who might want you dead. And why they'd go to such lengths as kidnapping my daughter and ordering me to kill you if I ever want to see her again."

The man's mouth moved, but no words emerged.

Okay, maybe Blake could have softened that a bit, but he was ready for something solid to chew on. Finally, the judge snapped his jaw shut. "Kidnapped your daughter?"

"Yes. She's . . ." He couldn't say "fine" because she wasn't. ". . . not with them anymore, but the fact is, someone tried to use her for leverage to get me to kill you."

"I . . . I don't know what to say."

"We need names," Jo said. "We need to go through your case files." She paused. "And I think we can narrow that down to anyone involved in human trafficking."

Judge Worthington rubbed a hand down the side of his face, and Blake figured he was working on processing what had just been thrown at him. The man gave a short nod. "Fine. I'll pull any files from my office that I think will be a possibility and we'll go through them."

"They're not digital?"

"Sure, but I keep a hard copy in my office," he said. "I'm not a digital guy, other than my smartphone."

"The hard copies might be better," Jo said. "It'll be easier to go through them. And less strain on the eyes."

"True. Let's get him into the courthouse. We'll grab the files on our way out. I'll let Linc know and he can pull in some agents to help us."

"Right," Jo said, "since he's the lead on the investigation, I would think he might appreciate being informed of what you're doing."

He scowled at her in the rearview mirror. She simply raised a brow. Of course he knew he was overstepping slightly.

JoAnn pulled under the covered area at the back door. Since the threats had started, the marshals made sure the judge entered and exited the building through the protected entrance.

Once inside, they passed through security with the judge nodding to the guard monitoring the metal detector. "You're new here."

"Yes, sir."

"Glad to have you. Keep up the good work."

"Will do, sir."

The three of them cleared, they walked single file down the hallway to the elevator that would take them up to the second floor where the judge's office was located.

He waited outside his office with Jo while Blake cleared the area. Blake noted that nothing looked out of place. All was in order. He returned to the hallway. "It's clear."

Judge Worthington entered and removed his robe from the back of the door. He slipped into it, then nodded to the outer office. "Lila has the hard copies of the files. I'll have her pull the ones related to human trafficking."

"That would be very helpful," Jo said, "thanks."

"Now, it's time for me to head to court."

"We're right behind you."

Back in the hall, JoAnn led the way while Blake brought up the rear.

Just as they approached the back entrance to the courtroom, a door pushed open at the end of the hall. Blake looked up to see a security guard step through and let the door shut behind him. He pocketed the key card that had allowed him access. "Y'all need any help?"

"We've got it, thanks," Jo said without looking at the man.

Blake frowned and met the brown eyes under the ball cap. He'd left strict orders that no one was to have access to the hall during specific times. Apparently, this guy didn't get the memo. "This hall is off limits. Can you make sure no one comes back this way?"

"Oh right. Sure." The security guard lifted a hand in a wave and turned to leave. Blake made a mental note to reinforce the no-access request. Or change it to an order.

Blake turned back to Jo and the judge and held the door open for the man to step through.

Movement from the corner of his eye brought his attention back around. And time slowed.

The security guard raised his arm, the weapon in his right hand shifted to aim at the judge.

"Gun!" Blake shouted and shoved JoAnn into Judge Worthington as the crack of the weapon filled the hall. The bullet slammed into the door. The second bullet whizzed past Blake and hit Jo.

She cried out and went down, her Glock clattering to the tile floor. Blake fired three rounds at the disappearing figure. All three bullets hit the door. He could only pray one made it through to hit the man he'd been aiming at. And hadn't hit any innocent person beyond.

He whirled back to his partner. "Jo!"

She waved at him with a grimace. "Got my vest," she gasped. "Check him. Is he hit?"

Judge Worthington. The man lay on the floor just inside the courtroom door. Blake stepped over Jo who struggled to get her breath and knelt beside the judge. "Sir? Are you all right?"

"I'm fine," he said and rolled to his feet. "Just landed pretty hard on my wrist. How's Jo?"

Law enforcement had already descended. Cory Little, a fellow deputy marshal who had been on the judge's detail, dropped beside them. Blake caught his eyes. "He's not hit. Stay here and cover him. I'm going after the shooter."

"Blake—"

"I saw his face. Put out a description." He rattled it off.

"Right. Go. I've got him."

Blake stopped for one brief second to check on Jo, who once again motioned that she was fine. "Okay, hang tight."

"Yep."

He sprinted down the hallway. The man had pulled his ball cap low, but thanks to that nanosecond glimpse, his face was now imprinted on Blake's memory.

His footsteps pounded down the hall and he slammed through the door the shooter had slipped back through after firing his shots. The stairwell echoed its emptiness and Blake breathed a relieved and grateful thanks that no one other than the shooter had violated the no-access request.

Relief quickly turned to angst.

The ball cap lay on the floor, a bullet hole in the middle of the bill.

But no blood, and no shooter, were to be seen. Blake texted an update.

Hat recovered. Everything else the same.

He caught his breath for a split second. Which way? He spun in a circle and growled. He'd lost the shooter.

Chloe dove for the floor when the first gunshot rang out. In the split second it took for her to realize that the bullets weren't coming her way, she had her weapon out. Hank pulled on his leash and she was actually surprised to find herself still holding it.

Huddled on the floor, she now waited, noting others in the same position around the lobby of the courthouse. When no more shots sounded, law enforcement bolted into action.

And Chloe with them.

She shot to her feet, weapon in her right hand, Hank at her side. Court security officers would handle the other courts, securing the doors and locking their areas down. The Special US Marshals at the magnetometers, the ones at the elevators, and those roaming the halls would handle the perimeter doors. Chloe blended with the rest of the officers, looking for the shooter and pointing frightened people toward safe areas.

Where was he? *Who* was he? Or she?

Whoever it was could be anyone and anywhere at this point. Had he hit his target? How did he get a gun inside?

Security was beyond tight. They checked everything. Weapons, IDs, *everything*. There was no way he could have snuck a gun past the checkpoints.

So, maybe he didn't bring the gun inside but acquired it once he was already in the building?

From who? It wasn't like the list of armed people in the courthouse was very long.

Her heart pounded in time with her feet. She hadn't planned on being here today, but thanks to Brady's announcement, she decided to find out if they'd learned anything from the judge. And now someone was shooting.

"Chloe!"

She pulled up short. Hank skidded beside her on the slick floor. She spun. "Blake? Did you see him?"

"He was after Worthington. The judge is safe, but I need you. Bring Hank."

Chloe raced after him, stopping only when he reached the

door to the back hall that led to the courtroom she figured Judge Worthington was supposed to be sitting in. He pointed. "Can Hank track whoever was wearing that hat?"

"Of course."

"Let him get a sniff and let's go."

Chloe reached for the hat, wishing for a set of gloves. It was evidence, but it could also lead them to an active shooter. She'd ask forgiveness later. She let Hank get a good whiff. "Hank, *zoek*!" The command to track.

Hank put his nose to the floor, then lifted it in the air and took off, nearly jerking her arm from the socket. Chloe hurried after him, spotting the FBI agents now on the scene. With her badge in plain sight and Blake on her heels shouting at people to clear the way, she stayed with Hank, letting him have his way.

He led them to a stairwell at the end of the lobby. Blake pushed the door open and up they went. Out on the second floor, down the hall, and back into the stairwell at the other end. Then up. "What's he doing?" Chloe demanded.

"Trying to make sure no one is following him."

"He wasn't counting on Hank being here."

"Exactly."

On the third floor, Hank wanted out of the stairwell. She let him have his head once more and they slipped onto the floor, weapons drawn, her nerves about as tight as they'd been when she'd faced the muzzle end of the gun yesterday.

A flash of movement at the other end of the building caught her eye. "There he is! Police! Stop!"

But her words spurred him on.

"He's going for the roof access," Blake said and peeled around her. Hank didn't seem to like that and put on an extra burst of speed. Chloe's lungs burned and her side ached as she kept pace behind the dog until they came to a stop just outside the door. Chloe grabbed a few quick breaths.

Blake opened the door and gave a quick look. A bullet pinged off the doorjamb and he jerked his head back inside. "Gotta get this guy."

"I'm right behind you," Chloe said.

Blake rolled out the door and Chloe followed, her weapon aimed, looking for a target.

No more bullets came their way. Hank strained to go, but Chloe wasn't ready to release him. Not yet. On the roof, her feet crunched the gravel. She turned her back to Blake's and watched for the shooter.

Hank barked and lunged toward the air-conditioning unit.

They ran toward it, skidding to a halt at the corner. Blake nodded to her and she nodded back. They buttonhooked around the edge to see . . .

. . . nothing.

Chloe turned to watch their backs.

"Stop! Federal Agent!" Blake's shout pulled her back to see the man at the edge of the building. Very near the end of the roof. And still holding his weapon.

Chloe released the leash. "Hank, *stellen*!" The command to bite—or take down. Hank zipped from her side, heading straight for the suspect.

The man stumbled back, lifted his weapon at the exact moment Hank's jaws clamped around his forearm. The gun fell to the surface of the roof and the shooter's harsh scream scraped across her ears. Chloe ran toward him. "Get down! Get down!"

Hank didn't give the man much choice. Within a second, his knees kissed the rooftop, his cries of pain still ringing. Blake kicked the weapon out of the man's reach.

"Hank! *Loslaten*!"

Hank detached his teeth from the forearm and the shooter curled into a fetal position, his arm tucked into his midsection.

"Show your hands!"

Quick as a snake, the suspect brought a knife around and missed Chloe's cheek by a fraction. She launched herself backward as he sprang to his feet. The crack of a gun sounded behind her. Another cry from the man in front of her ripped through the air. Blood sprayed from the wound in his shoulder. His heels hit the edge of the roof.

"No!" Chloe cried. She lunged for him and her fingers grazed his foot as he disappeared over the side.

A hard hand on her belt was the only thing that kept her from losing her balance and going headfirst after him. Chloe heard the sickening thud as the shooter landed on the concrete below. Bystander screams reached her and her knees went weak.

She slid to the gravel. Hank hurried to her side.

"You okay?" Blake asked while Hank tried to get closer.

"Yes. Just a little shaky."

"Understandable."

She pressed her palms to her eyes for a moment. Hank settled his nose on her shoulder and she instantly took comfort from his furry presence. Drawing in a breath, she let it out slowly. "Nice shooting."

"Wasn't me."

"It was me."

Chloe looked up. The officer with the Kevlar vest and the dark hair looked vaguely familiar. Quinn something? She'd seen him a few times at some stings when Hank had been called in to do his thing.

He stepped closer. "Detective Quinn Holcombe. I saw you two heading this way and followed."

Other officers poured onto the gravel roof.

Chloe met the detective's eyes. "I'm glad you did. Thanks. I'm Chloe St. John. This is Deputy US Marshal Blake MacCallum."

Detective Holcombe waved to the others that everything was all right. "Any relation to Linc St. John?"

"I plead the fifth."

His eyes glinted for a moment before the brief flash of humor faded and grim intensity took its place. He walked to the edge and looked over.

"He's dead," she told him. She didn't need to see it, she'd heard it.

"Yep, he's definitely very dead," Detective Holcombe said. She caught the flash of grief before he covered it up, and her heart went out to him. She'd never shot anyone and prayed she never had to. Killing someone was a heavy burden. No matter that the shooter had brought it on himself.

"Anyone else hurt?" Blake asked, placing a hand on Chloe's shoulder.

Hank whined and nudged her. She scratched his ears reassuring him that she was fine.

"I don't know," the detective said. "Don't think so."

Chloe gathered her strength and lifted a hand to Blake. "Let's go find out." He grasped her fingers and she let him help her to her feet.

9

Blake, Chloe, Detective Holcombe, and Hank made their way back down the stairs to the lobby level, empty except for law enforcement. Blake looked for other victims. When he didn't spot any bodies or blood, he released a breath. Maybe no one else had fallen victim to the shooter's bullets. Except Jo. And her vest had probably saved her life. He headed to check on her, but stopped when Izzy hurried over to them. "Guess you found the shooter."

"Hank did," Chloe said.

"And Detective Holcombe shot him before he could kill Chloe," Blake said.

Izzy blanched and Blake wished he'd softened the news a bit. Twice in one day his words had gotten past the filter. He was going to have to work on that.

"Actually, Blake was the one who saved me from going off the roof," Chloe said.

Another flinch from Izzy. She held up her hand. "That's all I need to know. I'm glad you're okay. Don't tell Mom about any roof diving. She still hasn't recovered from my death-defying experiences. On another note," Izzy continued, "first responders are here, but they won't be any help to him. Do you know who he was?"

"I've never seen him before," Blake said.

Chloe shook her head. "I only got a brief look at his face before he went over. I don't recognize him either."

"I've got to check on Jo and Judge Worthington," Blake said. "Excuse me."

"She's in an ambulance," Izzy said.

Blake stopped. "And the judge?"

"He's secure and has two deputy marshals on him."

Okay, that was two things he could mark off his worry list. For now.

"Blake."

He turned to find Linc and his partner, Special Agent Travis Richfield, bearing down on them. "Good job," Linc said.

"Kudos go to Hank and Detective Holcombe here."

"Quinn," the detective said. "And I was hoping to take him alive, but he wasn't of the same mind."

"Yeah." No one was going to shed tears over the loss of the would-be killer. Linc turned to his sister. "Are you all right?"

"I'm fine."

"And Hank?" He scratched the animal's ears. Hank edged closer, encouraging him to continue.

"Happy with himself. He did his job too."

Linc nodded. "Travis and I are talking with other witnesses, but, as usual, stories are scattered and inconsistent. We'll focus on the consistencies and go from there." He eyed Blake. "As much as we can figure he somehow got his hands on a badge with his picture. Fake name, but the badge is real enough. He passed through security with no issues."

Chloe bit her lip. "This whole thing screams inside help."

Linc raised a brow. "Thanks, we've come to that conclusion as well."

Blake thought Chloe might stick her tongue out at her older brother, but being the professional she was, she refrained. He knew she wanted to, though.

"I've got to go do all of the shooting protocol paperwork and figure out what I'm going to do with myself for the next few days," Quinn said with a sigh. "Let me know if you need anything else."

"Will do," Blake said.

An officer, wearing the SLED logo on her vest, approached Linc. "Are you Special Agent in Charge Linc St. John?"

"I am."

"I'm SLED Special Agent Jessie Parrish."

SLED. South Carolina Law Enforcement Division. The two shook hands, then Linc introduced Blake and Chloe. "What can I do for you?" Linc asked.

"We've just gotten notice that the name on the badge the shooter used is legit. Matthew Neighbors is a guard here. But he doesn't look anything like the shooter." She passed her iPhone to Linc to take a look. Blake peered over his shoulder. Definitely not the shooter.

"So, where's this guy?" Linc asked.

"We're looking for him. He's not answering his phone, but his wife said he left for work this morning, just like every day."

"I've got a bad feeling about this," Chloe muttered.

Blake raised a brow and Linc frowned. "What do you mean?" Linc asked.

"Is there anything that belongs to this man that Hank could use?" Chloe asked.

"Why? You want Hank to track him? You think he's here in the building?" Blake said.

"Yes. Don't you?"

He sighed. "I'd say it's a distinct possibility. Which would mean our shooter came in through security with no weapon. Found the armed guard and took his weapon."

"And his uniform."

"But not his badge," Linc said. "Our shooter had that made long before he got here."

"This was a well-planned attack," Chloe said.

"But why, when they had Rachel?"

"Backup," Blake said. "And when she escaped, they decided to go with Plan B."

"All right," Linc said, "let me get someone who works here to show us where employees stash their stuff while on the job." He pulled his phone out and dialed a number.

Within a minute, a courthouse employee hurried forward. He shook hands as he introduced himself. "I'm Danny Frank with First Defense Security. My company is in charge of the courthouse security here. I'd apologize more if I thought it would make a difference, but it won't." His pale face and tight jaw said he wasn't happy at all with the incident. "Just tell me what I can do to help."

"Can you show us where employees would leave personal items and such while working?" Blake asked.

"Of course, follow me."

He led the way down the stairs to the basement and swiped his card across the pad. The lock clicked and he pushed the door open. Empty, the room echoed with their footsteps as they crossed the floor. Danny looked at his phone. "Says here, his locker is number 56."

"Combination?"

"No, he's got a padlock. Uses a key." He tapped the screen. When he looked up, he nodded to the far end of the room. "Over there. I've got someone bringing a tool to cut the lock off." He shook his head. "I don't understand this. I don't understand where we went wrong or where the gap was in security."

"There always seems to be a way around the tightest security," Blake murmured.

Chloe raised a brow but didn't comment. Hank shifted at her side, restless. She placed a hand on his head and he settled.

The door opened and an officer dressed in tactical gear entered. "Here you go." He hefted the bolt cutters. Blake took the device

111

and hooked the ends around one side of the lock. He squeezed and the hasp split apart.

Blake handed the tool back to Linc and opened the door. Matthew Neighbors faced him with the blank stare only the dead had. The black hole in his forehead told a lot of the story.

"Blake?"

He stepped back. "Guess we don't need Hank for this one."

10

Rachel took one more step, then sank to the log on the ground beside her. She'd been walking forever and was cold. Very cold. The sun tried to reach through the trees but wasn't having much success.

The old horse blanket around her shoulders helped, but the temperature had dropped with each passing hour, and now she sat shivering, the dark woods pressing in on her from all sides.

She had no idea how far she'd gone or even in which direction. Who knew there was this much wooded area thirty minutes outside of Columbia?

Think, Rach, think.

She'd followed a path. At least a rough one. But it *had* been a path. Surely it had to lead to *somewhere*.

"And you're not going to get anywhere sitting here like a bump on a log." She sighed. "Pun intended." She couldn't laugh at her misplaced wit. And she didn't dare cry because she'd never stop.

So she stood and continued her trek on the sort-of-maybe-path. Truthfully, it did look like someone had cleared it at some point, but it had grown back over from lack of use. Placing one foot after the other, she kept walking, praying for the end of the trees. However, they seemed to go on forever.

Was Blake looking for her? Was he worried about her? She shuffled, her heart heavy, grief mingling with the fear that had been her constant companion for the past week. He seemed to care, but she knew he didn't. She'd found the proof shortly after she'd moved in with him.

So, why the act? Why would he be so frantic on the phone? Why race to the hospital?

Or *was* it an act?

She scoffed. Of course it was. He'd turned down the opportunity for full custody when presented with it. So . . .

Rachel sighed. She was so confused. And hungry. So very hungry. She'd eaten the second protein bar a good hour ago. Thankfully, she'd found a small creek with flowing water and that quenched her thirst. She figured since it was moving, it wouldn't be stagnant and give her some kind of parasite. She hoped so anyway. Her stomach rumbled. She wanted a hamburger and fries and a shake.

A branch snapped behind her and she spun to see nothing.

She slipped off the trail and scrambled behind one of the large oaks that towered above her. Heart crashing in her chest, she held her breath, waiting. Listening.

Another crunch of dried wood. Then another. Whoever was out there wasn't even trying to be quiet. Rachel peered around the edge of the trunk and spotted the doe munching on green leaves.

Her breath whooshed out and she let her forehead fall to her upraised knees. Tears sprang to her eyes and she stuffed a fist into her mouth to keep the sobs from escaping. *God, why is this happening? Why do you hate me? What did I ever do to you?*

"'Even though I walk through the darkest valley, I will fear no evil, for you are with me; your rod and your staff, they comfort me.'" She whispered the verse aloud, wondering how she'd pulled it from the recesses of her memory. Probably all those times her mother had dropped her at some summer church camp. "'I will fear no evil.'" This time her voice rang stronger, but the words didn't penetrate.

Because she did fear evil. She feared it very much. She was terrified of the men who'd taken her and still held Lindsey and the others. She wanted to sink into the ground, pull the horse blanket over her head, and sob out her anger and fear.

But more than that, she wanted to see the men, the people doing this to girls like her, punished.

And that wasn't going to happen if she didn't get up and push on. Just like with swimming. Each time she pushed herself to go farther, dig deeper into the water with her strokes. Each time she succeeded, the rush was there. With swimming, she very rarely failed. The gold medals hanging in her bedroom testified to that.

But this was different. This was life or death. No lifeguard was standing by ready to jump in and save her. Nope. This one was on her.

Rachel stood . . .

. . . and walked.

One foot after the other.

Until, finally, she saw a break in the trees ahead. Heart in her throat, with renewed energy, she pressed forward, pushed through and came to a stunned halt.

The back of the barn she'd left earlier this morning loomed in front of her.

"No," she whispered. "No." How had she done that? How had she managed to walk in one big circle? It hit her then. The path had simply been skirting the edge of the property. Probably made by the previous owners who liked to walk in the woods, but didn't want to get lost or turned around.

Despair choked her.

A door slammed in the distance and voices reached her. She raced to the barn and found the back entrance.

She slipped inside and sat down in the warmest part she could find. Smoky Hope joined her, and with tears streaming down her chilled cheeks, Rachel curled under the blanket and closed her eyes.

C hloe scratched Hank's ears and stood back while the medical
examiner followed the paramedics rolling the poor security
guard's body from the employee room. The crime scene unit had
arrived and were doing their thing.

Even though the shooter was dead, they would cover the area
with a fine-tooth comb since they had to prove the guy was also
the killer of the guard and had been working alone. Chloe was
almost 100 percent sure of that fact, but wouldn't bet her career
on it. Neither would anyone else.

Security footage would help determine a lot of things once they
got a chance to take a look at it. She spotted Blake checking his
phone, then putting it away with a stony expression. No word on
Rachel, she assumed. Her heart went out to him. As devastated
as she had been at Penny's disappearance, she couldn't imagine
the emotions and pain going through him right now. And every
second of every day that Rachel remained out of reach, she remained in danger.

Blake caught her eye. "I'm going to go check on Jo."

"I'll go with you."

They made their way back up to the lobby of the courthouse.
As they got closer, Chloe could hear the strident voice of a young

woman coming from the door. "He's my father! Let me in. I have to check on him!"

"That's Paula," Blake said and picked up his pace.

Chloe rushed after him.

Blake reached Paula just as the cop she was shoving against looked ready to cuff her. No telling how long he'd been holding her back. The woman's blonde hair had probably started out in a stylish bun, but now strands hung down around the sides of her face and one piece trailed over her shoulder. She wore a two-piece gray suit with a pencil skirt and matching gray pumps.

"Paula?" Blake called.

She froze, her eyes widening, then locking on his. Chloe recognized intense relief when she saw it. "Blake! Tell them to let me in."

Blake stepped in and grasped her elbow. "I've got this," he said to the officer.

"You're welcome to her."

"Paula, come here, please," a deep male voice said.

A large man with emerald green eyes stood on the other side of the crime scene tape. Miles. He and Paula must have rushed over as soon as they heard about the shooting. And if the news vans were any indication, there'd been no time wasted in airing it. Chloe had yet to meet the man in person, but she recognized him from the family photos she'd studied when trying to familiarize herself with every facet of the investigation.

Paula hesitated, then stomped to her fiancé's side, arms crossed, lower lip pushed out like a petulant child.

Chloe followed Blake, Paula, and Miles outside. She'd gotten past the yellow crime scene line. Chloe frowned. She *should* be arrested. Then again, she was obviously frantic with worry about her father.

"Your dad's fine," Blake told Paula. "He's with two marshals and locked away in a safe place until everything calms down."

Paula stilled. "He's fine?"

"Yes."

"You're sure?" Miles demanded.

Blake flicked him a glance. "I'm positive. I was there. He wasn't hit."

Tears gathered in Paula's hazel eyes. "He was the target, wasn't he?"

"He was, but they didn't get him." Blake paused. "And the person who pulled the trigger is dead."

Paula's tears faded and she sniffed while she rummaged in her purse for a tissue. "The guy who took a nosedive off the roof?" She dabbed the moisture under her perfectly made-up eyes.

"That's the one."

She nodded. "Okay then. So, my dad's out of danger now? He can go back to living a normal life without people constantly invading his space?"

None of them took her words personally. It was extremely difficult to have to live with 24/7 supervision. "Unfortunately, I can't answer that question yet," Blake said. "My first guess is, no. I think this guy was just a hired hitman."

The woman shuddered. "I want to see my father."

"Let me find out where he is." He got on his phone. Chloe thought she heard him say Parker's name. When he hung up, he nodded. "He's in his office. Come on. Chloe and I can take you to him."

"I know the way."

He gave her a tight smile. "I know you do." Chloe raised a brow at the words he left unspoken. She may know the way, but she wasn't going alone. Blake belatedly introduced Chloe to the couple, then escorted them back through security, passing the cop Paula had tangled with earlier. He shot her a dark look but didn't say anything. Paula simply ignored him. He wasn't even on her radar. Chloe grimaced and tried not to hold the woman's attitude against her. Her father had come close to being killed. Chloe could extend a little grace.

The four of them walked through the lobby to the secure door that would lead them to the back of the courthouse. Blake swiped the key card and the door clicked open.

Paula hurried through, followed by Miles and Blake. Chloe and Hank pulled up the rear. Blake stepped ahead of Paula and led her to the judge's chambers. He rapped twice and identified himself, holding his badge up to the peep hole.

The door swung open and Paula pushed past the marshal, making a beeline for her father. She hugged him and Chloe held Hank's leash while she watched the reunion unfold. The judge still looked shell-shocked, but his arms came up and wrapped around his daughter.

When she pulled back, she touched his cheek. "Are you all right?"

"Yes, Paula." He blinked and shook his head. "I'm fine. I'm fine."

Paula planted her hands on her hips. "This time."

Judge Worthington sighed and closed his eyes. "Don't start. Not now."

Her fiancé had stepped up beside her and laid a hand on her arm. "Paula—"

She shrugged him off and glared at her father. "Fighting them is not worth your life!"

The shout echoed through the office.

All of the marshals found other things to do. They checked the windows, checked the doors, checked their phones. Even Miles backed up a few steps.

Chloe simply watched. Finally, she stepped forward. "You're talking about the bill you're pushing legislators to pass, aren't you? The one that cracks down on perpetrators of human trafficking."

Judge Worthington turned to her. "I'm working with House of Representatives member, Corrine Johnson. We wrote the bill and she introduced it. It's making its way through the steps and is at the stage where the House debates it and decides whether to send it on to the Senate. I've spoken to the Senate. They know it's coming. I'm slated to speak to the house—along with Corrine—next week."

"Has Mrs. Johnson had any threats against her?"

"Yes, as the marshals are aware. But we've agreed we're not backing down. We'll keep pushing until it becomes a law. We want the death penalty for those who are convicted of human trafficking. Do you know how much prison time an offender serves for enslaving a human being and selling her sometimes as often as twenty times a day?"

"Three years," Chloe said softly. "On average."

Her answer raised his brows—and slumped his shoulders. "Yes. Selling dope comes with a stiffer sentence than selling a human being. It's an outrage."

"And the shorter sentences mean victims are scared to come forward to testify," Chloe said.

"Or they've been brainwashed," Blake murmured.

"Exactly." Judge Worthington rubbed his hands together and crossed his arms. "So, the only way to make a difference is to change the law."

"And you have to be the one to do that?" Paula demanded.

"If not me, who?" he asked.

She stomped a foot and spun on her heel. Striding to the door, she tossed over her shoulder, "Then make sure your will is up to date if you continue down this path, because I'm afraid you're not going to live much longer." A tear trickled down her cheek and she swiped it away before stepping out of the chambers.

The slamming of the door echoed for long seconds after she was gone. Miles sighed. "I'm assuming there's an officer outside who'll stop her and hold her?"

"Yeah. She can't be loose in the building. It's a crime scene," Blake said.

"Then I'd better go rescue him and talk her into cooperating."

"That's a real good idea."

Chloe's buzzing phone jerked her from her stupor and she yanked it off the clip. Dispatch. "St. John here."

"You and Hank are needed. Are you free?"

"I can be. Where?" Chloe noted the address and typed it into the GPS app on her phone after she hung up. "Hank and I have got to go."

Blake nodded, his brow furrowed, eyes thoughtful. "Text me when you're finished. I've got an idea."

Curious, she nodded. "Will do." Chloe said her goodbyes and led Hank out of the chambers, down the hall, and out of the building.

Blake sat in the parking lot of A Taste of Yesterday restaurant and pressed the palms of his hands to his eyes. It was nearly 6:30 on this chilly Friday evening. Another day had passed with no sign of Rachel. How could she have just disappeared? Again. He slammed a fist against the steering wheel. Once. Twice. Three times. It didn't help.

Tears swept past his lashes and he pressed his thumb against his eyelids as memories of her toddler days blipped like an old movie through the front of his mind. Her tight hugs and cute lisp. The way she said, "I love you, Daddy," before planting a wet kiss on his nose. And then all of a sudden, she was calling him Blake. What was up with that? He wasn't Blake. He was Dad. Daddy.

Sobs threatened. With mammoth effort, he held them back. What was he doing? Big boys didn't cry. Men didn't show emotion or let the tears fall. His father had beaten that into him at a young age. Blake immediately snipped that train of thought off and focused on the building in front of him while he swiped at the tears on his cheeks. He found a napkin, blew his nose and cleared his throat.

Distraction would be good, food would be good. But he would only allow himself to be distracted for a short time. Then he would be searching once more.

Linc was on his way, as well as Chloe, Izzy, Brady, Ruthie, and Derek. All of the St. John siblings under one roof. It could be a bit overwhelming, but he was grateful for the short respite before he went back to searching for Rachel. His stomach had been growling at him all day, since he'd barely eaten anything and had consumed entirely too much coffee.

Too much caffeine. Too much emotion. Too much stress. At the rate he was going, he'd be gray and nursing an ulcer by this time next week.

Chloe's SUV pulled into the spot beside him and she climbed out. He couldn't help noticing once again that she was extremely pretty.

And he was *extremely* annoyed with himself for being drawn to her. She was Linc's sister, for crying out loud.

But she'd been on his attraction radar from the moment he'd seen her at the hospital. He'd just been so focused on finding Rachel, he hadn't addressed it.

And besides, why would she be interested in a guy with as much baggage as he had attached to him? No, it wouldn't be fair to ask someone else to hook on to that baggage. Once he got himself free of it, cleaned up, so to speak, then maybe he'd be ready to find someone to settle down with. Give marriage another try. Maybe. Not necessarily with Chloe—he wasn't that far gone to start thinking along those lines—but marriage in general.

Then again, after his ex-wife's betrayal, trusting someone else to that extent—to actually be willing to marry again—would take a lot of . . . something.

Maybe prayer.

Chloe slammed the door and the frown on her face said something was on her mind and it wasn't good.

He rolled down the passenger window. Cold air rushed in, but he ignored it. At least it wasn't raining. "What's wrong?"

Startled, she turned. "Blake. You scared me."

"Sorry." He leaned over and opened the passenger door and she slid in. He rolled the window up and cranked the heat up a notch. "What's on your mind?"

"Nothing. Just thinking." She held her hands against the nearest vent. "It's cold."

"Thinking about the weather put that frown on your face?"

She shot him a small, tight smile. "No, not really." Her lips turned down again. "I was thinking about Penny. Is she okay? Is she alive? Does she wish she was—" Her mouth snapped shut and she glanced at him. "Never mind."

"Does she wish she was dead?"

"Yeah."

"It's okay, Chloe. I'm scared to death for Rachel, and I can't say I haven't had those same questions when it comes to her."

"I'm sorry," she whispered. "I can't believe this whole human trafficking thing has touched both of us in such a personal way. I mean, as a cop, yeah, of course, I expect to come across it. But with Penny . . ." A sigh slipped out.

He sighed. "I don't think Rachel's started out as a human trafficking thing. They took her to get to me."

"So you'd kill the judge?"

"Yeah."

She pulled the mirror down and scrubbed at the eyeliner below her left eye. Or what was left of it. "They say it's all-day makeup, but I haven't found that to be the case. I should sue them for false advertising."

"How long has your day been?"

She scrunched up her nose at him. "Going on sixteen hours, I think."

"I doubt you'd win the lawsuit."

"Yeah. Probably not." She shut the mirror. "You really think if the judge was dead, the legislation would stop? That the bill would be dismissed?"

"Maybe. Between him and the congresswoman, they're generating new support for it every day."

"True." She bit her lip. "So, what was your idea? What's up?"

He shot her a blank look.

"At the courthouse, you said to text you when I was done. Well, I just got done and am asking in person."

"Oh. I think we should put dogs on the judge."

"K-9 teams?"

"Yeah. States are using K-9s in courthouses to detect things that shouldn't be there. Why not use them for protection too?"

"I don't think the lieutenant would go for that idea. That's not what the teams are for. US Marshals have their own teams. Why not call them in for this?"

"I've thought about that. But this situation. It's . . . different."

She raised a brow. "Different how? I mean, I know it's personal with Rachel's situation and all, but . . ."

He shook his head. "No, I mean . . ." He sighed. "I don't know what I mean. I can't explain it. Something just feels . . . off."

"A lot of things feel off," she muttered. "But all you can do is ask. I'm happy to be a part of it if the lieutenant says yes."

"Good. And if he wants to bring in the US Marshal K-9s, I'm cool with that too. The more the better, but I want you in the house with us. You know this case—and Hank is trained to protect as well as detect."

"Yep, and to trail. He's a triple-trained animal. All of the shepherds are because they excel at it."

He nodded.

She paused. "Can I ask you a personal question?"

"Sure."

"What happened with you and Aimee?"

He winced. "Ah, that's kind of a long story."

"I'm not trying to be nosey, just trying to understand Rachel."

"You and me both." He fought with the memories of his dead wife, trying to figure out which ones to pull forward and vocalize. While he was searching for words, Linc's blue truck pulled into the parking lot. Soon, more vehicles followed. "Let's save that for another time. Ready?" he asked.

"Yep. Let's go. I'm hungry."

Grateful she followed his lead on the change of subject, he smirked. "If I remember correctly, you're always hungry."

She rolled her eyes at him and he grinned. Then felt the slam of guilt. How could he smile when Rachel was still out there? How could he eat when he didn't know if she had eaten? How could he keep going?

Because he had to.

He needed to be at the top of his game in order to do everything possible to bring Rachel home.

Once inside, out of the cold, he shed his jacket and helped Chloe off with hers. They hung them on the rack of pegs just inside the door and waited for a waitress dressed in 1800s attire to approach. "How many?"

"Seven," Blake said.

"Blake? That you?"

He turned to see Daniel Matthews, owner of the restaurant, walking toward him. He held out a hand and Blake shook it. "Hey, man, how are you doing?"

"Just fine. Haven't seen you in here in a while. You getting your home cooking somewhere else?"

"What? You really think I'd betray you like that?" Blake had to force the smile. Even joking with a friend seemed wrong. "Work is pretty crazy right now."

Daniel frowned. "Everything all right?"

"Nope, but I'll have to fill you in later." The rest of the St. John siblings were behind him, and while he trusted Daniel, he didn't want to get into everything right here. The man had a restaurant to run. Blake forced a smile. "We'll catch up later, though."

"Sure thing. Where's Rachel? Riley's been asking about her. Said she hasn't seen her in a while."

Riley was the man's nineteen-year-old niece. He'd taken her in when his brother and sister-in-law were killed while on the mission field. "Rachel's been busy. Tell Riley I'll have her call as soon as she can."

"Sounds good." Daniel nodded to the young woman who'd been standing off to the side. "Take them to the back room where they'll have a bit of a quieter atmosphere."

"Of course, Mr. Matthews." She smiled at Blake. "This way."

He knew the way but fell in behind her. Chloe stayed beside him and the scent of her strawberry shampoo wafted toward him. He drew in a deep breath and tried to ignore the fact that he wished they were headed for a table for two instead of seven.

Once they were all seated, Blake was gratified to find Chloe next to him, with Hank at her feet. Linc sat on his other side, scrolling through something on his phone.

Blake leaned over to Chloe. "Thanks for letting me join in."

She raised a brow at him. "Of course."

"Why haven't we seen each other much since I've been back?"

The raised brow stayed up. "What do you mean?"

He shook his head. "I'm not even sure. I guess I've just seen so much of Linc. I just wondered why I hadn't run into you."

She shrugged. "Linc and I don't really run in the same circles."

"I suppose."

"Hey, Chloe."

She looked past him to the end of the table where Ruthie sat. "What?"

"Guess who was in my OR today?"

"Are you about to break some HIPAA law by telling me?"

"Not at all. He told me to tell you hi."

"Who?"

"Jordan Crestwood."

Blake paid close attention to the fact that Chloe's face went blank. "Oh, is that right? Well, how's ol' Jordan doing these days?" Her voice was chilly enough to send goose bumps pebbling his arms.

"Not happy to hear from him?" Blake murmured so only she could hear.

"Not in the least," she muttered back. To her sister, she smiled. "What rock did he crawl out from under this time?"

Ruthie blinked. "Ah . . . I don't know. I thought you two were an item."

"Not for a while now," Derek answered for her then thumped the table with a fist. "Are we going to order or what? I'm starving."

Everyone turned their attention to the waitress, who stood poised with pen over pad. All except Blake. He reached for Chloe's hand. "You all right?"

She drew in a deep breath and gave him a short nod. "Fine." Once she gave her order, she took a sip of water and he tried to read her expression. "Is Ruthie talking about the Jordan Crestwood on the SWAT team?"

"Yep."

"Derek's friend?"

"Ex-friend, I think, but yep."

"And you don't want to talk about this, do you?"

"Nope."

He paused. "Do I need to hurt him?"

Her laughter turned heads and drew speculative looks from the others at the table. But his comment had the desired effect. Her countenance lightened and the gentle squeeze of her fingers on his eased the pain in his own heart a fraction.

"Nah. He's probably going to self-destruct, thanks to his mega

127

ego. You might want to make sure to stay out of range of the explosion, though. It'll be massive with the aftershocks."

"Isn't that an earthquake that has aftershocks?"

"Same idea."

"Ah. Gotcha."

The fabulous food and good-natured teasing that went on between the siblings helped as well. It didn't take him long to down his burger and fries. When he finished, he stared at his plate, wondering what Rachel had eaten. *If* she'd eaten. If she was cold. If she was—

Any semblance of peace fled and his heart throbbed a painful beat as he shut off the direction of his thoughts.

Linc's phone rang. He spoke into it, then leaned over to nudge Blake. "That was Monique Pascal from hospital security. We might have some more information on Rachel."

"What?"

"Monique wants us to come in and look at some more footage she managed to find."

Blake tossed down his napkin and rose. "Let's go."

12

Chloe hurried after the men. She'd overheard the conversation between Linc and Blake and she wasn't going to miss this one. "I want to go."

"Well, come on," Linc said.

In her vehicle, with Hank in his area, she pulled out of the parking lot. The drive to the hospital only took her about fifteen minutes, then she was following the two men inside while Hank stayed in the vehicle.

The tension radiated from Blake, and Chloe found herself wishing she could do something to ease it. But she had a feeling that only finding Rachel would do that.

They found the security office and Monique was waiting for them. Her dark brown eyes glinted when they walked in. "Glad you could make it on such short notice."

"Thanks for calling," Linc said.

"This won't take long." She motioned them toward the display of monitors and clicked on the mouse. A video Chloe thought they'd seen before jumped onto the nearest screen. Monique pointed. "This was the side view of the truck. I really wanted to see what was inside the back of the vehicle, so I started going through each and every camera, trying to find the right angle. I think I did." She clicked through another series and finally got a shot of the back of the Suburban. The window was down, as they'd noted before. "I just thought it was really weird that he'd have the window down in November. It's not freezing during the day, but still . . ."

"So, what did you find?" Blake asked.

"Here. In the back. What does that look like to you?" Monique zoomed closer.

Chloe squinted. "Looks like some kind of rack or something. Like a super large dish rack?"

"Good description. And in that super large dish rack are paintings."

Blake blinked. "Paintings? As in pictures? And stuff?"

"Yes," Monique said. "My guess is the oil still had a strong odor, so he left the window down."

"And Rachel just helped herself," Blake muttered.

"Rachel mentioned the girls were going to be sold at an auction," Chloe said. "Let's see if there are any auctions scheduled soon."

"Rachel wasn't talking about an art auction."

"Maybe not, but wouldn't hurt to check, would it? The fact is, she heard the word 'auction.' The guy she hitched a ride with had oil paintings in the back of his vehicle. I'm thinking there could be a connection."

"I agree," Blake said.

"So, we need to check art supply stores around here too," Chloe said. "Track down the driver of the Suburban. If he paints, he's got to purchase his supplies from somewhere."

Linc nodded. "I'd say that's our best bet." He blew out a breath. "You have a picture of this guy, Monique?"

A few more clicks on the keyboard and she brought up a close-up of the young man who looked to be in his late twenties or midthirties. "This is the best one I could get. It's not bad if I do say so myself."

"I think that'll work just fine."

Monique moved back to her keyboard. "All right," she said and looked at Linc. "I have your number so I'm going to send this picture to you. Feel free to share it with whoever you need to."

"Thanks."

Within seconds, the three of them had the man's picture on their devices. "Anyone want to try again with the facial recognition software?" Chloe asked.

Linc shot her a tight smile. "I'm already on it." He tapped the screen. "The bureau's resources are faster."

Blake snorted and Chloe rolled her eyes. "Whatever."

"As long as it gets results, I don't care which agency does it," Blake said.

Linc tucked his phone into its clip and stood. "Thanks, Monique."

"Hold on, not so fast. I've got one more thing."

Linc raised a brow and settled back into his chair. "What's that?"

"In finding that segment, I also found this one." She clicked a few keys and the footage rolled.

Their man had just come out of the stairwell and walked toward a car that had stopped. "What's he doing?"

"They talk for forty-five seconds, then the driver leaves. I figured you might want the license plate on that nice Mercedes S550."

"Yes," Blake said. "That would be awesome."

She tapped another few keys and everyone's phone buzzed. Chloe looked at hers. "Well, well. Linc, guess you'd better send that off as well."

Linc worked the screen. "Done." He tucked his phone back into the clip. "Those are some seriously good investigative skills you've got there. Thank you."

Monique batted her long lashes at him. "Any time."

Chloe raised a brow when her brother's cheeks turned an interesting shade of pink. She locked her gaze on his and he scowled at her, daring her to say one word. She bit her lip on a smile, but filed away the information for use later. When she needed it. She so rarely had anything on Linc that she could use as leverage for . . . whatever. But she knew *he* knew this would come up again.

And probably soon.

When she turned her attention back to Blake, all thoughts of teasing her brother dissipated. The mixture of raw grief and fear in his eyes sent shafts of compassion through her. Her heart actually hurt for him and for Rachel. He was studying the picture of the man who owned the Suburban. "We need to find this guy like yesterday."

"Agreed," Chloe said, "but this is going to take some manpower."

"We'll round up volunteers to hit the pavement with this guy's face," Linc said. "Surely someone's seen him. Even if Rachel just hitched a ride with him due to the convenience of the open window, I want to know where he went."

"Exactly. The more stops he made, the more chance that someone spotted Rachel."

Linc's phone rang. "St. John." He listened, his eyes snagging hers and Blake's. "I see. Thanks for the update. Email me everything." He hung up. "Fingerprints came back on our courthouse shooter. Noah Hampton. He's in the system. In fact, he was just released from prison about four weeks ago."

"Let me guess," Chloe said. "The judge put him away."

"Excellent guess. Ten years behind bars for being in a bar fight that resulted in a broken bottle hitting a young man in the face. He lost an eye."

"Ouch," Blake said. "That's serious, but ten years?"

"Maximum sentence and Judge Worthington gave it to him."

"That could make someone mad. Ten years' worth of rage and planning to kill the man who put him in prison?"

"It's possible," Linc said.

"Then it could really be over?" Chloe said.

Linc shook his head. "Not until we have hard evidence that he's the one who sent the threatening letters and kidnapped Rachel."

"Well, he sure fired the bullets."

"That he did. We've got a team over at his place. He was staying at his mother's house. She's in a retirement home now, but the house was sitting empty. When Hampton was released, that's where he went. We're checking to see who he's had contact with since his release."

Chloe rubbed her eyes and fought off the weariness that pressed in on her. "Okay, let us know what you find. If anything. And if you get a name on the Suburban driver." She tapped her phone that held the mystery man's picture. "In the meantime, Blake and I are going to get to work as soon as businesses open in the morning."

"Let me go!"

Rachel jerked fully awake at the shout. She pushed the blanket off and hurried to look out the cracked door. Even though it let in the cold air, keeping it shut didn't make it much warmer in the barn. And this way she could hear better when something was going on outside.

"I said let me go!" The scream that followed was high-pitched and ear-shattering. Rachel flinched.

"Shut her up," a harsh voice said.

"You heard him," Carson said. "Shut up."

A twin scream to the first one ripped through the night air. A sharp smack sounded and the pained cry that followed made Rachel wince again.

Then silence.

Finally, the men attached to the voices came into view, thanks to the motion light that came on. One of them had a young teen tossed over his left shoulder. Probably the one who'd been uncooperative. She didn't recognize him or the girl, but she saw Carson come

133

around from behind them, a key ring jangling in his fist. At the side of the house, he stopped, then bent over at the waist.

Rachel's breath caught when she realized what he was doing.

And frowned. That's not where the girls were kept. What was he doing with her?

Taking deep breaths in order to slow her pounding heart, she continued to watch. He opened the double doors that were attached to the cellar-like opening, and the man carrying the girl disappeared down the steps.

Within a minute or two, he returned empty-handed and Carson shut the doors, then bolted them with a padlock.

"Leave her down there for a day or so and she'll break," the man said.

"Wish we could just drug 'em," Carson grumbled.

"Yeah, well, we can't. Not these girls. Not with these clients. Right now, the money's better than ever and that's the way I want to keep it." He paused. "And if you ever hit one again, I'll kill you."

"Like you killed Manny?"

"He was a liability. It was time for him to go."

Carson sighed. "You said to shut her up."

"Exactly. Didn't say to mark her up, did I?"

A slight pause. "No. You didn't. Sorry."

"This is your only pass. Don't screw it up again."

"Got it."

"Good. Now we've got a missing one to find. Let's get busy."

The two men rounded the side of the house and went inside.

Rachel let out a shallow breath and swallowed hard. She had to do something. They'd killed Manny. Not that she was upset about his death, but . . . she was. It hit home that these guys were serious. They didn't mess around and she didn't want to fall back into their hands.

And she had to find a way to get the other girls away from them. She needed a plan.

A better one than what she'd come up with just before she'd drifted off to sleep.

But as long and as hard as she thought, she couldn't figure out anything else.

So . . . plan A it would be. Go down the driveway, hit the road and follow it until she came to a store or a gas station that had a phone and call 911.

But first, she needed food. She stayed to such a strict diet that she didn't usually have issues with low blood sugar, but the beginning symptoms were there. Lightheaded and nauseous, heart palpitations, sleepiness. She drew in a deep breath, then blew it out. She pulled the pod off. No sense in pumping more insulin in if she wasn't eating.

Food. She had to find some. Now. Passing out wasn't an option, but her body wouldn't give her any choice if she didn't do something about it.

Keeping the horse blanket wrapped around her, she eased the door open and stepped into the wide-open-anyone-looking-toward-the-barn-would-see-her space. She shut the door with as little noise as possible and darted toward the driveway. Staying far enough away from the house so that she didn't trigger the light was extremely important.

With a pounding heart, she hurried as fast as she could without making any noise until she could run parallel to the drive. Once she reached the end, she was out of sight and surrounded by trees. Her absolute terror at being discovered faded slightly. Now, which way? Right or left?

She remembered turning right into the driveway so she decided to go the way they'd come.

Gripping the horse blanket tight, she started walking. If she saw a car, she'd have to find a way to hide. In the dark, it wouldn't be that hard. She could just drop to the ground. The wet, cold ground. But until she was far enough away from the house, she couldn't take the chance that a passing car might be someone involved with the rest of the people at that house of horrors.

Streetlights were few and far between, but they did pop up occasionally, causing her to have to walk farther from the road to avoid being cast in the light. Fortunately, trees lined both sides of the two-lane road, offering her plenty of places to duck into.

And each time a car passed, she did.

The passing cars were also few and far between. Scant enough that it made her nervous about flagging one for help. She knew not every one of the passing cars held someone who would hurt her, but she simply couldn't take the chance that the one who stopped would be the *wrong* one.

"Just keep walking," she whispered. Her stomach cramped and her throat felt dry. At the barn, she'd been able to use the water hose connected to it, but out here . . .

A car approached, the headlights sweeping across her before she could duck.

She dove into the protection of the trees as the vehicle slowed, then pulled to a stop. "Hey, anyone out there?"

Her stomach clenched. She couldn't be positive, but he sure sounded like one of the men from the cage room. Maybe. Or maybe she was just so scared that every voice she heard would sound like one of them.

Heart pounding, she closed her eyes. This was why she hadn't flagged down any passing cars. This was why the only person she would trust to help her was Blake. He might not want her, but he'd never do anything to put her in danger. And he would help. Surely he would.

Soon the man climbed back into the car and roared off down the road. Rachel let out a slow breath. She could do this. She would do this. Maybe if she rescued the girls, her father would love her. Just maybe.

Only one way to find out.

Pressing on, fighting the nausea and the desperate need for food, she walked, then stumbled. Gritting her teeth, she kept going. Passing out was not an option.

Five steps later, a light caught her attention. A house set back off the road. She knew she had to chance it—and maybe they had a phone.

Once she reached the front door, she noticed one car in the driveway, but other than the porch light, the rest of the house was dark. With a shaky finger, she pressed the doorbell then ran and hid behind the bushes.

She waited.

No one came. No dog barked.

Nothing.

Rachel made her way back up to the front door and rang the bell again. Then hurried to hide once more.

Again, no one came to the door.

"Okay, you can do this. Everyone leaves out a spare key. Just find it."

She made her way to the back door and tried the knob.

And found it unlocked. "Or they just don't bother to lock up out here in the middle of nowhere."

She gave a silent laugh and pushed the door open. Stepping inside, she stayed as silent as possible while the darkness pressed in on her.

Once her eyes adjusted, she moved into the kitchen and stopped when she found a bunch of bananas. She pulled two off and shoved them into her back pocket. She removed a third and ate it. A bowl of M&Ms sat on the counter and she stuffed three handfuls into her front pocket.

It might not be a good idea to open the refrigerator. Would someone be able to see the light from the road? Probably not, but why chance it?

Instead, she opened the pantry and found it a bit bare, but a jar of peanut butter and a package of crackers stared at her from the eye-level shelf.

"Marge, that you?"

Rachel froze, her breath caught in her throat as the light flicked on in the hallway and footsteps headed her way.

"When'd you get home? I didn't hear the car pull up."

Rachel grabbed the peanut butter and crackers and darted for the door.

13

At 9:00 a.m., Blake met Chloe and Hank outside the first place on the list they'd put together last night. She handed him a cup of coffee and he took a sip. Black, just like he liked it. "Thanks."

"Welcome. Did you sleep?"

"Nope. You?"

"Not much. A little."

He took another swig, ignoring the burn as it went down. He'd already gulped one cup before he left the house. After this one, he might consider himself appropriately caffeinated to work. "Did Linc call you this morning?"

"He did."

"So, you and Hank are officially Deputy US Marshals. Welcome to protection duty."

"Thanks. I suppose he told you that Hank and I were assigned to be with you and JoAnn. Stacy and her K-9, Max, are with Parker and Justin."

"Yes. I think the dogs are going to make a huge difference." He took another gulp of the coffee and then blew out a breath. "They tracked down the driver of the Mercedes. Linc called to tell me that too."

139

"No kidding? Did they talk to him?"

"Yes. His name is Gerald Atkinson. Said he was just asking our guy in the garage for directions. He'd never seen him before."

"Linc believed him?"

"No reason not to."

"What did his background check say?"

He smiled. "Don't miss a trick, do you?" She raised a brow and Blake said, "He checked out clean. Worked an IT gig for ten years before he jumped ship and started his own software company. His net worth is staggering, but there's nothing about him that sets off any need-to-investigate alarms."

She frowned. "Great."

"Yeah. Unfortunately. So . . . are you ready to do this?"

"Ready when you are."

Together, they walked into the shop that had just opened ten minutes earlier and Blake pulled his picture out of his pocket. Five minutes later, they walked back out with a negative on anyone recognizing the man in the picture. "How's Jo?" she asked.

"Doing okay. I talked to her this morning. She's got a cracked rib and some real sore muscles, but she's going to be okay. Better than taking a bullet in the flesh."

"Absolutely."

A long hour later, Blake pulled the picture of their "art man" out of his pocket. "How many times have we shown this picture to someone? Five hundred?"

"Probably only ten or twelve times."

"Right." But with each negative reaction to the photo, his hopes dropped lower and lower. "This is ridiculous."

"*This* is good old-fashioned police work, my friend."

He grimaced. "I know. I spent my time walking a beat for a couple of years before transferring to the marshals."

"You did? I didn't know that."

"Yep. Why? You respect me more now?"

Chloe stopped, looked him in the eye. "I have tons of respect for you, Blake. For a lot of reasons."

He lifted a hand and brushed a few stray hairs from her eyes. What did that mean? He almost asked, but needed to focus. Clearing his throat, he nodded. "Thanks."

"So, what's next?"

"Anyone who'll say yes, that they recognize this guy. I'm tired of nos."

"I understand." She reached over and squeezed his hand. He couldn't tell her how much her support meant to him.

"Well, I don't. He had to get his supplies from somewhere."

"Could have ordered them online and had them shipped."

He grunted. "True."

Chloe had decided they needed to question not only high-end art shops, but any place that looked like it might carry a painting, oils, or a drawing pencil.

He glanced at the list. "A museum? Really?"

"You don't like museums?"

"I mean, sure, they're fine. I'm just not into it like some people, I guess."

She rolled her eyes at him. "Well, if someone is into art, they're into museums. And besides, there's an art gallery in the back."

True. "Fine, let's check it out."

"10:15. It just opened."

"Awesome. We'll beat the rush."

He pulled open the door and let her precede him. Blake didn't like doing it, but he'd asked for a personal day. Chloe already had the day off and had agreed to spend it with him pounding the streets to see if they could ferret out at least one lead that would help them find Rachel.

Or a human trafficker or two.

Chloe plucked the picture from his fingers and walked up to the information desk with Hank padding along next to her. "Hi,

I'm Officer Chloe St. John. We're looking for a guy who may have some information on a case we're investigating. Do you know him?" She slid the photo in front of the well-dressed young man who was probably in his midthirties. He wore black pants with a white shirt and had the cuffs rolled to just above his wrists.

He glanced at the picture and lifted a brow. "It's not a very good likeness, but it could be Ethan."

Blake actually jerked, he was so surprised to hear the man say something besides "I've never seen him before." He cleared his throat. "Ethan? Does he have a last name?"

"Of course. Ethan Wright. If it's him," he squinted, "and I think it is. We have a rather large gallery in the back and he's one of our bestselling artists."

"Great," Chloe said. "Do you know where we can find him? Do you have his contact information?"

"I can't give that out. You'll have to talk to the gallery director. He's often in touch with Ethan, though."

"That'll be fine. Where can I find him?"

"Let me call him for you."

He picked up the phone and relayed the message. While they waited, Chloe wandered over to the display showing Ethan Wright's work. Boats on the water. The beach at sunset. A couple watching the sunrise while the waves washed over their feet. She had to admit, his paintings were gorgeous. "They're so lifelike. Almost like if I reach out and touch the water, my hand will get wet."

"That's why his work is selling so well."

She turned to see a man in his midsixties walking toward them, hand outstretched. When he smiled, he reminded Chloe of Bruce, the shark in the Disney movie, with his pearly whites and gleaming eyes. A predator all the way. "Neal," he said, "could you please help the delivery guys unload in the back? They're waiting."

Neal rolled his eyes. "Mr. Barlow would never have me do such a mundane task."

"Well, Mr. Barlow isn't here, is he?"

"No, he isn't. More's the pity," he muttered. But he rose and opened a drawer. Keys in hand, he disappeared down the hall, his steps quick and sure, yet silent on the tile floor.

"Sorry about that," the older man said. "I've been here for eight months, you would think I would have won over the staff by now. Unfortunately, Neal is pretty much my staff and I suppose he's still grieving poor Mr. Barlow's death."

"His death?"

"Car accident. Now, I'm Bryce Fleming, how can I help you?" He turned on a wide, toothy smile.

Chloe choked, then went into a coughing spasm. Blake slapped her on the back. "Chloe? You okay?"

"Yeah, yeah, sorry. I just swallowed wrong." She couldn't help the strangled sound to her words, but *Bryce*? One letter away from Bruce? She swallowed another giggle. She was either losing it or punchy from lack of sleep. Probably both. She needed to get it together.

Blake raised a brow at her before turning back to the director. "We need to find Ethan Wright. Do you know how we can get in touch with him?"

"Oh yes, Ethan. An amazing young man. From teacher to one of our bestselling local artists. While he's not yet well-known outside of our gallery or on a national level, I guarantee he soon will be."

"His work is going to be featured in this auction?" Blake asked. He pointed to the flyer taped to the welcome desk.

"Yes indeed."

"Good for him. Could you tell us how to find him?"

The man sighed and clasped his hands in front of his chest. "Alas, I wish I could help you, but unless I have permission to give out the contact information of our artists, I simply can't do it. I would never violate the trust that's been placed in me. I do hope you understand."

"And you do understand that we're cops, right?" Blake said. "We're not the general public or a fan who wishes to meet his favorite artist."

"Of course, of course." He frowned and his forehead creased in distress. "But it's just our policy. No matter who's asking."

"I guess I can always ask with a warrant." Blake's scowl would probably give most people nightmares. Mr. Fleming didn't even blink.

"By all means," he said, "please get the warrant if you feel it's necessary."

Chloe placed a hand on Blake's arm to hold him back. "That's fine. We certainly wouldn't want you to betray anyone's trust and we won't need the warrant. We have his name and probably won't have any trouble finding him. It's kind of what we do. Thank you for coming out to speak with us."

"Absolutely." His smile actually warmed a little.

Chloe dug a card out of her pocket. "But since you know how to contact him, do you mind passing a message on to him?"

"I'd be happy to." He took her proffered card and slid it into his front shirt pocket.

"Just let him know we have a couple of questions for him. He's not in any trouble, okay? Can you please make that clear?"

"Of course. You should expect to hear from him soon."

"Wonderful. Thank you." After he shook their hands, he turned on his super-shiny shoes and strode back down the hall where Chloe assumed his office was.

"What was that all about?" Blake hissed. "We need that contact information."

She gripped his arm and Hank's leash and led both of them out the door, stopping only to give the young man, Neal—who'd apparently finished his mundane task—a cheeky wave. Once outside, Chloe dropped Blake's arm, trying not to miss the feel of his bicep beneath her palm. "Chloe? Hello?"

"Oh." She blinked and flushed. What was he talking about? Oh yeah.

"Weren't you listening? We have Ethan's name. We don't need to fight *Bruce* to get the rest of the info on the guy. We'll just have Linc run him through the system."

"David, our tech guy, could do it just as easily, but I'm pretty sure he's still going through the footage from traffic cams trying to pick up the route of the semi that had the girls in them."

"I'll call Linc. Why don't you give David a call and see where he is on that?"

"Good idea."

Blake got on his phone while she dialed David's number. He answered on the fourth ring, just as she thought she was going to have to leave a message. "David here."

"Hey, it's Chloe. Have you managed to track down the route of the truck yet?"

"No," he sighed. "I've just decided that's pretty much a wash. I even consulted with Linc's tech girl FBI buddy, Annie, who's in agreement. She's incredibly smart, by the way."

"Smarter than you?"

He laughed. "Not likely, but that remains to be seen. Anyway, we caught up with the eighteen-wheeler on I-26 heading east where it crossed Broad River Road. A couple of the cameras before that were out, so we're not sure where it came from to enter the highway."

"Okay, thanks. At least that tells us they're coming from outside the city."

"Yeah, in other words, it's not much."

She sighed. "Right. Let me know if you get anything else."

"Will do."

She hung up and passed the information on to Blake, who shook his head. "Linc's having Annie run Ethan. Come on, we've got the task force meeting. We'll fill them in on this Ethan Wright character and see if we can get some answers."

Rachel stomped her feet, impatient with the cold and the slow passing of time. Wasn't anyone going to come open the store?

She had no idea how far she'd walked last night. But she'd counted six cars that had passed her before she'd come across the small gas station–slash–general store. It had felt like forever, but had probably only been about five or six miles. She'd run that far before during training. And she wouldn't think twice about *swimming* a couple of miles. But walking in the dark, the cold, and the sometimes drizzle had been an excruciating experience.

The relief that had poured through her at the sight of the place had fizzled quickly when she'd realized it was closed. But the sign said it was supposed to open at eleven o'clock this morning.

She had no idea what time it was, but surely it had to be getting close to eleven, didn't it? Last night, the walking and the horse blanket had kept her pretty warm, but once she stopped, she'd quickly cooled. Shivering, desperate for her bedroom and snuggly down comforter, she'd had no choice except to take shelter in an unlocked storage building behind a small farmhouse. She'd huddled under the horse blanket and slept deeply, waking shortly with the sun already high in the sky. She considered continuing her march, but the road seemed to go on forever with no other stopping place in sight. Her captors had chosen well for their little house of horrors. Out in the middle of practically nowhere, she had no idea where she was. Thirty minutes from Columbia. That was all she knew.

And just past the store, the area opened up with pastures and farmland. If she were to keep walking, she'd be exposed for who knew how long? From what she'd figured while listening from her spot in the cage, Carson and his cohorts traveled this road almost every day.

No, she was right to stop and wait for the store to open. The only way not to be caught was not to be found.

One good thing, in her tour around the building, looking for a way in, she'd found a patch of wild blackberries and a garden growing in the back. Blackberries in November. She couldn't believe it, but supposed it had something to do with the unseasonably warm fall that had only turned cooler in the last week. Frankly, she didn't care what had caused them to grow, she was just glad to have them.

She'd eaten her fill and decided blackberries had never tasted so sweet or so good. She'd even scarfed down two carrots, not caring she couldn't get all the dirt off. She'd heard of fall carrots, but had never had a fresh one, straight from the ground. They'd been surprisingly good. One thing was for sure, she'd never take food for granted again. Or complain about the things she shouldn't eat because of her diabetes.

To top off her meal, she'd found a water hose that worked. Of course, the owner of the garden would have one. Not that he'd needed it over the last couple of weeks with all of the rain. She was surprised the garden hadn't been washed away, but grateful for small things. Now that her thirst was slaked and her belly full, she was starting to feel better and was ready to find a phone.

At the tail end of that thought, she heard a car turn into the parking lot. Rachel jumped to her feet and raced to the side of the building so she could have a good look at whoever had just arrived. A silver Ford Escape parked to the side and a woman in her early fifties climbed out of the vehicle. As if on cue, two more cars pulled up.

Good. That was good. They couldn't *all* be working for Carson and whoever else was involved with the operation.

Rachel waited, heart pounding. She desperately wanted to hear Blake's voice. Wanted him to come and rescue her. But would he? She didn't deserve his concern or even his love since she'd done nothing but be a total brat to him. But right now, she'd give anything to feel his arms wrapped around her with promises to make everything right.

A low grunt escaped her. Okay, she'd even take a chilly "I'll be there in a few minutes," if that was all he was willing to give. Then again, she might not be giving him enough credit. After all, he'd sounded frantic on the phone. And he'd said he'd drop everything to come to the hospital. For some reason, the doubts left her.

He'd come here. He'd find her. And he wouldn't hold her bratty attitude against her.

Whatever phone she used, he'd have to be able to track it.

Voices disappeared into the store. Rachel drew in a deep breath and let it out slowly. Excitement and desperation slugged it out in her midsection, battling the caution and fear that kept her from moving. She finally let the old horse blanket fall to the ground and shivered when a gust of wind whipped against her. Clasping her arms against her belly, she walked to the heavy glass door and pulled it open.

Stale smoke and fresh coffee greeted her. The coffee would be nice as it would warm her insides, but for now, she was grateful for the heated store.

So very grateful.

For a moment, she simply stood there trying to get a good look at all of the people inside. Besides the cashier, there were the other two. A woman in her sixties, maybe, and another who could be in her early thirties. She looked awful. Like she had a broken nose or something. Two green eyes with dark circles around them met hers before she turned away and opened the refrigerator holding drinks.

"Help you, hon?"

Rachel jerked. The woman behind the counter was eyeing her with a curious look on her face. Rachel flushed. "Um . . . could I use your phone?"

One over-arched eyebrow rose. "You don't have a cell phone?"

"No, ma'am."

She scoffed. "Come on. All you teens have cell phones."

"I don't have it with me and I need to call my dad. Please?"

She waved a hand. "All right, honey. I got a landline you can use. Help yourself. And girl, where is your coat? It's too cold to be walking around out there in that flimsy outfit." She pulled a handset off the base next to the cash register and handed it to Rachel. "Now, don't be taking off with it, you hear?"

Rachel blinked. Take off with it? "Of course not. I wouldn't." What in the world would she do with a handset?

"Hmm." The woman reached behind her. "And here. It'll be too big for you, but put this around you. You're practically blue."

Rachel took the heavy fleece-lined hoodie with a grateful smile. "Thank you. I'll give it back to you in just a few minutes. It won't take my dad long to get here." She hoped.

With a huge sigh of relief and on the edge of tears, she stepped to the side, put the warm coat tight around her, and leaned her forehead against the wall as she dialed her father's number.

Blake and Chloe had returned to the downtown headquarters office to meet with the rest of the task force. Impatience clawed at him. What was he doing to help find Rachel? What was he *not* doing that he *should* be doing?

Linc stood at the front of the room and faced the conference table, surrounded by those on the task force. "We've got a name we're going to follow up on," he was saying. "Ethan Wright. For some reason, Rachel MacCallum, who was on the truck with the other victims, left the hospital and climbed into the back of this man's SUV. We believe it was deliberate, that she followed him for a reason. I think once we find her—or him—we'll have a lead on our traffickers. David and his FBI counterpart are working together on this. Hopefully, they'll have something for us to chase down soon. What we do know is that he's former Army turned bestselling artist for one of the local galleries. His work is in high demand. He's no longer living at the address indicated on his driver's license, but we don't have a forwarding address right now. Should have that soon. He's teaching several art classes at the university. He's supposed to be in class right this minute, but when we called to speak with him, we were told he'd called in sick this morning. And he might very well be sick. He's got no priors and is squeaky clean, so he's simply a person of interest we want to talk to."

Blake's phone buzzed. He didn't recognize the number but immediately answered, muscles bunching. "MacCallum here." He stood and motioned he was going to step out of the room. Linc nodded.

"Blake?"

He blinked and stopped. "Rachel? Is that you? Where are you?"

All talking ceased. Every eye was on him. He hit the speaker button. "Hang on one second." He motioned to Linc. "Record this."

Linc nodded and immediately had his phone next to Blake's, the record app going. "Where are you, Rachel?"

"I don't know," she said, her voice raspy and hurried. "I'm at a gas station. Hold on, I'll ask." He didn't want her to stop talking, but at least he could still hear her. "What's the address here?"

Blake heard whoever Rachel was talking to give the street address. "Chapin, South Carolina, honey," the woman said.

"Chapin?" Blake nearly shouted. "How did you get there? In the back of that Suburban?"

She sucked in a breath. "How'd you know about that?"

"Got it on hospital security footage, kiddo."

"Come get me, Blake—*Dad*—please. I'm scared. I know I've been rotten to you and I don't deserve for you to come to the rescue, that I'm . . . I'm not really yours, but I'm—"

"I'm already on the way," he said, grabbing his keys from his pocket and heading for the door.

Linc immediately mobilized the team and within seconds, they were out the door. Chloe headed to her vehicle and Blake stayed on her heels.

"I'll drive you, get in," she said.

He didn't argue.

Hank hopped in his area and Chloe cranked the SUV. She was pulling out of the parking lot before he had his seatbelt fastened. "Rach, you still with me?"

"Yes, I'm here."

In the rearview mirror, Blake saw Linc fall in behind them. "We're on the way, but it's going to be about thirty minutes before I can get there. I'm going to send some local officers to stay with you until then, okay?"

"Okay."

Chloe was already on her Bluetooth with the dispatcher. She listened, then nodded. "Someone should be there within ten minutes."

"You get that?" Blake asked.

"Ten minutes. Okay, Dad, I'll be here. Dad?"

"Yes?"

"The house is near here. It's where they're holding the girls. I walked from the house to the street, but there are other girls there right now. We have to rescue them. Lindsey's there and—" Her voice rose with each sentence, her hysteria rising.

"What's the address?"

"I don't know. I never saw a street sign. I just know it's not too far from here. And it's got a barn. And . . . and . . . a walking path thing that goes in a circle around the whole property through the woods. But that's all I know. I just can't . . . I don't know—"

"It's okay, Rach. We'll figure that out when we get there." He needed her to stay calm. "Who's the guy in the Suburban? Do you know him? His name is Ethan Wright."

"Who? No, I've never heard of him."

"Then why were you following him?"

Silence.

"Rachel? You there?"

More silence. He looked at his phone and saw the call had been disconnected.

Rachel looked down at the handset, then put it back to her ear. "Blake? Dad?"

Had his cell phone dropped the call?

She looked back at the counter only to find no one there. Where had the woman gone?

And the others? She swept her gaze around the store. Then moved down the aisle only to stop with a gasp.

Two customers lay unmoving on the floor and there was no sign of the woman behind the counter.

A chill zipped up her spine. She looked at the handset as though it would have the answers. "Dad? Answer me."

"He can't, Rachel," the voice said.

She spun to the right.

And screamed.

A man with a ski mask stepped out from behind a tall display of cokes.

"No," she whispered. "No, I'm not going back!"

Dark eyes gleamed at her from behind the ski mask. A cruel mouth grinned at her and advanced, the spray bottle in his right hand. "Yes, I'm afraid you are. Landlines don't work very well when they're not pugged in." He held up the base. The unplugged base.

"My dad knows where I am. I told him about you. I told him about the house with the barn and the girls—"

He said nothing and she could tell he didn't care. How had he found her? How had he known she was here?

He advanced, and with a sick twist in her belly, she realized that when she'd leaned against the wall, she turned her back on the door . . . and everything that went on behind her. So stupid. How many times had her dad warned her to keep her eyes open and on her surroundings.

Despair and fury raced through her. She could *not* let him take her.

Rachel lunged at him. His eyes widened at her charge, his surprise causing him to stumble backward. She intended to use the phone as a weapon and lashed out, catching the side of his head, not with the phone but with her knuckles. Pain radiated from her fingers up her arm and she dropped the handset. It clattered to the floor and bounced off the wall.

He cried out and went to his knees, the spray bottle hitting the floor and skidding under the nearest display rack.

With a howl of rage, he dove for it while Rachel raced out of the front of the store.

Heart pounding, she headed for the woods, spurred on by the sound of the back door of the building opening. A glance over her shoulder sent panic racing. It was *him* and he'd spotted her.

She tripped over an exposed root and stumbled. Tried to catch herself and failed. She fell to her knees. Scrambling, crab crawling, she tried to get to her feet while moving, but lost her momentum. A foot caught her in the ribs, and with a gasp of pain, she rolled to her back to get away from another kick.

And felt the liquid hit her in the face.

"No." Tears leaked down her cheeks even as the darkness closed in.

———

Fifteen minutes out, Blake's phone rang. "Yeah."

"This is Chief Sharpton. Two of my officers responded and are currently at the address you reported your daughter to be."

"Is she all right?"

"We're not sure. She's not here."

"What do you mean she's not there?" Though his voice was low and even, Blake seriously thought his head might explode.

"Two people are on the floor unconscious. No visible wounds, but none of them resemble your daughter. We've got EMS en route and officers searching the perimeter. We've also got tire tracks at the back of the store that are fresh. The rain hasn't washed them away and the mud has left a good outline. I've got a crime scene unit on the way. We'll get a cast of that tire print."

"They got to her," he whispered. "They got her again. How?" He punched the dash. Ignored the pain that shot up his arm.

"Sir?"

"I'm going to need any security footage you may have."

"I don't think we're going to have much. I'll have to check with Deb when she wakes up."

"Deb?"

"Deborah Mann. She's the owner and was hit with whatever stuff this guy is using. Chloroform, is my first guess. I see two cameras. One facing the gas pumps. The other one facing the front of the store. We'll see if we can get anything, but don't hold your breath. This is a sleepy little town and this gas station is literally in the middle of nowhere. Not much goes on out here."

That he knew about anyway. Blake pinched the bridge of his nose and prayed silently while he tried to corral his fear. "Any idea where they could have gone?"

"No. Unfortunately, we weren't looking for anyone, so they could have passed us on the way here and we never would have known it."

Blake ended the call and started tapping into the notes section of his phone. He wanted to get down the conversation he'd just had with Rachel to the best of his ability. She'd given clues. A few anyway. A house with a barn and a walking trail that went in circles. How common could that be?

Several minutes later, they pulled into the middle of organized chaos. Two ambulances sped out of the parking lot. No doubt headed to the nearest hospital. Blake jumped out of the SUV before Chloe even had it in park. He ran to the officer who looked like he might be in charge. "Chief?"

"Yeah." The officer turned. A man in his early sixties with sharp blue eyes peered at him.

"I'm Blake MacCallum."

"The dad?"

"Yes, sir."

The man nodded. "This way."

Chloe slipped silently up beside them and followed them inside. Linc did too. Blake paused at the entrance. To the right was the counter.

"That's where we found Deb."

He pointed to the other side of the counter in front of the register. "Maya Manning was paying for her goods. Krissy Austin was in here as well, in the aisle across from the register. He got her last. She said her back was to him, but when she heard the other two drop, she turned and he sprayed her."

"Wait a minute, she's awake and talking?"

"Yep. But still on her way to the hospital. Bobby, her husband, broke her nose. Which was why she was in here looking for some pain medication."

"And she didn't breathe in the spray because she *couldn't.*"

"Right. Completely clogged. She got a little through her mouth, but not a full dose. She went ahead and dropped to the floor so he wouldn't realize the spray had almost no affect."

"Quick thinking."

"She's had to learn to think on her feet." The man scowled.

"Can't talk her into leaving him?"

"Nope."

"So, she heard everything that went on with Rachel?"

"Probably. I tried to get it out of her, but she was in so much pain, she just kept asking for someone to make it stop. Figured I'd let her get on to the hospital and get that nose taken care of. You can question her once she's seen to."

"I'll plan on that. One more question."

"Sure."

"Do you know of a property around here that's got a barn and a walking trail that circles the property?"

Chief Sharpton rubbed his forehead. "Not right offhand. I can ask around, though. I've got a friend who's a realtor. She might have some suggestions."

"Good. Try her and let me know."

"Will do." The chief's phone rang. "As soon as I get this. Excuse me."

"Of course."

Linc stood looking at the back door.

Blake stepped over to him. "What is it?"

"How did he manage to incapacitate three people without Rachel seeing him or you hearing anything on the phone?"

Blake's eyes landed on the device resting on the floor near the wall adjacent to the checkout counter. Rachel had been on that phone. And when her attacker had overpowered her, she'd dropped it. He wanted to grab it but knew CSU would need it for evidence. He curled his fingers into fists.

"I don't know." He shook his head. "I need to get to the hospital to talk to this Krissy person."

"We've got officers going door-to-door, checking homes around here. Not sure how big of a radius to cover though," the chief said.

"Do at least five miles," Blake said.

Linc nodded. "That's what I was thinking. Maybe even six or seven."

The chief nodded and went back to his phone.

Blake raked a hand through his hair. "We need a chopper in the air. See if they can spot a property that sounds similar to what Rachel described."

"Yeah. Let's do that. They can cover more area faster." He walked off, phone pressed to his ear.

A soft hand landed on his bicep and he turned to see Chloe looking at him with those blue eyes of hers. "I want to ask if you're okay, but I already know the answer. I guess I'll ask what's going on behind the tough cop facade."

"I'm terrified." His voice shook and he cleared his throat. "I'm scared I'm not doing enough, that I'm missing something, that I'm never going to see her again because we won't figure everything out before it's too late." He needed to stop talking. Airing his fears wouldn't do him or anyone else any good.

"Yeah. That's kind of what I figured." She squeezed his hand. "Don't give up. We're going to find her."

"Like you've found Penny?"

She flinched and stepped back.

He moved forward and grasped her arm. "I'm sorry. You didn't deserve that."

"No, I didn't, but that doesn't mean I don't understand what you're saying. And this situation is very different from Penny's in a lot of ways."

"Like what?"

"Like we haven't heard from Penny in almost six months. You talked to Rachel today. We have video footage of her getting into the back of a vehicle. We're tracking down Ethan Wright, who could be a very good lead. We don't have anything like that with Penny. Except for the fact that Rachel had on her blouse. I find that encouraging in some weird way. Like if we can find a dumb shirt, we'll find Penny."

"You're right. Very right. It's just, that's twice now that I feel like she's been within reach and then . . . she's not. This shattered hope is killing me."

"I imagine she feels the same."

He blinked, then groaned and dropped his face into his palms. "I'm a selfish pig, aren't I? Only thinking about myself and how this is affecting me." He looked up to find Linc striding toward him.

"We've got a chopper in the air. Should be in the area within the next five minutes or so."

"Good. Let's figure out where Rachel was trying to send us and get there."

"Wait a minute," Chloe said. "I have an idea. It's been forming since we found out Rachel was missing, but I wasn't sure it would be possible. I mean, it's a long shot, but . . ."

"What?" The sparkle in her eyes sent hope surging.

"Do you have anything that belongs to Rachel?"

Blake's eyes narrowed. "No, not with me. Why?"

"Because Hank might be able to follow her trail."

"But they took her in a vehicle."

"Yes, but she arrived at the store on foot. It's possible Hank can trace her steps back to the place she started walking from. Like I said, it's a definite long shot, but I think it's worth a try."

This time hope ruptured. He grabbed her and planted a kiss on her lips, then pulled back. "You're a genius."

With bright red cheeks, she blinked at him. "Um . . . thanks?"

Blake didn't even care that Linc was looking at him with equal parts amusement and exasperation. "I need a glove and an evidence bag."

Linc cleared his throat. "Why?"

"Because I'd be willing to bet my next paycheck that Rachel used that cordless handset sitting over there near the wall. I'm also willing to bet that she was the last one to use it and dropped it when she was attacked. If I'm right and she did, it's got her scent all over it."

Chloe nodded. "Doesn't look like anyone's touched anything since the incident. I think that handset would make a great scent-article." She walked to the back door, opened it, and stepped outside. Hank followed her. "Not much wind. That's helpful. We've got cooler temps and it's damp, which hold the scent closer to the ground. As long as the wind stays dormant, I think we might actually have a chance."

"All right," Linc said. "Let's get Blake here fitted with an earpiece in case Hank needs to travel a bit."

They followed Linc back to his vehicle and he pulled out the equipment needed for Blake. Chloe made sure she had her own earpiece on the right channel with the others. Once Blake had the earpiece in and verified it was working, he gave her a short nod.

She turned to Hank, who'd settled on the ground next to her, his eyes never leaving her. "Hank, you ready to get to work?"

His ears perked and he leaped to his feet. She looked at Blake. "We're ready."

With the phone in her gloved hand, Chloe held it out to Hank. "Hank, *zoek*!" The well-trained dog knew what to do and took a whiff. His nose immediately went to the floor and then the air. He trotted to the back door and waited for Chloe to open it for him. "Good boy, Hank." Chloe wrapped her fingers around the toy rope and Hank pranced ahead, anxious to find the person attached to the scent so he could play. He went straight to the side of the building and sat next to an item lying on the ground.

"That's a horse blanket," Blake said. "She said there was a barn. She must have used it for warmth while she was walking and left it here when she went into the store."

Chloe threw the rope and let Hank chase it. When he brought it back, she praised him, took him from the area away from the scent of the blanket, and let him have another whiff of the phone. He went back into work mode and took off.

She trotted along behind him and Blake stayed right with them. A police cruiser rolled at a slow pace in the lane closest to them. Hank pulled on the leash, wanting to run full out. Once again she congratulated herself on investing in the top-notch equipment for the animal.

As much as he may pull on the lead, he couldn't hurt or choke himself. The large draft-horse-style leather harness allowed the force of resistance to spread over the dog's chest. Using this style of harness rather than a simple collar cut down on fatigue and kept him from experiencing irritation around his neck. Especially if they were going to be going for a long stretch of time.

And this looked like it might be one of those times.

Blake carried the phone in the bag in case she needed to let Hank take another sniff, but so far, the dog didn't look close to slowing down.

When they'd gone at least two miles, Chloe glanced at Blake. "This is a thirty-foot lead, but he's raring to go. The conditions are just right for him to track long distance. Can you run faster?"

"Of course. I can do about four miles alternating between flat-out running and jogging, but after that I'll have to slow."

"I can do five." She tossed him a grim smile. "On a day when I've had a good protein shake anyway."

He nodded. "Let's pick up the pace."

After about a mile, Hank sped up and swerved right into a driveway, bolted around the back of the house and to an old storage shed.

"Rachel!" Blake swerved around them and yanked the door open.

"What's going on out here?"

A woman in her forties stood on the back porch, eyeing them. The officer who'd been trailing them in the vehicle came around the corner. "Just hold tight, ma'am, we're looking for a girl who was kidnapped. Do you mind if they continue?"

"Oh my stars. Of course. Is she in there?"

"No," Blake said. "She's not. But there are crackers, a peanut butter jar, and some banana peels in here."

Chloe nodded. "She was here."

Hank wagged his tail, and once again Chloe went through the game, which delighted the animal. "Let's keep going," she said. "Rachel said she walked all the way to the store. She must have stopped here to eat and rest."

"Where'd she get the food?"

"No idea."

"I might can help you with that," the woman said. "My neighbor up the street called and asked me if I'd heard anything weird last night."

"Weird?"

"He said he thought he heard someone in his house. At first he thought it was his wife, but she wasn't home yet. By the time he got the lights on, no one was there, but he said he was missing some food. Said three bananas were gone as well as his jar of peanut butter. Might not have noticed the crackers."

"That had to be Rachel," Blake said.

"Let's keep going up this road and see where it leads."

"Thank you very much," Blake called to the woman.

"I hope you find her!"

Hank found the house, but they already knew Rachel wasn't there and Chloe helped the dog get back on the scent farther up the road. "He's got it," she said.

For the next two miles they ran with Hank veering to the left, sometimes into the road, then back, weaving through the trees. But for the most part, he continued down the grassy area near the

161

road. Chloe figured they looked a little crazy to the casual observer. Definitely not a couple out for a run with their dog.

Instead, Blake wore his khakis and comfortable black loafers and Chloe, her uniform. When she started to lag, Blake slowed and she pulled Hank to a reluctant stop. "Okay," she gasped. "When I said I could do five miles, I meant with jogging shorts and a T-shirt. Definitely not in this gear." She wiped a trickle of sweat from her temple. Although, she thought she'd done pretty well for as long as she had.

The cruiser pulled to a stop beside them and directed a green pickup truck to go around. "You big-city cops spend most of your time in cafés and doughnut shops, or what?"

Blake shot him a dark look and Chloe had a few choice words she could have spat at him. What was his name? Officer Rickie Monroe. Chloe decided she'd offer grace instead of releasing her anger.

They were all tense and he was probably just letting off some stress by trying to be funny. And truly, if she wasn't so worried about Rachel and the other girls, she would have just laughed. Right now, she didn't feel like laughing. From Blake's expression, he didn't either.

Officer Monroe waved a hand with a sheepish smile. "Sorry. Didn't mean anything by that. I sure couldn't have kept up if I wasn't behind the wheel."

Blake's expression softened. "Forget it."

Hank wandered back and forth for a few seconds nose in the air as though looking for the scent. Chloe called to him and when he trotted over, she opened the bag with the phone to let him take another sniff. Within seconds, Hank had the scent again and was at the end of the lead ready to keep going.

Thirty minutes later, they'd passed several houses and Hank never once showed any interest in veering from his path. And then he went to the right. His new direction took them next to a gravel driveway.

"Look," Chloe panted. "There. A barn." She pulled Hank to a stop. "Good job, boy." She scratched his ears and praised him to let him know he'd done his job well. Hank's entire body vibrated with happiness while Chloe's muscles added another layer of tension.

Oh please, God, let Rachel be in there.

15

"T hink there's a walking trail around it?" Blake asked as they
moved back and out of sight should anyone look out a window.

"Only one way to find out. But I don't want to scare them. I
think we need to keep a low profile until we canvass the place. They
might have it rigged to alert them if anyone comes up the drive. I
wouldn't think they do, though, if Rachel was able to walk away
without alerting them. Still need to check."

Blake nodded and planted his hands on his hips. Sweat ringed
his armpits and dripped down the side of his face. He lifted the
hem of his now untucked shirt to wipe it off while he fought the
urge to storm the house, yelling Rachel's name. "Good idea. You
and Hank stay here. I'll go find a window."

"They'll have cameras," Chloe said. "You can't just walk up
to the front door—or even around the house. They'll spot you in
a heartbeat."

"I agree," Linc said, his voice echoing in Blake's ear and sounding like he was standing right next to him. "About six miles from
the store. Impressive dog you've got there, Chloe."

"I know." But she smiled.

"Humble handler too." He paused. "All right, here's what we're going to do. Stay out of sight for now. The chopper is going to make a pass and see what's on the other side of the house, around the barn, and if there's a walking trail that can be seen from the air. If so, I'd say it's likely we've got the right place. Backup is on the way, but coming in quiet."

Blake chafed at the waiting. Rachel was probably in that house and he wanted to go get her. Now.

He caught Chloe's gaze with his. She'd been watching for a few seconds, he realized. And knew exactly what he was thinking. With a quick shake of her head, she expressed what she thought. He grimaced and nodded.

Federal agents arrived in force. Linc stepped out of his sedan and approached them. "ERT is en route," he said. "They'll be ready to take over to find all the evidence we need to put these guys away for good once any arrests and rescues are made."

"Good," Blake said, bouncing on his toes. Several ambulances were on standby and out of sight, but would arrive within seconds of being notified they had victims ready for transport. He prayed Rachel didn't need one—or any of the other girls.

"Chloe," Linc said.

"Yes?"

"You and Hank be ready. We'll want him to help clear the house. Might as well use him while we have him."

"We'll be ready. Just let us know."

Blake shook his head. Chloe had given Hank his rope and he sat at her feet chewing on it, happy to be right where he was. They could all learn a lesson from the dog.

Linc pressed a finger to his ear and listened. Blake could hear every word through his own earpiece. "This is Chopper Two. There are no vehicles on the property. No visible weapons. No sign of movement from the house." A pause. "And there appears to be something that could be a walking trail that circles the property."

"This is it," Blake said. "It has to be."

Chloe nodded. "Hank wanted to keep going, but I didn't want to let him, in case someone saw him. This is the place. I can feel it in my gut."

"Me too." Blake shifted, never taking his eyes from the front door.

Linc tilted his head at Chloe. "Stay behind us as we approach, okay?"

"Got it."

His gaze shifted to Blake. "You can listen in. When we find Rachel, we'll send her out to you."

Blake started to protest, but Linc's hard-eyed stare said it would fall on deaf ears. He clenched his jaw, but nodded his assent.

Linc raised his arm and motioned for the team to move in, slowly.

Heart in his throat, Blake watched them go. All he could do was pray that no one started shooting.

Chloe stayed behind the line of special agents until they started breaking off into different directions. Thanks to the earpiece Linc had given her, she could hear the commands being given by her brother. She stayed with the two agents ordered to cover the door. They took up posts on opposite sides. Chloe shadowed the agent on the right, staying behind him. He'd be first through the door and she and Hank would be right behind.

Chloe followed the soft chatter coming through the earpiece. She looked back over her shoulder but could see nothing. If anyone had missed their arrival but were now looking out a window, they'd never know a team of agents had them surrounded. The agent in front of her reached out and tried the knob. He nodded. "It's open."

"We're ready here in the back. On three," came the voice through the earpiece.

"One . . . two . . . three."

And then they were inside. Chloe held Hank back for just a moment before rounding the doorjamb and stepping into the foyer. Weapon in her right hand, leash in her left, she followed, eyes scanning. Hank knew the drill, they'd practiced this very type of exercise over and over. And done it again. His ears swiveled and his nose twitched as they walked through the home.

"Clear!"

"Clear!"

"Barn's clear too," someone else said.

"She's not there?" Blake's quiet voice came through the earpiece. So did his despair.

"We're not done yet, Blake," Chloe said.

Linc exited the kitchen and nodded to her. "Let Hank do his thing."

Chloe nodded and holstered her weapon. "Hank, *volg*."

Hank came right to her left side and looked up at her.

"Hank, find the dope."

The animal went to work, his lead running through her hands as she let him have his freedom to roam at will, looking for any drugs. Chloe monitored his behavior closely. His mouth was mostly closed, which meant he was using his nose to take up scents. And his ears. Hank's ears always told her if he found something. Over the years, she'd learned to read him, know his traits, and know when he was on the trail. Right now, something had caught his attention. But what?

He went through the kitchen to the back door of the house and sat. "What's he doing?" Linc asked.

Chloe opened the door. "He wants out." She followed Hank out into the backyard to a wooden porch with a large outdoor rug. He pawed at it, then sat and looked at Chloe. "Guys? Come over here."

Linc jogged over to her. "What is it?"

She pointed. "Can you move that?"

"Why?"

"Because Hank says to."

"Right."

From the corner of her eye, she saw Blake approach, followed by two other special agents. His fists opened and closed at his sides.

They'd probably taken pity on him once they cleared the house and let him come closer.

His eyes locked on hers and the desperation there nearly took her to her knees. She had to find *something* that would help lead them to Rachel and, hopefully, Penny as well.

Linc and another agent moved the heavy rug, exposing a double door.

"A cellar," she said. "Get this lock off."

Hank paced, nosing at the door, then walked back to her to sit at her side.

"Hold on, boy. We're getting there."

Within seconds, someone passed Linc a tool and he cut the lock off the doors. With gloved hands, he pulled the first door up and laid it on the side. Chloe did the same with the opposite door. Hank lunged for the steps and Chloe let him go. The thirty-foot lead would allow him to reach the bottom.

Linc shoved past her, the heavy beam of a flashlight lighting the way, weapon held ready. Chloe eased down the stairs behind him, her weapon also out and ready. Hank barked once as Chloe reached the bottom. Linc stood still. Silent. Staring. And then he was moving. Checking the area in the back while Chloe did the same at the entrance. She caught a glimpse of the chain-link cages to her right and sucked in a harsh breath, but kept going. The last thing she needed was a surprise with a gun.

"Clear!" Linc called.

"Clear!" she echoed.

Linc hurried back toward her and they headed to the cages together. "I need paramedics down here, now!" he barked.

Six cages lined the wall.

Three of them held girls who appeared to be unconscious.

Hank was already pacing in front of the cages as Chloe rushed over. "Are they alive?"

"I can't tell."

"Hank says there's dope down here too. Or was at some point."

"If they're gone, they took it with them. We've got to get these girls out of here."

Her gaze swept each girl, sprawled on the floor, eyes closed. Each had a bluish tint to their lips. Like Linc, she couldn't tell if they were breathing or not. She jerked the door of the first cage, but it held fast. Linc spoke into his radio. "Need paramedics and something to cut a padlock off."

Footsteps pounded down the steps. Chloe moved out of the way while four paramedics entered the area. One passed Linc a tool and he moved quickly to cut the locks off the cages, one by one.

As the doors opened, the paramedics went for the girls, who lay on the hard concrete floor.

"This one's alive," called the first paramedic. A female in her early thirties.

The second one looked up. Another female about the same age. "This one is too." She went to work checking the victim's vitals.

"This one's not." The third paramedic's voice was flat. No emotion colored her words, but Chloe could tell the death affected her. Affected them all. The woman moved to help her partner in the second cage.

Priorities. Keep the ones alive, alive. Grieve the ones you couldn't help later.

"Chloe?" Blake's whisper reminded her that he could hear what was going on. And he'd just heard there was a dead girl in the hole in the ground.

"It's not Rachel," she said softly. "None of them are Rachel."

His breath whooshed in her ear.

"Syringes are on the floor," the lone male paramedic noted.

Linc stepped forward and pulled an evidence bag from his

169

pocket. "I'll collect those. We'll test them and see what drug was used and if there are any prints on the plastic." With a gloved hand, he collected the syringes and dropped them in the bags.

Chloe gripped Hank's lead. "Come on, boy, do your thing. Is there anyone else here?" She led him through the basement, checking every nook and cranny, looking for secret rooms, booby traps, and anything else he might alert on. He sat next to one of the doors that Linc had opened and cleared, but there was nothing there. "Probably had drugs in this area," she said.

And that was it.

She gave him his toy and he settled down with delight to give it a good workout. Chloe turned her attention to the medical personnel working on the girls. The Evidence Response Team had arrived and was getting to work.

"Come on, honey, wake up. My name's Pete and I'd really like to see what color your eyes are." When he got no response, he looked up. "I think we're dealing with opioid overdoses here. Breathing is shallow, pulse is slow and erratic. Pale and clammy skin." His light flicked across his victim's hands. "Purple fingernails. Yeah. Let's give them a dose of naloxone and get them out of here. Be ready to give another dose if necessary." The three women paramedics nodded and went to work.

Linc stepped forward. "We need sheets from the ambulance. We need to contain any evidence."

"I've got them." One of the woman paramedics rushed up the stairs. When she returned, she had three sheets.

They spread them next to each girl. "Now roll them on gently. We'll collect their clothes and the sheets at the hospital." He nodded to Pete. "I can carry one if you can get the other." The medical examiner would take care of the deceased teen.

"We'll have to," Pete said. "There's no way to get a gurney down here. I don't see any sign of neck or bone trauma. We'll put collars on them and get them out of here."

"Let's do it."

Chloe gathered Hank and ran up the steps, her heart in her throat. She didn't want to be the one to tell Blake about their find, but knew he'd been listening in on the conversation and figured he was chomping at the bit to know the details. He already knew that Rachel wasn't there. And if the three girls left to die in the cages were any indication, that was probably a good thing.

16

Blake could easily let himself tumble headlong into a major depression, but knew that wouldn't help him bring Rachel home. Right now, he would be grateful that the dead victim wasn't Rachel even while his heart grieved for the parents who would soon learn of her demise. He briefly wondered if they'd care. He hoped so. She deserved to have parents who would miss her, mourn her, and hound the police until they found her killers. He blew out a breath and clamped down on the surge of rage that wanted to spill out. No time for that.

Chloe approached with Hank. She'd taken him out to the edge of the woods to do his business, and he now trotted happily at her side, his toy once again clenched in those powerful jaws.

And then she hugged Blake.

Surprised, he froze, then wrapped his arms around her and squeezed until she gasped. Loosening his hold, he rested his forehead on hers. "Sorry. I didn't mean to hurt you."

"You didn't. Not really. Want me to take you to pick up your truck?" she asked.

He'd left it at the office that morning. It seemed like a lifetime ago. "Yes."

His phone rang and he grabbed it, not recognizing the number.

Rachel? Did he dare hope? Blake pulled the earpiece out of his ear and lifted his phone. "Hello? Rachel?"

Chloe's eyes widened.

"It's me. I'm sorry." Rachel's sobs wrenched at his heart.

"Where are you?"

"They caught me, Dad. I wasn't smart enough. I'm sorry."

"Tell me where you are."

"I don't know where I am. They want you to kill that judge, Dad, or they're going to kill me." He was having a hard time discerning her words through her tears, but he got it. "I don't want to die, Daddy! Help me! But don't do it! Don't kill him. Just find me!"

His heart shattered. "Rachel—"

"You're the only one who can save me, Daddy."

"I will, Rachel, I'll find you, I promise."

"Sorry, Rachel's gone now," a hard voice said. "And I really doubt you'll find her."

Blake flinched. "You're asking the impossible." He kept his voice low, aware of Chloe's watchful eyes.

"Nothing's impossible. It's simply a choice. Kill the judge or your daughter dies. She was supposed to encourage you to follow through. She disobeyed, so now she'll have to be punished. You have twenty-four hours. And that's a gift you should be grateful for. She should already be dead. Twenty-four hours. Once I get word of his death, I'll let Rachel go."

Punished? Because she wouldn't tell him to kill someone. "You touch her and I'll kill *you*."

"Don't make threats or promises you can't keep."

"I always keep my promises." The line went silent and Blake decided not to push. "How will you know he's dead?"

A low laugh filtered to him. "I'll know. Tomorrow, Deputy US Marshal Blake MacCallum. Tomorrow's the day. We'll be waiting."

Click.

Blake held the phone to his ear a little longer, then lowered it slowly. "It's not over yet," he said. "Noah Hampton may have wanted the judge dead, but so does someone else."

"What do you mean?"

"I mean, we're back to square one." He filled her in.

She blew out a breath. "Well, at least we know she's alive."

"Yes. At least we know that. For now. The punishment comment scares me just about more than anything."

The last ambulance pulled away from the back of the house, and Blake watched it go as the coroner pulled in. Sickness coiled in his belly at the thought of Rachel in the hands of the monsters who thought life was something to be bought and sold—or simply ended. The very idea infuriated him and made him want to smash someone's face. But he'd settle for simply stopping them and having Rachel home safe. "I've got to find her."

"I know," Chloe said. She squeezed his forearm. "Let's go."

With his hands shoved in his front pockets, he shook his head. "How did they know where she was? What tipped them off that she was at the store?"

Chloe placed a hand on his arm and curled her fingers around it. Now that the adrenaline was starting to wear off, the cold was seeping through her coat. Sweat and a cold breeze mixing together produced a massive shudder. She led him to the officer's patrol car—the one who'd driven alongside them. "I don't know. Could have been a fluke thing. Could have been someone was watching the area and spotted her."

"But who?"

"No telling." She tilted her head. "Linc and the other agents—as well as the local officers—will make sure everyone who was in the store at the time is interviewed, but you know it could have been someone outside, someone who never set foot in the store, who saw her go in."

"True."

"For now, why don't we grab some food, go over what we know, what we don't know, and what we can do with what we know."

He blinked. "Huh?"

"Let's eat and talk."

"Right." Blake drew in a deep breath. "I just realized I really am back at square one. No one knows Rachel is missing. Really missing. Except you and the team here. And I can't let on that she is. Which means I have to work tomorrow."

"Or call in."

"No. I did that today." He ran a hand down the side of his face. "They're watching me. They're watching the judge. If I stay home, they'll know and it might make them mad. And if I make them mad, they may take it out on Rachel."

"Right." They climbed into the back of the cruiser. With Hank against the door, that left Chloe in the middle. Blake took up the rest of the back seat, his right leg snugged up to her left. She tried to inch over closer to Hank, but it wasn't like he was the size of a schnauzer or something. Blake raised a brow at her and she flushed. She didn't mind being this close to him. Didn't mind at all. But Rachel was missing.

Officer Monroe headed back to the store.

"Six miles," he said. "That's impressive. Not just the fact that y'all practically ran the whole way, but that Hank there was able to track backwards. I don't think I've ever seen a dog do that before."

Chloe allowed a smile to curve her lips and scratched Hank's ears. "Just one of the many exercises that we've trained on over the last couple of years. Today the conditions couldn't have been more perfect for it." Although, they'd trained in less-than-ideal conditions as well. "He's a special guy for sure." Her mind flashed to Jordan Crestwood and she grimaced. Too bad she couldn't seem to fall for a special two-legged male as easily as she'd fallen for Hank. Then again, Hank had never ditched her for another woman. Or made her feel less of a woman because of her profession.

The painful memories settled themselves right in the middle of her heart and she blinked. Why was she thinking about that now? Her gaze slid to the man at her left. Blake MacCallum. She had a feeling he'd never treat a woman the way Jordan had.

Then again, it didn't matter. Right now, the focus was Rachel and the human traffickers. Not her romantic baggage.

Officer Monroe pulled into the parking lot of the gas station and rolled up next to Chloe's SUV. "Thanks for the ride back," she said.

"Anytime. I'd love to stay updated on this."

"Of course. Text me your number. I'll give you an update when we find her." Once Chloe had the man's number in her phone, she waited for Blake to exit the vehicle and she followed, clutching Hank's leash.

When they were settled in her Tahoe with Hank in his area, Blake let out a low breath. "Well. That was a bust."

"Yes, for Rachel. But because of her, we found two girls alive, who, if they make it, will owe their lives to her."

He paused, then gave a slow nod. "I guess that's a really good way to look at it."

"It's the only way to look at it." She caught him looking at her from the corner of his eye. "What?"

"What happened with you and Crestwood?"

"Huh . . . what?" Where had that come from?

"I need to think about something else. So . . . he hurt you."

"Um. Yes, he sure did. Not physically, but definitely emotionally." Why did he want to talk about *that*?

"Why?"

She gave a humorless laugh and started the vehicle. "I don't know why. I guess because he found someone he liked better than me." She pulled out of the lot and made a left. They had about a thirty-minute ride back to the office where he'd left his vehicle.

"I know the feeling."

"Your wife?"

"Yes."

176

"Right. I heard."

He sighed. "Linc?"

"Yes. He wasn't gossiping," she hurried to say, "just mentioned you'd gotten a lousy deal, especially when it came to sharing custody with your ex."

"It was lousy, all right." He fell silent for a few moments before clearing his throat. "So, any word on our artist friend, Mr. Wright?"

"Nothing that I've heard. Been a little busy."

"Right. He's next on the list, though."

"Someone is tracking him down, I'm sure. Why don't you check with David? It looks like he and Annie are working together now, so nothing will fall through the cracks with all of us investigating and going in different directions."

Blake dialed David's number and put it on speaker.

"David here."

"Hey, it's Blake, any information on the whereabouts of Ethan Wright?"

"His last known address was vacant. Looks like they tore down the apartment building to put up a grocery store six months ago. We're still working on it on this end, but as soon as we locate him, you'll know."

"Perfect. Talk to you soon."

"Sooner rather than later, I hope."

"Yeah," Blake said, "me too."

Rachel woke slowly, awareness of the cold hitting her first. She was so tired of being cold. Voices reached her and memory returned. Fear clawed at her, but fury burned bright. A soul-deep anger at the people who had no respect for human life—and at herself for getting caught. She'd been so close.

She refused to open her eyes. Not yet. Let them think she was still unconscious. She wished she was. After she'd awakened the first time, they'd forced her to make that awful call to her father. And then they'd sprayed her again. Afraid she would cause them trouble, no doubt.

They were right to be afraid.

While she lay there, she engaged her senses and took inventory. When she'd called her father, she'd been in the back of a large van. After knocking her out, they must have moved her here. The question was, where was *here*?

The room was cold, but there was a mattress beneath her. And a thin blanket over her shoulders. So she wasn't in a cage. That was only a slight comfort, but she'd take comfort where she could.

". . . got her back. Now we're in business again. He'll kill the judge or she dies. Simple." A voice she didn't recognize.

"Not simple. If you kill her, that's good money down the tubes." A voice that sounded familiar. "Have you taken a good look at her? You know as well as I do this business is all about the looks. She's magazine-worthy gorgeous and she's never been touched. Top-dollar goods there."

"Who's going to buy her with the medical issues?"

"I've got someone in mind."

"Then sell her. Whatever. I don't care. But unless MacCallum follows orders, he'll never see her again."

"He's not going to see her again anyway," the second voice said softly. "And he knows it. I don't see him killing the judge. We're going to have to come up with another plan."

"He's a father. Fathers do desperate things for their kids."

"Hmm. Guess we'll see."

She almost laughed. Like her dad would kill someone for her. Especially someone he was protecting.

But he had tried to come to her rescue. The thought resonated and her heart swelled.

Maybe he did care. A little anyway.

Shivers wracked her and she let her eyes open into slits. The room spun and she swallowed the hit of nausea. She remembered the feeling and knew to just stay still until it passed.

When she could open her eyes without wanting to heave, she did so. Slowly. Making sure no one was watching. The voices had stopped. A foot nudged her back and she slammed her eyes shut again. "This one's going to sleep a little longer, I guess. I'm going to grab some food. I'll be back to check on her before too long. Don't let her out of your sight."

"She's not going anywhere."

"And check her sugar again. It was too high earlier."

"The drug probably affects it. She'll be fine."

"I said check it."

"I will." Footsteps faded. And a hand touched her cheek. "Yeah," the voice whispered. "So pretty." Fingers trailed over her cheekbone to her collarbone and slipped under the edge of her shirt.

Rachel held herself rigid, forcing herself not to respond, to keep her breathing even. Just like when she used to avoid her mother and her incessant harping.

A chuckle. "You know, you don't fool me. I know you're awake." His breath whispered across her cheek. She didn't move. "If I thought you wouldn't cause me no end of trouble, I'd be tempted to fork over the money and take you for myself. Unfortunately, I have other issues that demand my attention for now." A pause and Rachel knew her heartbeat was visible in her throat. But still, she lay otherwise motionless, refusing to give him the satisfaction of seeing her terror. "All right, then. I see how you want to play it. And if I didn't have a problem to take care of, I'd call you on your little bluff. But I must go handle a rather explosive situation. Wish me luck." His lips pressed ever so softly against her temple. "Until we meet again."

And then he was walking away and Rachel's breath left her in a whoosh that turned into a sob.

Tears leaked onto the mattress as her prayers for rescue whispered toward the heavens.

17

SUNDAY

Chloe let Hank take the lead on their route around the perimeter of the judge's property. The Worthingtons had a beautiful estate, well maintained, and mostly green even in the middle of November. At least the rain had stopped. Hank trotted along beside her, his manner alert, but not alarmed.

So far, so good.

She made her way back to the house, unlocked the kitchen door, and slipped inside.

Files spread from one end of the massive twelve-person table to the other, spilling over onto the floor and the large island.

Blake, Linc, and the judge sat at the far end of the table discussing the three girls found in the house. "You have an update?" she asked Linc.

"Yeah. First, the three women who were knocked out at the store are awake and talking. Two, Deb and another, said the guy walked into the store with a gun. He pointed it at Deb and held a finger to his lips. So she didn't make a sound. The other woman didn't either. The third woman with the broken nose said she heard the whole thing go down, but was too scared to look."

"So, she's not really going to be any help, is she?" Chloe asked.

"No. Unfortunately. The guy walked in with a mask on. No one even got a look at his face."

Chloe rubbed her eyes and nodded. "What about the girls at the house?"

"The one who didn't make it is Katherine Moore. The other two—Nancy Littlejohn and Rhys Bolton—they're in ICU. They're clinging to life right now, but it's not looking good for either of them. Nancy's mother is with her and Rhys's grandparents flew in to stay with her. Rhys lives with her dad and he's out of the country on business."

"Out of the country? When your kid is missing?" Chloe asked.

"She's been missing for six weeks. The man had to keep his job in order to keep funding the search."

"Right," Chloe said. "Of course." She knew better than to judge too quickly. "Where's her mother?"

"Dead."

She winced.

"Also, another body was found in a back room."

"What? Who? We searched that place and it was clear."

"He was wrapped in plastic and buried under a pile of mattresses. His prints came back belonging to a guy by the name of Manuel Garcia. Long rap sheet. Was busted for human trafficking four years ago. Did two years and got out on parole for good behavior. Looks like he made someone mad, though. He was beat to a pulp."

"Manuel?" Chloe said. "Could be the one who pushed Skye down the stairs and kicked her. Rachel called him Manny. She said it made one of the other guys mad."

"Mad enough to kill him."

The judge slapped the table. "Those poor girls. It's not right."

"No," Blake said, "it's not." He sighed. "Are you sure you don't have any idea who could have it in for you like this?"

"No idea," the man said. He gestured to the stack of files. "The answer could be here, but it's impossible to pick one or the other out of the choices. These are all cases that I've passed sentencing on that have dealt with human trafficking."

Chloe counted twenty files. She picked up the nearest one. "I can't believe there's not more than this."

"Exactly. Why do you think I've been fighting so hard on this? Last year there were about fifty cases that came through the courts in South Carolina. Fifty. Nationwide there were about seventy-five hundred." He swept a hand at the small pile of files. "There should be hundreds of cases coming through my court, but because most of the victims are afraid to come forward for various reasons, this is what happens. And then when there *is* a case, the sentences are so minor that the traffickers don't really fear getting caught. I always give the maximum I can give, but I'm only one judge in a sea of them. We need to be consistent. We have to make it so that getting caught is not worth the risk. Right now, it is."

Blake ran a hand over his face. "I had no idea."

The judge shook his head. "It's not your area. No need for you to keep up with the statistics. But I've made this my passion."

"What got you so fired up about this particular issue?" Linc asked.

The man froze, his eyes narrowing and focusing on something over Chloe's shoulder.

"Tell them, honey."

Chloe turned to find the judge's wife, Lucy, standing at the entrance to the kitchen.

"I . . ." His mouth worked. "No. It's not important."

"So, it's personal?" Chloe asked.

"Yes."

"Then it might be important," Linc said.

"It's not." He brushed past his wife without looking at her as he left the room.

"What is it?" Linc asked. "Anything you tell us, any small detail might help us find who's doing this."

"It's not my story to tell, it's his. And I was hoping he would share it with you."

"Do you think knowing his story would make a difference in finding the person who wants him dead?"

"It's . . . possible." A frown. "But not likely."

"Then you need to tell us," Blake said. "Because whoever has my daughter wants your husband dead."

She blinked. "Someone has your daughter?"

"Yes. The same person who's making the threats against the judge. If he doesn't die, my daughter does. And we're running out of time." He explained the situation in more detail with a final plea. "Please . . . help us."

Pale, trembling, she took a seat at the table. "Oh my." She glanced over her shoulder then back at them. "Oh dear. And they let you continue to stay near my husband?"

"I'm not committing murder, ma'am." He rubbed his eyes and looked at her. "No matter the . . . cost."

Chloe's heart lurched. He knew they were going to kill Rachel regardless. The only way to get her back was to outsmart them and rescue her or pray she could find a way to escape again.

After studying Blake's dark eyes for a moment, Lucy bit her bottom lip and she sat there for what seemed like an eternity. Finally, she sighed. "All right. Ben's father left when he was ten and his sister was fourteen. Things were tough. He had no other family that could help—or *would* help. His mother slipped into a depression and started prostituting herself to make ends meet. And then . . ." She paused with another look over her shoulder.

"Then?" Chloe asked.

Deep breath. Her eyes slid to the stairs where her husband had vanished moments before. "Then, she started selling his sister."

Chloe swallowed a gasp. She'd seen a lot in her years in law enforcement. The fact that she could still be shocked surprised her. "How old was he when he figured this out?"

"Close to three years ago."

"What?" Linc blurted.

"But how?"

"Vicky committed suicide and left a note detailing everything. Including the fact that she'd only cooperated with their mother because if she didn't, she'd sell Ben instead. So Vicky cooperated. Three years ago, Vicky didn't show up for dinner one night and her phone kept going to voicemail. Ben went over to her house and found her. She'd swallowed a bottle of pills. The note was on the end table beside her."

"How horrible," Chloe whispered.

"It's changed everything around here. Changed him, changed us." She shook her head. "He won't talk about it. To anyone. Even now, three years later."

Linc sighed. "Where's his mother now?"

"I don't know. Probably shacked up with her latest. Ben hasn't talked to her in years. She didn't even come to Vicky's funeral." Lucy cleared her throat. "But it sparked something in him. Once he recovered from his shock and grief, he decided to do something about the human trafficking business around here. Not just in South Carolina, but nationwide. Every time he had a trafficking case come into his courtroom, he would come home depressed—and more determined than ever. Seeing the scumbags get a slap on the wrist for selling someone into slavery or the sex trade fired him up. Seeing the victims, those who were able to, gather their courage and put aside their trauma to come testify in court would stay with him for weeks. Their stories broke his heart. Because every one of them was his sister. And every time he put a guilty person away, he was getting justice for Vicky."

"Wow," Chloe said.

Linc nodded. "It certainly explains the motivation behind his passion, but not the who behind the threats."

"I don't know. He's a good husband and good father. His past haunts his dreams sometimes, but he never let that bleed over into our family. And he was always determined that our kids understand that exploiting others was wrong. That money wasn't to be gained by using others. We raised our kids to work for everything and not expect handouts just because we could give it to them. As a result, they both worked and put themselves through college and have good jobs, doing their best to give back to those less fortunate."

"Mom? Dad?"

Lucy's brows rose. "That's Paula." She stood and went into the den. Chloe and Hank followed her.

Lucy hugged her daughter. "Honey, what are you doing here? I thought you'd be in court?"

"We're recessed right now. The defense attorney had some kind of medical issue. We reconvene in two hours. I wanted to come by and check on Dad. I . . . said some pretty harsh things to him and want to apologize."

"No wonder he's been in such a bad mood."

Paula grimaced. "Yeah."

"Have you seen your brother lately? He's being evasive and not answering my calls."

"I talked to him earlier. He said he was coming by to see Dad too. That he was worried about him."

"Good. I'll talk to him when he stops in."

"Miles sends his love as well."

"Does he plan to join us tonight for dinner?"

"We'll see. He's meeting a client who's interested in the new drug that's being marketed for dementia."

"Does it really work?"

"Miles says it does. If he didn't think it was worth it, he wouldn't bother."

"Good to know they're making progress in treating that horrible disease." She sighed and waved a hand toward the back of the house. "Now, go see your father. He's in the bedroom."

Paula turned and noticed Chloe and Hank for the first time.
"Oh. Hi."

"Hello."

"I'm just here to see my dad." Her gaze landed on the file folders spread across the table. "What's going on?"

"Just looking for someone who would have a reason to want your father dead."

"I thought it was because of his stance on human trafficking."

"It is, but we need a name to put to the person behind the threats. Someone willing to kill to make sure your dad is silenced. Someone who has a lot at stake."

"I see. Of course."

"Can you think of anyone like that?"

Paula shook her head, but pulled file after file from the stack to glance through it. Chloe raised a brow at Blake, who nodded at the folder.

"Any of those ring any bells for you?" he said.

"No. I don't think so." Paula frowned. Studied one of the files a little closer, then set it aside to pick up the next. "It's like looking for the proverbial needle in a haystack."

"No kidding," Blake said.

With a deep breath, she set the file she was holding back on the table. "I'm procrastinating. It's time to face the music."

"Good luck," her mother said.

Paula grimaced and headed down the hall toward the master bedroom.

Lucy shook her head. "She's always had a bad temper. And then she regrets it and has to apologize. Sometimes I wonder if my future son-in-law isn't slated for sainthood."

Chloe smiled. "I understand. I know a few people like that myself."

"I'm sure."

Linc waved her back into the kitchen even as he spoke into the phone. She walked toward him. "What is it?"

"Annie called. She and David got a hit on Ethan Wright's whereabouts."

"Where?" Blake asked.

"Not too far from here. Looks like he moved into his aunt's house after his apartment building was scheduled for demolition. He's still using his old address, which was why it was so hard to track him down. Yesterday, he applied for a credit card with this current address and we got an alert. I've got a team meeting me there. We still don't know what his role is in everything, so we're just going to question him. But because we don't know his role, I want backup in place." He looked at Chloe. "Bring Hank."

"Why?"

"I just want him there. We have the video showing Rachel getting into the back of his vehicle. She was following him for a reason. I want to take every precaution to ensure he doesn't get away from us."

"All right."

Blake rose. "I want to come too. Just let me find someone to cover for me here."

"It's already been taken care of. Parker and Justin are on the way." Linc scowled. "And I only took care of that because I knew you'd insist on it."

"Thanks, man."

Linc grunted his acknowledgment of the gratitude. "All right. Things are moving fast. As soon as we know the judge is covered, we'll head out."

Blake's heart pounded. He could only pray that Wright could give them a clue as to why Rachel would have been in the back of his car. Why she'd followed him.

The guy had no priors. That reassured Blake somewhat. But that didn't let him off the hook. Everyone's life of crime started with

the first one and sometimes they weren't caught until the tenth—or more. And Rachel had chosen to follow him for some reason.

Blake sat in the passenger seat of Chloe's SUV. She'd parked it across the street from the house but down about three doors where they had a good view of the front door and the side. A team of agents and other law enforcement stood ready to move in should they need to, but for now everything remained quiet.

Linc approached the house and knocked on the door. If Wright was home and looked out the window, he'd see a man dressed in khakis and a dark blue collared shirt. Linc would identify himself as FBI when Wright opened the door.

Only no one answered.

Linc knocked again.

Still nothing.

Chloe chewed her bottom lip.

"What is it?" Blake asked her.

"I don't know. It's almost too quiet."

He glanced around. "Yeah, I know what you mean."

"Bryce would have told Wright that two cops came to the museum asking about him, right?"

"Probably." He paused. "Unless he didn't."

She rolled her eyes. "You're a big help. So, let's say he told him for the sake of argument. If Wright's guilty of something, he's going to wonder if we've found anything. And if he's not guilty, he should wonder what we wanted. The fact that he hasn't called makes my skin itch."

Blake raised a brow. "But you're assuming Bryce told him about our visit."

"True." She paused. "But why would he *not* tell him? He has to know we'll be back if we don't hear from Wright."

"Having two cops show up could rattle anyone. Maybe he doesn't want to rock the boat. Maybe he's worried his client is in trouble with the police and he's got that auction coming up. If his most sought-after artist gets arrested, where's that going to leave his precious auction?"

"In which case, he'd probably tell him to lay low until after the auction."

"I keep coming back to that."

"What?"

"The auction. Rachel mentioned the girls being sold at an auction. I think we should check into the possibility that there's a connection between that auction and the art auction."

"We can discuss that in more detail after we deal with this."

"Fine."

Linc had walked the perimeter of the house by this point and was now making his way back toward them. He stopped at Chloe's window and she rolled it down. "He's not here," Linc said. "Or, at least he's not answering the door. All the blinds are shut. There's an outbuilding in the back, but just looks like storage."

Chloe frowned. "The Suburban's in the drive."

"Might not mean much," Linc said. "Someone could have picked him up."

"Could have," she said.

Linc raised a brow. "But?"

But for some reason, she didn't think so. "You know, we were looking for him the other day. It's possible someone might be upset about that. You think Wright might be in some kind of danger?"

Her brother paused, studied her. Then gave a slow nod. "I think it's possible. If he's involved in the trafficking business and someone found out you two were asking around about him, then yeah, I'd say it's a real possibility. I might even say there are exigent circumstances warranting an immediate search of the property to ensure the safety of the occupant."

With exigent circumstances, they wouldn't need a warrant to

search. This might be stretching it a bit, but then again, there was no way to know for sure. "Great. Let's take a look and make sure Mr. Wright isn't in any immediate danger."

She climbed out of the SUV, slipped on a heavier coat to ward off the chill, and let Hank out of his area. She clipped the lead on his harness and walked toward the house. If the man had anything to do with the drugs being moved in the trailer where they'd found the girls, it's possible there would be traces of it on the property. She tucked the rope toy into her belt. But first, she really was rather concerned for the man. Linc's assessment could be spot-on. They needed to check on Ethan.

And find out why he hadn't called them. She, Hank, Blake, and Linc walked the perimeter of the home. Linc was on his phone getting background on the aunt.

"I don't see any sign of trouble, do you guys?" Blake asked.

"No, but . . ." Chloe shook her head. "He called in sick yesterday, but he's not at home. That's a red flag."

"Wouldn't be the first time someone's played hooky."

"True." But . . . "Hank, find the dope."

The dog went to work. She shortened the lead to about fifteen feet and let him have his way. Hank led her to the corner of the house, then around to the back and up on the deck. Hank took her back down the steps and across the yard to the outbuilding. He nosed the door, then sat. Chloe glanced through the only clean spot on the window and couldn't see much. She turned the knob and heard a slight snick that didn't sound anything like a simple door opening. She knew that sound. Or a similar sound. It could be nothing. Or it could be something big.

She froze. Her heart rate picked up and she blew out a slow breath while keeping the knob in the turned position. "Guys?"

Chloe turned her head slowly and spotted Linc walking toward her. She lifted the hand that held Hank's leash. "Stay back." He frowned and jogged toward her, followed by Blake. She scowled. "You don't listen very well, do you?"

"What's wrong?"

"There might be drugs inside the building. Hank says so anyway. But we'll have to do something about the bomb first. Now get back and call the bomb squad, would you?"

Her brother stilled and Blake jerked. "What?" he said.

She tilted her head toward her hand. "Something clicked when I turned the knob. I'm assuming it's rigged to blow when I either open the door or release the knob."

All color drained from his face. "You're sure? It wasn't just the release of the plunger?"

"I guess I could let go and find out."

Linc shot her a black look.

Blake was on the phone. She heard the words "bomb squad," then the address.

"Switch places with me," Linc said. "Let me have the knob."

"No way. Now back off and let the bomb squad come do their job."

"Chloe, I'm not kidding—"

"I'm not either. What if the only reason it didn't blow is because I have the right amount of pressure on the knob? If we try to change places, you could change that dynamic and blow us all up." Truthfully, she had no idea if that argument carried any weight at all, but it sounded good and might get him out of the way.

He winced, but didn't argue. He didn't move back either. Neither did Blake. She handed the leash to Blake. "Will you put Hank in his area in the truck?"

Blake took the leash, hesitated only a brief moment, then nodded. "Fine, but I'm coming back."

When he left, she looked at Linc. "Ethan Wright is former Army. What'd he do in the Army?"

"Not explosives, if that's what you're wondering. At least that wasn't in the file. He was a first lieutenant. Saw some action in Afghanistan, but was honorably discharged after being wounded by a roadside IED. Came back to the States and took up teaching and art."

All innocent enough. So, why rig his outbuilding to blow? It was locked. The knob turned easily, but there were two deadbolts that she could see were engaged.

The bomb squad chose that moment to roll to a stop just beyond the front of the house. Chloe's hand began to cramp and she clamped her lips together until the spasm passed.

Two bomb squad team members clad in their protective gear descended the sloping yard. One led an explosive ordnance detection K-9 who had his nose to the ground when they reached her. The handler looked at Chloe. "I'm Brad and this is K-9 Lulu. My friend there is Mitch."

Chloe nodded. She didn't recognize either of these guys and figured they were probably new. She hoped they weren't new when it came to explosives.

Mitch motioned for Blake and Linc to get out of the way. Linc grasped her free hand. "Don't let go of that knob until they give you the all clear."

"I don't plan on it."

Blake eyed her as well. She saw him swallow. "Go. Now," she said. "Both of you, get out of here." Neither man moved. "Please, Blake, Linc."

Blake shook his head. "I'm not leaving you."

Linc planted himself off to the side and crossed his arms. "I'm not leaving you either. Mom would kill me."

"Get out of here, guys," Brad said. "This is our scene and you're not welcome on it."

"Not leaving," Blake said.

"Me neither," Linc said.

"I don't have time to argue, but you guys are in serious trouble when this is over."

"As long as you make sure we live to face the trouble," Linc said, "I'm fine with that."

Brad snorted.

Tears gathered in Chloe's eyes as the two bomb squad members went to work. She was grateful for their support and furious at their stubbornness. "There's no reason for us all to be in danger. You guys need to move. Please." She honed in on Blake. "Rachel needs you around."

He flinched. "It's okay. It's not going to blow."

Brad's EOD dog alerted immediately on the door and Chloe let out a slow breath. "Well, I guess that answers that question."

"How much longer can you hold that knob?" Brad asked.

"As long as I have to." When she'd gripped the knob, she'd grabbed it with a tight hold, using muscles all the way up in to her forearm. Afraid to loosen her grip to give those muscles some relief, she simply endured.

She couldn't see Mitch's face through his mask, but she could imagine him frowning. "We need to see inside the building," he said, "but we've got to be careful how we do it." He pointed to the bottom of the door. "I'd try running a tiny camera under there, but it's flush to the ground and no way it would fit."

Chloe could read between the lines. He needed eyes in the building to make sure there weren't any other explosives rigged to blow if someone opened a window or drilled their way in. For the next few minutes, they worked on a way to get inside. Chloe alternated between praying and not letting the cramp in her hand get the best of her.

Mitch came back around. "We're going through the roof. There's a skylight we can get around and there's no sign of explosives attached to it. So hold tight."

"I'm holding." Tight. These guys were trusting her with their lives. There was no way she was going to blow them up. No matter how bad the cramp in her hand got. The only problem was her fingers were starting to go numb. Who would have thought holding a doorknob could turn into an act of sheer will?

18

Blake paced in front of the building where the bomb squad members worked quickly and efficiently to get inside. Normally, they used robots to handle the explosives, but there was no way to send a robot into this situation. It required putting human lives on the line.

Another member approached, finger pressed against his ear. Blake assumed he was listening to someone. The man's eyes slid to Chloe. "Mitch says they're inside. The door is rigged to blow with C-4. If you'd managed to push it in, you'd be dead."

"The deadbolts are on, so that wasn't even a possibility," she said. "Maybe he only wanted to kill if someone actually got the deadbolts open."

"What about the knob?" Blake asked.

"There's no lock on it. Someone put the deadbolts on there instead of just changing the doorknob, I guess. Anyway, looks like that was the trigger for the C-4 should the door actually open." He gave her a half smile. "Like if someone were to get the deadbolts open. They're pretty sure if you just let go, everything will be all right."

"Pretty sure?" she asked. "I'm not risking my life—and these crazy people who won't back away—on a 'pretty sure.' Could we get a hundred percent positive instead?"

194

"That's what we're working on, so even though it might be okay to let go, don't."

She scowled at him, and Blake figured Chloe didn't have any immediate plans to relax her grip.

A black sedan pulled to a stop behind the bomb squad's command center and a woman dressed in a dark blue pantsuit exited the vehicle. She swept her sunglasses down over her eyes and planted her hands on her hips.

Tabitha St. John. The chief of police—and Chloe's mother.

"Oh boy," he breathed.

She hesitated only a fraction of a second, taking in the scene, before she started their way. An officer laid a hand on her arm and she paused. Said something to him. He backed off and she continued down the slight slope of front yard.

She stopped when she saw Chloe, Blake, and Linc—and the bomb squad members on top of the building. Blake nudged Linc, who turned, spotted his mother, and jogged toward her. "What are you doing here?"

Chloe followed him with her eyes. That widened when they landed on her mother. "Oh, great."

Mitch came around from the side of the building and nodded to Chloe. "You still doing okay?"

"Just peachy."

The words were spoken through gritted teeth. She'd been holding the knob now for a good twenty minutes.

"We're inside and working," he said. "Shouldn't be too much longer."

"Chloe?"

"A little busy right now, Mom. Why don't you head back to the car and I'll let you know when I can talk."

The woman stopped her approach, standing a good distance away, but not far enough. "Glad to see you're holding steady."

"Oh yeah," she said, "holding steady. *Very* steady."

"How much longer?" Blake asked Mitch.

Mitch shook his head. "As long as it takes."

Blake wanted to punch the man, but since he knew the situation wasn't his fault, he held his temper and focused on the woman he was coming to care way too much about. "You can do this, Chloe," he said, his voice low and meant for her ears only.

She shot him a glare. "Y'all really aren't giving me much choice. I'd feel a lot better if everyone would just clear out."

"Can't do that and leave you here alone."

"Exactly," the chief said. She might have agreed with him, but he could tell she didn't like so many people in such proximity to a possible explosion.

The St. John family stood together. Blake knew that. Envied that. Chloe's relationship with her brothers and sisters were a source of fascination for him. Being friends with Linc meant having an open invitation into the St. John home. And it didn't take long to note that when one of them was in trouble, the rest came running to help.

A shiver wracked her and Chloe's gaze held his. "Hold on," he said. "Not much longer."

The chief's phone rang and she grabbed it. A helicopter hovered overhead and Blake figured it was a news crew. Awesome. How had they gotten ahold of this already? "Yes, she's fine, honey." Her eyes went to the chopper. "I know what's playing out on the news, but it's being handled. She's fine. Uh-huh. I will. Love you too. Bye."

"Dad?" Chloe asked.

"Yes. He wanted to know that you were okay." Chief St. John stepped closer, her face pinched. Blake thought she actually vibrated with the tension running through her. "You're okay, right?"

Chloe swallowed. Despite the "pretty sure it won't blow" reassurances, she was so scared she wanted to puke, but since that would up the possibility of getting her—and all of the people trying to help her—killed, she drew in a deep breath. "I'm okay, Mom. Scared, but okay." She couldn't break down yet.

"I am too, baby. But you know you've got the best working on it. Nothing's going to happen. We've just postponed the meal, but I expect you to be there for dinner."

"Sure. Absolutely. Wouldn't miss it."

"I mean it."

"I know you do, Mom, but I'd still feel better if you weren't quite so close. Can't you back up a little?"

"Nope. Linc," her mother said, "why are you standing so close? You too, Blake. You need to get out of range."

"We're not leaving her," Linc said.

"Yes, you are. And that's an order."

Linc blinked. Hesitated. Her mother removed her sunglasses and stared at the two men.

Still they didn't move, just stared back.

Her mother's gaze grew even frostier. Linc finally sighed. "Come on, Mom . . ."

She didn't waver.

Linc's jaw tightened, but he nodded. "Fine. Let's go, Blake."

"No."

Chloe sucked in a breath. Another one. Shivers hit her in spite of the heavier coat she'd put on. Fire flowed through her forearm. She desperately wanted to adjust her hold, but didn't dare. She wasn't comfortable with pretty sure. *Come on, come on, guys.*

Linc backed up while Blake continued to stare down her mother. "Blake—"

"She has no authority over me. I'm staying."

Chloe winced.

"Clear!"

The call came. Mitch came around the side of the building. "You can let go now."

Chloe tried to.

And couldn't.

"Chloe?" Blake stepped forward and placed his hand on hers. "You can let go."

She caught his eye. "You're sure?" Her gaze slid to Mitch. "You're absolutely sure?"

"Yes." He'd pulled his head gear off and his compassionate green eyes held hers. "I'm one hundred percent sure."

Chloe slowly let go of the knob.

When the plunger settled back into place, the explosion knocked her to her knees.

Blake yelled, something slammed into her, and Chloe found herself facedown on the wooden porch with a heavy body on top of hers. Stunned, unable to move for a brief second, she finally gathered her wits and her breath. "Blake," she managed to gasp, "are you all right?"

For a moment, he didn't answer. Smoke swirled around them. "Blake?"

"Yeah." He coughed. "I'm okay. Ears are ringing, but okay."

"Good, then get off of me, please."

He rolled and she helped him with a shove to his shoulders. When he landed beside her, he dragged in a long breath and stayed still. "You're okay? You're sure?" she asked.

"I think so."

Chloe looked to see her mother rising to her feet. One of the officers had tackled her too. "Sorry, ma'am. I didn't mean to hurt you, I just reacted. I'm really sorry. I—"

She patted his arm and raked a hand through her now mussed hair. "You're forgiven. As long as you're not hurt."

"No, ma'am."

"Good." She locked her eyes on Chloe's. "You're okay?"

Chloe pulled herself to her feet. "I'm fine, I think." Mitch lay on the other end of the porch. Chloe went to him, Blake on her heels. She dropped to her knees beside him. "Mitch?"

He groaned and sat up rubbing his ears. "What happened?"

"You said it was clear."

"It *was* clear." He stood, blinking. Grabbed the rail. "I'll find out what happened. Is everyone okay? Anyone hurt?"

"Not on our end. Not sure about your guy if he's still in the building."

Mitch went to the door. "Not a very big blast. Door is still there."

"Felt big enough to me," Chloe muttered.

Mitch examined the area that had been blown out by the explosion. He tried the door, then shook his head. "Deadbolts are still holding. The door is solid. That blow was meant to scare someone off and keep the door still in one piece. Kind of like a flash bang. Really masterful, if you ask me."

"Masterful," Chloe muttered. "Nice."

Brad rounded the corner, looking dusty, but still in one piece. "Sorry about that. He had the inside rigged as well. Just that small part where the plunger fits. When the plunger slid back into its resting place, it triggered the small blast. It wasn't meant to maim or kill, just to scare someone off. Just so you know, I ran the X-ray over the area. It didn't look like bomb material." He dropped his gaze. "It was so small, I never saw it."

"Not your fault," Chloe said. "Like you said, it was small. Big enough to scare, but not enough to do much damage."

Her mother approached once again and hugged Chloe. "Who's responsible for this?" she asked when she pulled away.

"A guy by the name of Ethan Wright."

She nodded. "Where is he?"

"That's what we're trying to find out."

She turned to Linc. "Get a warrant and search this place from top to bottom. Then find this joker and charge him with attempted murder."

Chloe realized the incident had shaken her mother. Badly.

"We'll find him, Mom," she said. "We need him found for more than one reason."

From the corner of her eye she spotted Brad talking to Linc. He nodded and approached. "Get away from the building. One of the other dogs alerted to the back."

They moved fast, heading toward the road where the other emergency vehicles were pulling back to a safe distance. Linc stopped Mitch. "Tell us what you find."

"Will do. Stay near your radio."

Sitting in the back of one of the ambulances, Blake massaged Chloe's arm while they waited.

Minutes crept past and Chloe closed her eyes while his fingers soothed her sore muscles.

Linc straightened and listened.

"What is it?" Blake asked.

"They managed to get some eyes inside," he said. "Brad just said the building is loaded with explosives. And drugs. There's enough street dope in there to fund a small city. My guess is he's holding it for someone."

"Drugs, human trafficking, probably weapons," Chloe said. She shook her head. "It never ends. No matter how hard we try, they just keep coming."

"Yeah," Blake said, "but this is going to put a hurt on someone."

"Probably Ethan Wright if he isn't already dead," Linc said. "When the owners of these drugs find out they've been confiscated, Ethan might just wind up a dead man."

Blake drew in a deep breath. "Then we need to find him first. Rachel's life may depend on it."

Rachel ate the apple slowly, savoring the sweetness on her tongue even as her gaze swept the small room she had yet to leave. When the man she could identify only by his voice had left, she'd sat up, used the restroom that was attached to the bedroom, and tried the door.

Locked.

Of course.

Instead of panicking, she'd sat on the bed, thinking. Planning. Praying. Wondering where Lindsey was and how she was faring. She prayed her friend was still alive.

When the lock had nicked open, she'd immediately lain back down on the bed and shut her eyes.

When she opened them—after being sure the person was gone— she'd seen the lunch tray. A chicken salad sandwich, two apples, a bag of chips—and a blood sugar monitor. She sighed and used the monitor. Her blood sugar was a little high, but she figured it was about right with all the stress running through her right now.

Starving, she'd polished off the sandwich, then the chips, and finally the apple. The second apple she decided to save for later. Halfway through the apple, the thought occurred to her that the food could be drugged, but she felt no effects so far, so she was going to assume she was fine.

The door opened midbite.

Rachel left the bite and lowered the apple.

Dark eyes glittered at her from behind the ski mask. "Looks like we're going to need you to move after all," he said.

"Move?"

"Back to the cages for now."

The food churned in her belly, but protest would be fruitless. They would just drug her or beat her into submission. Rachel reached for the other apple and slid it into the pocket of her jacket. She had no idea how she came to be wearing it, but it was warm, so she left it on.

She stood. "Okay."

Surprise flickered in the eyes. "If you're not going to give me any trouble, I'll let you walk."

"I won't give you any trouble." Yet.

"Good. Then walk."

Rachel walked. He placed a hand on her shoulder and she let him, proud of herself for not flinching away from him, as was her first inclination.

Out of the room, they walked down a hallway, through a kitchen, and down a set of stairs leading off from that kitchen.

A cement-walled basement. Probably soundproof.

Cages lined the far wall. Just like in the other house. Only these were smaller and held more girls. Eyes reflecting various emotions, the most prominent ones anger and fear, followed her progress across the floor.

He stopped at one cage. Hesitated, then directed her to the one at the end instead. "You can stay with your friend since you didn't give me any grief."

When he opened the door, Rachel's fear clawed at her. She sucked it down and stepped inside. The door banged shut and she couldn't help the flinch that shook her. She turned and met her captor's gaze.

He looked away. "Don't worry, you won't be in here long. It'll be time to load up in a bit."

"Load up to go where?"

His eyes reconnected with hers. "The auction."

When the lock clicked, he paused as though wanting to say something else—or waiting for her to respond. After several seconds ticked past, he shrugged and headed back toward the stairs.

Rachel knelt beside a shivering Lindsey. "Hey."

"Hey." Her friend's voice held no life. Just a resigned dullness that shook Rachel to the core, but at least she was speaking.

"Are you okay? Have they hurt you?"

"No and no."

Rachel slid down the wire wall of the cage to the cement floor. "My dad's looking for us."

"What do you mean? Where'd you go? Why are you back? No

one else has come back. I didn't think you were coming back. I didn't think I'd ever see you again. I want my mom." The last word ended on a sob and Rachel wrapped her arms around her friend's shoulders and pulled her close. Lindsey rested her head against Rachel's.

"I got away, but they caught me," she whispered. Why go into the details? Just thinking about her near escape and recapture brought tears to the surface. She should never have followed Carson from the hospital. All of her efforts to help had failed. But that didn't mean she was giving up. "We'll find a way to get out, Linds. We will."

Lindsey's tears soaked Rachel's shirt and Rachel couldn't find it in her to encourage her friend to stop crying, to have hope.

Because she didn't have it either.

19

After a dinner worthy of a gourmet chef, Blake now sat at the kitchen table of Chloe's parents' house, clicking through the latest information on Alessandro Russo. The man had grown up on the streets of Atlanta. Had gotten involved with the Leonardo Basico family who, at the time, had been the most feared Sicilian mafia family in the area. At the age of twenty-four, he'd married Veru Gallo, the only child of his boss, and had taken to crime like he'd invented it.

When Leonardo had died, Alessandro had stepped into the leadership role of the family. Since that time, he'd taken his involvement in crime to a new level. Gun running, extortion, murder, gambling, drugs, black market art, black market babies, and human trafficking. Just to name a few. The crime family had expanded from Georgia to South Carolina, North Carolina, and on into Virginia.

Busts had led to the arrest of a number of Alessandro's minions, those on the lower rungs of the crime ladder. But not once had anyone come close to capturing Alessandro Russo himself.

Blake wanted to be the one to do so.

His phone buzzed.

Frank
Dad's fading pretty fast. It won't be long now.
You need to come see him soon.

With a sigh, Blake texted back.

He was dead to me long ago. Quit asking me to
come. He wouldn't know me anyway.

But you still know him. I'm not asking for his
sake. I'm asking for yours.

Why?

You need to face him and then let him go.

Like you have?

Actually, yes.

Blake stared at the screen, then rubbed his eyes.

I'll think about it. I have more to worry about
than him.

It was a harsh response and he almost apologized for it, but couldn't force himself to type the words. If his brother felt the need to be with their father in his last days, that was his choice, his decision. Blake felt no such compunction.

Even though a little niggling of something started in the vicinity of his heart. Doing his best to ignore it, he looked up.

Chloe rinsed the next dish while her mother dried. Blake was having a hard time concentrating in the kitchen of the chief of police. A few years ago, he wouldn't have thought anything about it, but now, the fact that he'd been a bit rude to her during the whole Chloe-might-get-blown-up-by-a-bomb scare, his conscience nagged at him. But since she hadn't brought it up and had treated him as she always had, Blake kept his mouth shut. The ladies finished and the chief walked out of the kitchen without a word.

Linc entered the kitchen on the phone. "Yeah. Call me with anything else." He hung up and sat next to Blake.

"News?" Blake asked.

"Yeah. ERT finished processing Ethan Wright's house. They found something interesting."

"What's that?"

"A lot of fake IDs. Including one that belongs to Carson Langston—with Ethan's picture on it."

Blake's eyes widened. "So, Ethan and Carson are one and the same?"

"It appears that way."

"We need to find him. I want just three minutes alone with him."

Derek pointed his fork at Blake. "That's not going to happen."

Blake raised a brow. "We'll see about that."

Derek snorted. He had arrived ten minutes ago and filled his plate. The others were expected to show up any minute.

"They find anything else?" Blake asked.

"Nothing that directly relates to the case, but they're going through the evidence as we speak. You know, the usual. Phone records, bank accounts, real estate holdings, cell phone bills. So maybe something else will turn up." Linc stood. "I'm going to fill Mom in."

He left and Derek sat down across from Blake and proceeded to attack his food as though something weighed heavily on his mind—or it had been awhile since his last meal.

"You okay?" Blake asked him.

"Yes. Just not catching any breaks when it comes to finding Russo or those connected to the trafficking ring. I'm frustrated."

Blake waved a hand at the laptop. "I know what you mean."

The man paused midshovel and his eyes met Blake's. "Yeah, I guess you do. In spades."

Blake looked away, his throat going tight. Would he ever see Rachel again?

"Any word from Rachel?" Derek asked.

"No."

"I'm sorry."

"I am too."

Chief St. John reentered the kitchen and wiped her hands on a towel. "Have you been able to connect Ethan Wright—or Carson Langston or whoever he is—to Alessandro Russo? Seems like if we could track down Russo, who we know is involved in human trafficking, we could locate the victims."

Like Penny. He could tell her niece was in her thoughts.

"No, ma'am," Derek said. "And Van Stillman, the man we *did* manage to connect to him, is so low on the food chain, there's no hope of him knowing anything. He's an errand boy. Follows orders without asking questions and takes his pay." He sighed. "He's not talking anyway."

The back door opened and Brady, Ruthie, and Izzy stepped into the kitchen. They told Blake hello and hugged their mother. "Sorry we're late," Ruthie said. "We were all at the hospital. I just finished a surgery, Brady was checking on someone who'd done a nosedive off the Gervais Street Bridge, and Izzy was there questioning a victim of something."

"A mugging," Izzy said. "She gave us a good description so I think we'll be able to get the guy sometime soon. I can't believe we all managed to leave at the same time."

"Well, grab a plate. There's plenty. I've kept it warm for you." Eating in shifts was as natural as breathing to this family. Blake had learned to go with it a long time ago. Which was why he had a full belly and Derek was still eating.

"Thank you for the meal, Mrs. St. John."

She walked over and rested a hand on his shoulder. "You're welcome, Blake."

207

He cleared his throat. "Um. I'm . . . uh . . . sorry. About being disrespectful earlier today. I didn't mean . . ."

Everyone in the kitchen went still at his apology and all eyes turned on him and the chief.

"Don't worry about it," she said. "It was a tense situation." Her eyes flicked between Chloe and Blake. "I'm glad to know you have her back."

He held her gaze. "Yes, ma'am. I sure do."

A faint smile curved her lips. She gave his shoulder another pat, then kissed Chloe's head. "I'm going to join your father upstairs in the media room. He's had a movie he's wanted us to watch for the past two months. I think tonight's the first night we've had more than two hours together in a very long time. We're going to take advantage of that."

"Enjoy," Chloe said.

She left and Derek packed a plate to go. "I'm going over to see Elaine."

Chloe raised a brow. "I thought you two were broken up."

"We were. Are. Were."

"Which is it?" Ruthie asked. She set her plate on the table and sat down.

He rolled his eyes. "I don't know. I'm going to find out. See you."

"Right."

The door shut behind him.

Chloe stared at the door for a good five seconds before she blinked and turned her attention back to Blake. "Want to take a walk?"

"It's freezing outside," Izzy said. "Better just find a cozy spot in the den or on the sunporch."

"Fine. Want to join me in the den?"

Curious, but feeling like a bug under a microscope, Blake closed his laptop and stood. "Sure."

Once they were out of hearing range of her siblings and seated comfortably on the L-shaped couch, Chloe laid a hand on his arm and left it there. "Do you mind if I ask you a pretty personal question?"

A little shocked at the intimate gesture, he hesitated, then gave a small shrug. "I guess not."

"What did Rachel mean when she said, 'I know I'm not really yours'?"

He sucked in a sharp breath. "You caught that, huh?"

"Yes."

Blake stood, feeling a momentary pang at dislodging her hand. He liked her nearness. He liked the way she smelled, with her vanilla bean and strawberry fragrance that was as much a part of her as the dark curls she kept in a ponytail 99 percent of the time. If he was honest, he pretty much liked everything about her. Except maybe her nosiness sometimes. And her questions that probed at wounds that seemed healed but could be ripped open with one sharp tug.

He paced to the window that overlooked the large backyard. If he could see them, he knew the trees would be bare of leaves and the pool would be covered. "She's not my biological child." He turned to look her in the eye. "But she's mine in every way that counts."

She blinked. "Of course."

"When Aimee found out she was pregnant, she went ballistic. She was terrified of what her parents were going to say."

"Where's Rachel's father?"

"He bailed on Aimee as soon as she told him. Told her to get an abortion. He enlisted in the Army and was later killed in Afghanistan."

"Oh no. Even jerks like a deadbeat dad don't deserve that."

"I agree. I knew the guy and he really wasn't an awful person, just immature and irresponsible. If he'd had the chance to grow up, he might have turned out okay." He blew out a breath. "Anyway, ironically enough, in spite of the fact that her mother was a physician, Aimee was scared to death of doctors." And that was the only thing that had saved Rachel from being aborted. "Aimee and I were friends—and I'll admit to a slight crush on her. So, when she came to me, desperate and scared, I offered to marry her." He scowled and slid his eyes from Chloe's. "I was young and stupid and thought I could convince her to love me in time. But she didn't. When I changed my focus from law and decided to go to the police academy, she was furious. She didn't want to be married to a cop, she wanted someone with the potential to make a lot of money. So, she found someone else."

"So, basically, she used you. Used your feelings for her."

"Pretty much."

"I'm so sorry, Blake."

"I am too. And while I didn't think I'd ever recover from the pain, I have. I was over Aimee before she died. But Rachel, she's mine as sure as the sun will rise in the morning." He gave her a sad smile and pressed his fingers against his lips.

"What did your parents think of you getting married so young?"

He stiffened. "My mother was buried at the bottom of a bottle, so I'm not sure she was even aware. And my dad? Well, he didn't seem happy about it, but since his opinion meant nothing to me at the time, I didn't care."

"Wow. I didn't realize your relationship with your parents was so . . ."

"Awful?"

"Tense."

He let out a low, humorless laugh. "Awful. Yeah. It was tough growing up, but we survived."

"How?" she whispered.

"My uncle's a cop. He was one of the good guys and did his best to make sure he influenced me in a positive way. He also beat my dad within an inch of his life and told him if he ever laid a hand on me or my brother again, he'd arrest him and throw away the key."

"Whoa."

"Yep. That was when I was fourteen and Frank was ten. Mom had taken off about a year earlier and Dad wasn't so careful about where he left the bruises. Uncle Greg figured it out one afternoon and that was that."

"Did your dad ever hit you after that?"

"Nope. Punched a lot of walls, but not us."

"Good," she whispered.

Tears swam in her eyes and he swallowed at the responding lump in his throat. Clearing it away, he shook his head. "There's just one thing I can't figure out."

"What's that?"

"How Rachel knows I'm not her biological father. I've never told her."

"Did Aimee?"

He shook his head. "I mean, as far as I know she didn't. She was the one who was so adamant that we keep it between us." His eyes narrowed. "But someone told her and I plan to find out who. As soon as I get Rachel back." Getting her back was the priority. His heart ached. She might not have his blood running through her, but he loved her with every fiber of his being and he'd do whatever it took to get her back safe.

He rubbed his cheek and caught Chloe's gaze. "How do you feel about helping me kill the judge?"

Chloe blinked. "Um . . . what?"

"It's the only way I'm going to get her back."

"Blake, you're scaring me."

He grimaced. "I don't mean actually *kill him*, kill him. But what if we faked it? What if we explained everything to him and asked him to help us out?"

She gave a slow nod. "Maybe."

211

"The thing that gets me is that the guy who called was very confident that he would know when the judge was dead. Like he would be informed immediately."

"Like by someone close to the judge?"

"Exactly."

"But . . . who? We've vetted them all. Every coworker, every person he comes into contact with on a daily basis. Everyone. Including his family."

He frowned. "I don't know."

"And that could backfire too," she said.

"What do you mean?"

"If they believe he's dead, they won't have any need for Rachel anymore."

He hung his head. "I thought of that, but I don't think they'll kill her."

"Why not?"

His eyes met hers. "I think they'll sell her."

"Even with her medical issues?"

"I think so. It's a gamble, I know, but I just don't see these people passing up tens of thousands of dollars."

She bit her lip and nodded. He was probably right.

"I think, from what you said Rachel told you in the hospital, that they're going to be moving fairly quickly."

"The auction."

"Yeah. And if that's the case, if the judge isn't dead, they'll hold on to her and continue with their threats." He swallowed. "Or start sending me pieces of her."

She winced.

"So," he said, "I think I have to take a chance on this and act. These people are greedy. They're not going to kill a beautiful girl who could bring them top dollar in the market—even if she does have diabetes." His voice roughened as he fought the emotions running through him. Chloe covered his hand and squeezed. He cleared his throat. "I think if we make it seem like the judge is dead, then they may send her with the other girls going to the auction."

"Speaking of *that* auction, I think it's time to go with my first instinct and dig into the fact that it could actually be connected to the museum."

"I agree. We need to at least rule it out."

"Everything keeps circling back to that place. Ethan Wright, who we know is involved somehow . . . the flyer with the auction date," she frowned, "I don't know. I think they're connected."

Blake rubbed his chin. "Maybe. The guy did paint for the place. It has regular auctions or sales all the time, though. Could just be a coincidence. I mean, there's nothing else that points to it being an auction house for girls."

"True—although that Bryce dude was slimy. So where? If they send her and we don't know where and we miss the window of rescue—"

"I know. I know. That's what we have to find out."

"But how?"

"I'm working on that part."

Linc walked into the den and slumped into the chair next to Blake. "Well, we found our artist."

Chloe sat up straight. "Where?"

"Brady just fished him out of Lake Murray."

"What?" Chloe's and Blake's voices blended as one.

Blake dropped his chin to his chest. "Unbelievable."

"They're scared," Linc said. "We're putting pressure on someone. They knew Wright was the lead we were chasing and they got rid of him."

"Great," Blake said. "Just great."

Chloe felt his pain. She closed her fingers around his and squeezed. Then turned to Linc. "And they didn't find anything at his house?"

"That's part of the update. They found a file cabinet in the home office. A search turned up some letters from Ethan to his mother when he was in a foster home. His mom had lost custody for neglect and he ended up in the system for a while. He eventually went back to his mother, but he wrote her a couple of letters, talking a little about the different people he was meeting, how he hated school, and how he wanted to go home. Typical teenage boy stuff. We ran all the names he mentioned in the letters and one raised a red flag."

"Which one?" Chloe asked.

"A guy named Alan Garrett."

"Who's Alan Garrett?" Blake asked.

"He was a prisoner who was killed a couple of years ago by another inmate."

Chloe tilted her head. "What was he in for?"

His eyes met hers. "Human trafficking. One of the victims identified him in a lineup."

"Whoa."

"Turns out, he was innocent, though. Three days after he was killed, the victim recanted and said she'd picked the wrong guy. Six months later, she was found in a back alley with her throat slit. We still don't know who did it."

Chloe gasped and Blake's fingers tightened around hers.

"So, what's Ethan's connection to this guy?"

"From what I gathered from the letter, they shared a foster home and went to the same high school. I tried tracking down a couple of relatives of Ethan's and all I could come up with was an uncle in Charleston who owns a company named All the Wright Exports. I gave him a call and he said he saw Ethan on a regular basis and was hoping to see him this weekend. I had to tell the man that wasn't going to happen. He's on his way to identify the body."

Blake winced. "Ah man, that's tough."

Linc nodded. "He was pretty devastated. Apparently, after Ethan left the foster home to move back with his mother, things didn't work out too well. This uncle stepped in and took him in his last year of high school. He said he saw the talent in Ethan and sent him to art school. We're also looking into Alan Garrett's family and background. I want to know who his parents are, if he has any siblings, friends, whoever. From there, we might be able to get a little bit more information on the connection between the two."

"Back to the girl who accused Alan of trafficking her," Blake said. "What about Ethan Wright? If he and Alan were friends or something, he might have killed her because of her faulty testimony against Alan."

"I would be all over that except he has an airtight alibi."

"What's that?" Blake asked.

"He was in the hospital having his gall bladder removed at the time of her death."

Chloe sighed and rubbed her temples. "This case is giving me a headache."

"Anyway, I just wanted to run this by you. I've got Annie searching for more. And I think David's volunteered to help her. Over dinner, if I'm not mistaken." He smiled, then sighed. "I'll let you know if I find out anything else."

"Thanks, Linc," Chloe said.

Blake pressed his palms to his eyes. "I'm running out of time." He dropped his hands and shot a look at Chloe. "It's time to see if the judge is willing to play dead for a little while."

"What are you talking about?" Linc asked.

They shared their idea with Linc, and by the time Blake finished spilling his plan, her brother was nodding. "That might work. If he'll agree to it."

"The fact that it might save Rachel's life isn't motivation enough?" Linc raised a brow. "All we can do is ask."

Blake picked up his phone.

"What are you doing?" Chloe asked.

"Letting the kidnappers know the judge is about to die."

Linc frowned. "But he hasn't agreed yet."

"I'm not really interested in giving him a choice. We need to buy time. This is the way to do it. He'll agree."

Chloe met Linc's gaze and could see the concern there. She knew he was thinking the same thing she was.

It was probably time for Blake to be pulled from having anything to do with the case.

When she looked back at him, his glare singed her, then jumped to Linc. "Don't even think about it. I'm not going off the deep end. I just think this is the best plan for now."

Chloe sighed. "Do you know how much paperwork this is going to require?"

"A lot," Linc said.

"More than a lot," she said. "How fast can it be done?"

"After we get the judge on board, hopefully, fast."

Looked like they were going to find out.

Blake stood in the den of the judge's home and tried to read the man's expression. It was dark and it was late and everyone just wanted to get some sleep, but Blake was running out of time.

Ben finally walked to the fireplace and looked into the flames. The artfully arranged gas logs made a pretty picture. A direct contrast to the one Blake had just painted for the man. "They found your daughter and told you to kill me or they'll kill her."

"That's the sum of it. Yes. But since killing you for real is not an option, I need for you to simply play dead for a few days. At least until we catch these people."

"But you don't know who *these people* are, do you?"

"No. Not entirely. We do have some good leads that give us hope that we'll get this wrapped up soon."

Chloe cleared her throat. "We do think it's someone close to you. Someone who knows you well and is aware of your every move.

So, if you agree to the plan, you'll have to let everyone, including your wife, believe you're dead."

He drew in a deep breath. "Not Lucy. I can't let her believe that. And my children? No, not them either. But everyone else, fine. I don't like it, but . . . fine."

Blake pinched the bridge of his nose. "Sir, if your wife knows you're alive, she's not going to respond appropriately. People will know."

"Then no. I won't do it."

A yell welled in Blake's throat. With effort, he swallowed it.

"What about this," Ben said. "What if Lucy knows the truth, but takes to her room and refuses to see anyone except the kids? Then she won't have to put on an act and that's probably what she would do anyway should I die."

"Not the kids," Blake said. "Please. My getting Rachel back hinges on everyone believing you're dead."

Ben's gaze met his. "They're not going to let her go," he said softly.

"I have to believe—and act—like they will. Not in the hopes that they'll really release her, but with the intent of buying time so I can find her."

The man nodded. "I understand that. All right. For Rachel. But only for a couple of days."

"Thank you," Blake whispered.

The front door opened. "Mom? Dad?"

"In here, Paula," Ben called to his daughter.

Paula stepped into the den, her purse swinging on her elbow. She was a truly striking woman. Her professional dress fit her to perfection and her makeup could have been done by an expert.

"Wow. Do you ever get to be alone?" She raised a brow as she took in the scene.

"No. Not right now." He didn't sound like he cared.

She acknowledged each of them, then focused back on her father.

217

"Good, I'm glad. After the shooting at the courthouse, you need people watching your back for sure." She frowned. "Have you seen Stan?"

"No, not lately. He called to check on me after the shooting, but hasn't been by. Why?"

"He was supposed to get me in to see an inmate and hasn't gotten back to me."

"Who's the inmate?"

Paula waved a hand. "It doesn't matter. What's the latest on the bill?"

"You know the latest, Paula. There's nothing else to report."

"Fine. Where's Mom? I need to talk to her about that charity event she wants me to attend with her. I'm not sure I'll be able to, but Stan said he'd go in my place."

"I don't care which one of you goes, just as long as one of you does. I can't. I'm not taking a chance on bringing danger to the people there."

Paula's jaw tightened. "You think someone would actually do that?"

"Why not? They shot at me in a busy courthouse."

"Yes, they did. You're probably right. I get it, Dad, but that doesn't mean I have to like it."

The judge sighed. "Check the sitting area in the bedroom. Last I saw her, she was curled up with a book."

"Thanks." Paula nodded to them and headed down the hallway to her parents' bedroom.

Blake watched her go, then turned back to the judge. "Here's what I have in mind."

20

MONDAY MORNING

The man in the recliner aimed the remote at the television and powered it off. So. It was done. Judge Benjamin Worthington had died of a heart attack in his sleep. According to the reporter, the man had told his wife he was feeling ill and went to take a nap. He never woke up. His family, friends, and coworkers were in shock.

The marshal had done it.

If it was true. But his source was infallible. When she'd called him crying to tell him, he almost hadn't believed it. No, the judge was dead. Finally.

Too bad Rachel MacCallum would never see her father again. But that was fine. The brat. He'd like to wrap his hands around her throat and squeeze the life out of her, but that would be cutting off his nose to spite his face.

And that would be stupid.

She'd served her purpose and now she'd bring him a very large profit. He debated whether he should just kill her and be done with it, but the lure of the money was too great. As much grief as she'd caused him, he might as well make a profit off her. The fact of her diabetes wouldn't be an issue. He had a very special client in mind for her. He'd use her, then kill her. And he'd pay very handsomely to do so. So, Rachel would earn her keep and die in the process. It would all end well for him.

He picked up the phone from the end table and speed-dialed his contact.

"Yeah?"

"It's done. Put her in the next auction and get rid of her."

"You got it."

He hung up and leaned back with a deep breath. The stress of the last few weeks rolled off his shoulders.

"Who were you talking to?"

He looked up. "No one, honey. No one important. Just a business deal that needed some attention."

She smiled. When he'd gone looking for this woman, it was that beautiful smile that had stunned him. Attracted him. Even the realization that he could have made a lot of money with her hadn't motivated him to win her over. No, he'd had other plans in mind. Plans other than money.

When she'd responded positively to his flirtations, he'd been gratified, though not necessarily surprised. Most women found him attractive. He held out a hand. "Come sit with me. We should plan our next trip."

"I'm just so tired."

"I know. Can I do anything to help?"

"Yes." She curled her arms around his neck. "Just hold me."

He kissed her. "Italy?"

"Or France."

"Or both."

She smiled at him, then leaned over and nuzzled his neck. "Mm. Yes. Both." A sigh slipped from her. "Thank you for understanding. What would I do without you?"

He'd keep her.

For now.

Two hours ago, one of the captors had come into the room leading two women wearing ski masks and carrying large bags. "All right, everyone, listen up. Today is the big day. Thelma and Louise here are going to help you get ready for it. Thelma is in the red mask, Louise is in the blue. Thelma is hair and wardrobe, Louise is everything else. You'll be assigned outfits and makeup. From lingerie and dresses to heels to makeup to jewelry. You will look perfect in every way. Classy, not cheap. Is that understood?"

Even though her stomach was in knots, Rachel raised a brow and met his gaze. This was the man who'd snatched her from the store and from the edge of safety. He'd worn the ski mask in the store just like he wore one now, so she had no way of knowing who he was or what he looked like and she didn't recognize his voice. But she'd know those eyes anywhere. "Thelma and Louise? Let's hope so."

He scowled. "Not their real names. Can't take any chances now, can we, Houdini?"

Rachel snapped her lips shut. No need to antagonize the man. She'd been scared to death when she'd heard him talking to her father about "punishing" her, but he'd simply hung up the phone and stared at her before spraying her again.

He turned away and began his leisurely pace in front of the cages once more. "So, how many of you enjoy the beach?"

Silence.

"I said, how many of you enjoy the beach! Do you enjoy the beach? Answer the question!"

"Yes!" They answered in unison.

"Good, because we've got about a two-hour ride today. If you're good and cooperate, I might let you take a little walk in the sand. Would anyone like that?"

A few staggered yeses echoed in the cement room.

"I thought so. Now. Here are the rules. We'll be using a large cargo van. You will sit on the floor. You will not attempt to look out the back windows. You will not attempt to escape." His eyes locked on Rachel. "If you do, you will die and your family will die. You don't need to bother to think, you just need to follow orders. It's really that simple. Understood?"

He waited until she nodded with the others.

Keeping his eyes on hers, he said, "There's no one coming to rescue you, there's no Superman in Columbia, no knight on a white horse. It's just us. So, get hope out of your system and replace it with acceptance. It's the best way to stay alive and survive. There. That's my advice. I suggest you take it. Understood?"

Even though fury burned with every pulse of her heart, Rachel forced her face not to reflect it. She gave another slow nod along with the other girls. Seemingly satisfied, if slightly surprised, with her docile response, he tilted his head toward Thelma and Louise. "Get to work, ladies."

Sitting in the conference room of the FBI office once more, Chloe pushed the auction flyer across the table to Linc. Blake sat next to him. The other task force agents leaned in. "I think this whole auction thing is some kind of cover-up."

"It's an art auction," Linc said. "A real auction. People are coming from all over to buy paintings. And now that Ethan Wright is dead, his paintings are going to go for top dollar."

"I know. I think the auction is on the up-and-up. Mostly. I just think there's another facet and it's connected to the human trafficking ring somehow."

"Okay." He leaned back. "Connected how?"

"I don't know. I'm going on instinct. Did they find anything at Ethan's house?"

"Nothing that would lead us to where they're keeping the girls. Why?"

"Just curious." She frowned, her brain going faster than she could keep up with. When the meeting ended, Chloe blinked and realized she'd missed the end of it. About to ask Blake to fill her in, she snapped her lips shut when everyone stood and started to file out of the room.

Blake placed a hand on her arm. "I'm on Alessandro Russo duty today. The judge is covered with undercover officers posing as friends of the family. News crews got aerial footage of his 'body' being put into the back of the coroner's vehicle and taken to the morgue. It looks good, but we're going to have to move fast."

"What's our next step? I missed it."

"Jo and I are going to focus on Russo and—"

Her phone buzzed. "Hold that thought," she told him, then lifted her phone. "Hello?"

"Need you and Hank on a traffic stop. Drugs suspected."

"Address?"

The dispatcher passed it along to her and she wrote it down on the pad still on the conference table. "Got it. ETA is about ten minutes."

"I'll let the officer know."

Chloe hung up. "I've got to go. Keep me updated."

"I will. You do the same."

She nodded, clicked to Hank, and they headed for her vehicle.

Nine minutes later, she pulled to a stop behind two state troopers and a woman wearing a tank top and gym shorts in the fifty-degree weather. Chloe guessed the drugs were probably in the car and not on the woman.

Although, she'd been surprised before.

A man in his late twenties leaned against the car, his wrists cuffed behind him. Chloe left her red lights turning and climbed out.

When she had Hank beside her, she approached the others. The two state troopers were good buddies of Brady's. "Hi guys, what do we have?"

"Not sure. That's what Hank's going to tell us."

Chloe nodded and walked the dog over to the vehicle.

"Hey, there's nothing in there," the woman said. "You're, like, violating our rights or something. I want a lawyer."

Chloe raised a brow. The trooper nearest her, James Kincaid, held up a baggie that contained a joint. "Was in her right front pocket."

"Gotcha." She looked at the woman. "Probable cause. No rights violated."

"It's just one joint," the woman said. "That's it. There's nothing else."

Chloe scratched Hank's ears. "Hank, find the dope."

The dog went to work and in short order found an entire stash of joints and wads of cash in a hidden compartment in the trunk.

"Wow," Chloe said. "Looks like your instincts were right on. Probably five or ten grand there. Plus whatever the drugs are worth."

"Yep. Nice work, Chloe. Good job, Hank." James rubbed the dog's head and Chloe handed him his toy after she put him in his area of the vehicle.

Once the troopers had cleared out with their prisoners, Chloe sat on the side of the road thinking.

The auction was still niggling in the back of her mind. What was it? Something she'd seen. Something that she couldn't put her finger on but needed to.

She sighed. It would come to her. In the meantime, she had an idea she wanted to check out.

Fifteen minutes later, she pulled in front of the art museum where Ethan Wright's work was being showcased. The auction was to be held later this evening, but already people were there, eager to pick out which painting they planned to bid on. Chloe turned to Hank. "You get to stay here, my friend." She poured water into his bowl and scratched his ears. "I won't be long."

She went to the back of the vehicle and grabbed her "go bag."

Never sure where she would be from one moment to the next, she always carried several changes of clothing with her. In the bathroom of the restaurant across the street, she changed into khaki slacks, a pale pink shirt, and white blazer to hide her weapon she now sheathed in the shoulder holster.

Stashing her bag back in the vehicle, she paused a moment. What was bugging her? As she glanced at a car that had parked several spaces away, a flash blipped across the screen of her mind. She'd seen that car somewhere before. It wasn't exactly a popular model in Columbia. Only the very wealthy or the deeply in debt could afford a Mercedes like that. So. Where had she seen it?

The security footage of the SUV in the parking garage. The guy in the sedan. It was just like the one that had pulled to a stop in the parking garage. The driver and Ethan Wright had had a conversation. He'd asked for directions. There'd been a background check on him and it'd been clean. The details were coming back to her. His name was Atkinson, maybe? She snapped a picture of the car.

She stepped inside the building and simply wandered for a few moments, getting the feel for the place. Wright's paintings were prominently displayed just as she'd figured they would be.

She approached the first painting. "Number 7," she said and glanced at the man standing next to her. "What's the process for bidding on one of these?"

His eyes raked her, then narrowed. "There's an app. Download it."

"What's it called?"

"It's under the name of the museum."

"Thanks," she murmured. She continued her stroll, wanting to get away from his eyes. If she had to be in his presence too often, she'd like to do a background check on him. With a grimace, she ignored him and continued looking at each painting, taking in the details, the sheer talent. "Amazing," she whispered.

"I know," a voice said behind her. "I can't believe he's gone.

And just as he was about to break through into the big time. Such a shame."

Chloe turned to find a woman in her late twenties gazing at the picture. "Take that one," she said. "The waves are angry, lashing out at the shore, frothing and writhing in fury. It's one of his darker ones and I can't help but wonder what was going through his head at the time he painted it."

"You knew him?"

"In passing. I have some of my art on display here as well." She frowned.

"What is it?"

She gave a light shrug. "Nothing really. Ethan was an odd one. He had so much talent, but it was like he didn't really care."

Because he was making more money in the human trafficking arena?

"Did he ever say why he didn't care?" Chloe asked.

"No. And I could be wrong. We didn't talk that much. He would show up for the shows and be all charming and sell most of his stuff, then he'd just disappear until the next show."

"And that's unusual?"

"Very. Artists aren't like most people. We're just wired different. Which is why we like to hang out with others who are wired the same way. Usually, we meet once or twice a week to work or talk about the latest artistic medium, get feedback on a painting, whatever. Ethan wasn't ever interested in being a part of the group."

"Maybe he just didn't need that like others."

"Maybe. Then again, I know he spent a lot of time in Charleston. His uncle has a huge party yacht docked at one of the ports. I always hoped Ethan would issue an invitation, but he never did."

"Hmm. Interesting."

She rolled her eyes. "Weird." Then laughed. "I'm Serene, by the way."

"Serene?"

"Yes, it's my actual birth name."

"I like it."

"Thanks." She sighed. "Well, I suppose I need to go mingle. Maybe I can talk someone into buying art from a living artist instead of one who's no longer with us."

"I wish you all the best."

Serene smiled and glided away on silent feet. Chloe grimaced. She'd never been that graceful in her life.

She pulled her phone from her pocket and tapped in a group text to the task force agents.

> At the museum where Wright's auction is happening tonight. Check out his connections to an uncle in Charleston. Has a "party yacht" docked somewhere. No reason other than Ethan Wright appeared to spend a lot of time there. No other info. Will text if I get more.

21

Blake sat at his desk searching for and pulling every scrap of information he could find on Alessandro Russo, Van Stillman, and Ethan Wright. Probably a futile endeavor, but he was convinced he must have missed something that could help him. His phone buzzed and he read Chloe's text. "Party yacht, huh?" he muttered. Then typed back a text to Chloe.

> I'll ask him about that when he gets here to identify the body.

Here's another picture. That nice Mercedes from the hospital parking garage is here. I think. Check the plates and see if it's the same, will you?

> Will do.

He entered the information and had an answer within seconds.

> It's the same.

Could be coincidence.

Could be. Want to get some lunch later?

Sure. Text me when you're ready.

As his thoughts centered on Chloe, his attention moved from the case for just a brief moment to the huge influence the St. John family had had on him. With his abusive father and strung-out mother, he'd had a pretty dim view of marriage and family. Then Linc had wound up his best friend in seventh grade and taken him under his wing—and into his home.

A knock on the door brought his head up and his thoughts back to the case. He raised a brow when he saw Rachel's swim coach standing there. "Hi, Roger, what's up?" He kept his tone light, but dread filled him even as he scrambled for what to say to the man that wouldn't be a complete lie and wouldn't put Rachel at risk.

"All right if I sit down?"

"Of course."

Roger made himself comfortable in the older arm chair that faced Blake's desk. "I'm concerned about Rachel."

"I know. She's missed a few practices."

"Yes." He rubbed a hand down his cheek. "Blake, she's my best swimmer. Actually, she's the best I've ever coached in my twenty-two years. I never would have expected this from her, but if she doesn't have a good explanation for skipping practice, then I'm going to have to cut her from the team. And I *really* don't want to do that."

Blake sat for a moment trying to decide what to say. He finally nodded. "Look, Rachel is having some personal issues right now. I can't divulge any more than that. All I can say is that she loves being on your team just about more than anything, but is physically unable to participate right now."

Roger's brows dipped. "I'm so sorry. Why didn't you call me and let me know?"

"I was hoping the situation would be resolved by now. But it's not and to be honest, I'm not sure how much longer it's going to take."

"Is there anything I can do?"

Blake met the man's gaze. "Don't kick her off the team."

With a sigh, Roger leaned forward and clasped his hands between his knees. "I won't for as long as administration will let me get away with it." He paused. "You can't give me any more information that I can use to fight back with should they tell me I have no choice but to kick her off?"

"Let's just say that her safety hinges on me keeping her location quiet."

Sharp blue eyes studied him. "This have something to do with your job?"

"I can't say," Blake said. He kept his gaze steady on the coach's.

The man paled a shade and he swallowed. "Someone's threatened you. Or her," he said softly. "You've got her in hiding?"

It was a good guess. One that he'd let the man go with since Blake had deliberately steered him in that direction. "Like I said, I can't say anything else. Just that this is out of Rachel's hands, and if she could be at practice, she would."

"I can't believe this. First Lindsey and now Rachel. What's happening in this world?" It was a hypothetical question and Blake didn't bother to try and answer. Clearing his throat, Roger stood. "I'll be praying for her."

"Thank you. We'll take the prayers. And I would appreciate it if you'd keep this to yourself. If you absolutely have to share it with the principal, then you have my blessing. I've been fielding their calls about her absences but am going to have to offer an explanation before long. I've known you a while and I know you can keep your mouth shut. The principal at the high school is new this year. Can he keep it quiet?"

"Yes. Absolutely. We all think the world of him."

"Then I'll leave that in your hands."

The coach shook his head. "All right. Let me know something when you can."

"I will."

He paused. "Wow." Then left the office.

Blake shut his eyes. "Yeah," he whispered aloud. "Wow."

Chloe wandered through the multitude of rooms, noting that Ethan Wright had at least one painting on every wall. When she came to a closed door, she tried the handle and was surprised when it opened. She stepped through and let the door click shut behind her.

No heat blew through the vents in the floor, leaving the room chilled. A shiver wracked her even as her eyes traveled the room. They stopped on the wall opposite her. Smaller paintings, all the same size, covered the space.

Upon closer inspection, she made out that there were twenty-six total, each with a number in the bottom right-hand corner of the frame. "Huh." Maybe this was just a new way of doing things in art museums. It wasn't like she was an expert or anything. But it was strange that they were back in this room, shut off from everything else. What did it mean?

She downloaded the app and stood there a few moments, figuring out how it worked. Thankfully, it was simple and well organized. Each artist had his or her own page with a picture of their works. One simply had to tap on the picture to get information and place a bid. Chloe went to Ethan Wright's page and scrolled through his work.

But the paintings in front of her never showed up.

Maybe she could just ask.

Then again—

"What are you doing in here?"

She spun to see Bruce—*Bryce*—standing in the doorway. "Oh, hi. I thought this was a part of the show. The door was open."

"Well, it's not. This is a restricted area."

Tension threaded through his words and Chloe raised a brow. "I see. I'm sorry. Could I ask you a couple of questions, though?"

"Ma'am, I have a show and an auction to conduct. Can't your questions wait?"

Chloe lasered him with her best official look. "And I have a murder to solve. I'd really appreciate your cooperation."

"Very well. Ask away."

"Why are these paintings back here and what do the numbers represent?"

"They're back here because they're not for sale." He cleared his throat. "And the numbers . . . uh . . . represent the order each was painted in, I believe." He flushed. "I hate to admit that I'm not sure." He sighed. "You wouldn't believe the mess I inherited."

"So, is that why they don't come up on your handy little app here?" She waved the phone at him.

"Exactly. Well, because they're not for sale. I've never been told why and I've been so busy trying to get everything organized that this room has been low on my priority list."

"Interesting." She walked toward him. "So, Ethan spent a lot of time in Charleston. Do you know what he was doing there?"

"Spending time with family is what he told me. And painting." He swept a hand to the wall. "Doing a lot of painting as you can see. Now, please—" He motioned her to the door.

Chloe nodded. "Are you aware that we've connected Ethan to a human trafficking ring?"

He blanched. "A what? No. Absolutely not. He would never involve himself in something so awful."

"Well, unfortunately, the evidence shows that he did. Do you have the names of any of his contacts? Friends? Fellow artists?"

"I do not. Ethan and I weren't exactly close. He was a very talented artist—and the only portion of the deal that I was actually glad to have inherited. And now that he's gone, I'm going to have to find someone to replace him. If you find who killed him, I hope you put him away for a very long time."

He was truly upset. Whether it was about the loss of life or the loss of profit, she couldn't decide.

"Now, please," he said, "come enjoy the rest of the auction. I'll be sure to lock this room so no one else wanders astray."

"Yes. Do that. And thank you."

"Of course."

His cultured voice held an undertone of steel and Chloe figured he was more than capable of cleaning up the mess he'd been left with. Was that true or was he just feeding her a line? Something to distract her and take her attention from him and his gallery?

Ethan had been one of his artists. No doubt he had some kind of file or something in his office. She hoped he still used a file cabinet and didn't have everything computerized. That might make what she was planning a bit more difficult.

Chloe tracked the man as he turned on the charm and began to greet the people who would drop a lot of money on Wright's pieces in a couple of hours.

When she was sure he had lost interest in keeping up with her, she slipped through the growing crowd to the hallway. With a glance to the left, then to the right, and back over her shoulder just to double-check, she strolled through the area Bryce had come from the day she and Blake had first talked to him.

"Can I help you?"

She turned to find the young man who'd been behind the reception desk. Neal. No last name surfaced in her memory. "No, I'm fine, thanks. Just checking out the paintings." Fortunately for her, the walls of the hallway held several pieces of amazing artwork.

"Those aren't for sale, you know."

His superior attitude irked her. "Yes, but I can still appreciate beauty even if it's not for sale, can't I?"

"Ah, yes. Well . . ." He tilted his head toward the crowd. "If you'll excuse me?"

"Of course. It's been a lovely visit, but I guess I should get back to work."

He started to leave, then turned back. "You're a cop, right? You were here the other day."

So, he recognized her even without the uniform. "I am. And I was."

His gaze flicked past her then behind his shoulder. "Where's your partner and dog?"

"The dog *is* my partner. But if you're talking about the guy that was with me, he's working on something else right now. I'm just here to appreciate the art."

"Hmm. You really think you can afford anything on display?"

She raised a brow. "Wow. Judge much?"

He grimaced. "I know. You're right. I'm sorry."

Chloe frowned. She couldn't get a read on the guy and that bothered her. Part of her wanted to say he was a harmless snob. Snob? Yes. Harmless? She wasn't sure yet. "No problem."

"Okay, enjoy the art. I'm going to mix and see if I can sell a painting or two. Commission, you know."

She hadn't known. But okay.

He walked away and she headed for the offices. Spying the cameras in the ceiling, she paused while pretending to study another painting. Should she risk it? Did they have someone monitoring them? It was possible.

The security guards had been stationed in the other area with the more expensive work. Hopefully, that would be where the cameras were aimed today because she was going to chance it.

She knocked on the nearest door and waited. No answer. She tried the handle. Locked. A breath hissed between her teeth. Of course. The door next to it was also locked. *Rats.*

Looking back over her shoulder, she pondered her next move. When her gaze landed on the empty desk Neal had occupied the day she and Blake had been here an idea sparked. More like a long shot. She really shouldn't. It would be trespassing, and anything she found would be inadmissible in court. And if she were caught, she could be brought up on charges. But what if it helped her locate the girls?

Deciding it was worth the risk, Chloe hurried over to the desk, checked to make sure no one was looking, then ducked behind it. She opened the top drawer. "Well, well, what do you know?" she whispered.

Bingo. She snatched the keys and almost shut the drawer when her eyes landed on a picture of three boys. She pulled it out for a better look. One of the boys looked familiar, but she couldn't place him. On the back, someone had written "Hopkins family." She snapped a picture of both sides, then on silent feet, headed back to the office door, passing three newcomers who'd just stepped inside the museum. They ignored her and aimed their steps straight for the crowded gallery that held Wright's paintings.

In front of the office marked Director, she tried the keys until one turned in the lock. "Thank you," she whispered, then slipped inside and shut the door behind her. The office was large, probably twenty by fifteen, and held a desk with a leather chair, a laptop—and a file cabinet in the corner. A leather sofa sat against the far wall and a plush oriental rug covered most of the hardwood flooring between the sofa and the desk. Chloe moved to the file cabinet and opened the last drawer, labeled V–Z.

Quickly, she thumbed through the files, only to find nothing under Wright. "Of course. Couldn't be that easy." She turned to the desk and wiggled the mouse. Password protected. "Naturally."

She set the office keys on the desk and looked at the open folder sitting on top of the scattered papers on the desk. Fleming wasn't exactly the neatest freak in the place. With his uppity attitude and his perpetually curled upper lip, she would have figured him for one who thought everything had a place and everything should be in it. Then again, maybe he'd inherited the mess. But eight months seemed like enough time to get everything straight.

Shoving the folder aside, she found the flyer for the auction. Papers regarding sales of paintings, expense reports, and more. And something about a delivery to Charleston. To a port? Which one? She pulled the file folder closer and glanced at the door.

"What are you doing in here?"

Chloe flinched and looked up, pasting an innocent smile on her lips. "Oh, hello, Mr. . . . um, Neal, right? How are you?" She slipped a hand into her pocket and closed her fingers around her key fob. She didn't like the look in his eyes.

He stepped into the office. "How did you get in here?"

"The door was unlocked."

"No it wasn't." His focus dropped to the keys she'd placed next to the monitor. "Been snooping?"

She was so busted.

"Um. No, those were there, why?"

His eyes narrowed. "Are you looking for something?"

"Yes, you."

The direct approach seemed to surprise him. "Well, you've found me. What did you need?"

"Do you know a young man by the name of Carson Langston?"

He stiffened. "No. Why?" His body language shouted *liar*.

Her question had been a shot in the dark, a desperate grasp at *something*. Bull's-eye. "I think you do."

"And I figured you were going to be trouble the first time I laid eyes on you. Because of you, Ethan had to die."

Two of the security guards she'd noticed in the gallery area stepped into the room, weapons held at their sides. She noted the suppressors on each one. With a cold ball of fear growing in her gut, she knew they had experience in using them. She had the

236

brief thought of going for her weapon, but decided she'd be dead before her fingers touched it.

"Now, are you going to come nicely?" Neal asked. "Or does this have to get ugly?"

Chloe pressed the button on the fob and released Hank from the vehicle. He'd be confused, but at least he wouldn't be trapped. With a mixture of terror and determination, she realized she was going to find out exactly what happened to the girls and where they'd been taken—the hard way.

Rachel sat on the floor of the van and held Lindsey's cold hand in her own. They'd had their trial run of dress and makeup and practicing poses until Rachel wanted to puke. But she went along with it without protest, unlike one of the other girls who refused to cooperate. Rachel hadn't seen her since, but her screams would echo in Rachel's dreams for the rest of her life. She swallowed against the ever-present lump in her throat and shuddered, then looked around one more time, still not completely convinced they couldn't somehow escape.

The rear windows of the van had been blacked out, leaving the back dark and stuffy. She and the other girls were packed into the space, sitting on foam padding that covered the floor.

First, seventeen girls. Now twelve. Originally, she'd thought they'd only sent the seventeen in the trailer because they didn't have room for the others, but now, she wondered if they had originally only sent part of their "inventory" on purpose, thinking that if some were found or escaped, it wouldn't disrupt their "business" because they had more to replace them. Sick, sick, sick.

Shuddering, she saw that someone had rigged a spring rod and curtain so no one in the back could see the driver or the passenger. But the little camera in the back corner near the double doors said those in the front could see the girls.

Tears dripped and she swiped them away with a sharp flick. This was so wrong. No one should be allowed to do this to another person. And where was God in all of this anyway, that's what she wanted to know. Didn't he care? Or was this her punishment for being such a horrible daughter? *God, if you're there, I'm really sorry about everything. I don't want to be angry anymore. And I don't want to be afraid either. Please help me. Help all of us.*

"Yeah, I know. We'll be there in about an hour," the driver said. Rachel tuned in to the words that came from behind the curtain. "I know, man. You got the other girls?"

He must be on the phone.

"Tell him about the extra one we've got." The person in the passenger seat spoke for the first time. Not a voice she'd heard before. She let her gaze slide to the woman who lay unconscious near the back doors.

After loading the other girls, they'd added her. The *extra* one the passenger had referred to. Chloe St. John, the officer who'd been so kind to Rachel in the hospital. Hope had immediately blossomed when she'd realized who it was. They'd duct-taped her hands together, but otherwise she was free to move about.

If only she would wake up.

Inch by subtle inch, Rachel slid her foot across the van floor until it rested against Chloe's shoulder. Keeping her eyes on her hands as though subdued and without fight, she pressed with her foot. Once. Twice.

Chloe didn't move. How much of the drug had they sprayed her with? As best as she could calculate, they'd been moving for about an hour. She waited another thirty minutes and thought she saw Chloe's eyes begin to flutter. Rachel pressed the woman's shoulder again and she finally stirred. Then lifted her head. Blurry eyes locked on Rachel's and slowly cleared. Rachel knew the moment reality hit Chloe by the way she drew in a deep breath and stiffened. Rachel didn't look away until Chloe understood she wanted to tell her something. The woman dipped her head slightly.

Rachel slid her eyes to the camera in the corner.

Chloe's eyes narrowed and she rolled her head slightly, then back to Rachel. She gave another small nod.

She understood. Rachel sighed and pressed the palms of her hands against her eyes to relieve the pressure of the tears that wanted to fall. When she let her hands fall away, Chloe lay still, her eyes closed. What was she doing? Going back to sleep? Rachel knew she probably felt nauseated and was trying to keep her stomach where it belonged so she left her alone. The feeling would pass in about thirty minutes. About the time they should be arriving to their destination.

Rachel leaned back, tried to ignore the headache building behind her eyes, and began to pray once more.

22

Blake slammed a fist onto his desk. "Yes!"

A coworker looked up, caught a glimpse of the satisfied look on Blake's face, and shot him a thumbs up. "I know where you are now, you scumbag, and I'm going to get you."

Linc entered Blake's office with his own triumphant smile. "We got something off the GPS from the eighteen-wheeler involved in the crash on the bridge."

"And I know where Russo is."

"Where?"

"Charleston."

Linc's brows rose. "Well, well. Do you believe in coincidences?"

"Not really. Why?" Blake pushed aside the sandwich he'd forgotten to eat and waited as Linc cleaned off a chair to sit down. "And why'd it take so long to get the addresses off the GPS?"

"A bullet hit it. They basically had to rebuild it and hope for the best."

"And?"

"There were four addresses in there. One was the Chapin address that we already know is a dead end. Two are in Charleston and one is the museum—slash—art gallery place you and Chloe visited."

"Which seems to indicate that Wright drove the truck once upon a time."

"Could be. But why would he need the GPS? He knows where the place is."

"True. Could have been someone else."

"How long have the addresses been in the system?"

"Annie said they couldn't tell. She was just glad to get them for me."

"Right." Blake rubbed his eyes, his excitement growing. It felt like they were getting somewhere, and that if that was the case, it meant he was closer to finding Rachel. "All right, so we need someone in Charleston to check out these locations. Find out what they are. Businesses? Residences?"

Linc shot him a tense smile. "Annie's already on that. One is an export business. A warehouse full of cars waiting their turn to get shipped out of South Carolina."

"Cars, huh?"

"Looks legit too."

Blake frowned. "A lot of things can look legit without being so. What reason would human traffickers have in visiting a car export business?"

"Haven't figured that out yet. Want to take a chopper to Charleston? We've got agents on the ground there, of course, but this is my case. I want to be there so I've got the chopper lined up and waiting."

"Absolutely. I was just going to let my boss know I'm heading that way."

Linc stood. "Works for me."

Blake grabbed his phone. "I need to let Jo know too. She can cover for me where it's needed."

"How's she doing?"

"Still sore, but you know Jo. Nothing keeps her down for long. She's still at home, but wants to be kept in the loop."

"Of course."

"And Chloe. She'll want to go."

"Call her."

Once they were settled in Linc's SUV en route to meet the helicopter, Blake called Chloe. When her voicemail picked up, he frowned. "Linc's got a lead," he said after the tone. "Heading to Charleston and wanted to pick you up. Call me." He hung up. "Should we just go on?"

"Yeah, she must still be busy at the museum. We'll fill her in later."

Blake didn't like it, but agreed they didn't need to delay.

The chopper was warmed up and waiting when they pulled into a parking spot near the landing pad. The pilot waved them over and they ran for it. Only once seated with belts buckled and headgear pulled over their ears did Blake draw in a deep breath. His phone buzzed.

Frank
Please, Blake.

His brother. Once again pleading with Blake to visit their father. Blake sighed and dropped his head back against the headrest. The chopper took off and he shoved his phone into the clip on his belt. Would Frank hate him forever if he didn't at least put in an appearance before his old man's death? His younger brother meant everything to him, next to Rachel. Blake had taken more than one beating for him as a teen. If he could do that, why was it so hard to join him and support him while their father lay dying?

He didn't have an answer to the question. It just was.

Shooting a text to Chloe provided the distraction he needed.

Where are you? Still at the museum?

The helicopter ride passed quickly. Blake pulled his phone off his clip and checked for messages. Still no response from Chloe. "Chloe's still not answering," he said.

Linc frowned. "That's kind of odd. She always answers even when she's on a case. It's imperative that she keep her phone close by."

"No kidding. Which is why I'm concerned. I know she was at the museum. Maybe she got a call."

"Call her lieutenant and see if he can tell us where she is. I want Hank to be there should we need him."

Blake used the headphone jack to connect his phone in order to hear and dialed the number. Finally, he was put through to Chloe's boss.

"Sir, I'm looking for Chloe. Can you tell me where she is?"

"I sure wish I could. We found Hank and her vehicle outside the Palmetto Museum. Chloe's nowhere to be found. Can't raise her on her phone or her radio."

Chills swept him. "That's not like her, sir."

"Of course it's not. And she sure wouldn't let Hank loose."

"Loose?" Blake shouted. "I thought you meant someone found him inside the vehicle."

"No, looks like she remotely let him out. An officer passing by saw the door open and Hank jump out. He couldn't see where there was a problem, but called it in and started looking around. When he gave me the address, I sent him inside the museum to investigate. He initially didn't see anything that alarmed him but kept searching and found an office that looks like someone put up a struggle."

Not good. Very much not good. "What did they say happened?"

"Chalked it up to an irate buyer who lost out on the painting he wanted."

"They file a police report?" Blake asked.

"Nope. Said the man stormed out, and because of the computer smashed on the floor, they don't have access to his information to give us."

"That has the stench of a lie."

"Pretty much. The museum director stated they didn't want the negative publicity and they wouldn't be pressing charges."

"I don't buy that either. Chloe's in trouble."

"I agree, now let me go so I can get back to looking for her."

Blake hung up and found Linc watching him. "What is it? What's wrong?"

"Chloe's missing," Blake said.

"Missing? What do you mean, missing?"

"I mean she's missing and whoever has Rachel probably now has Chloe."

He wanted to throw up.

Chloe drew in a breath of fresh air when the back doors opened. It chased the last bit of nausea from her system, but she didn't let on to the masked man, who grabbed her by the forearm and pulled her into a sitting position, then out of the van. "Come on, you can sleep later." Neal's voice. Interesting. The other girls must not be able to identify him. Otherwise, why bother with the mask?

"Feel sick," she mumbled and let herself sag against him.

He gave an exasperated grunt and lowered her to the ground. "Puke on me and you'll regret it. The drug should have worn off by now anyway."

"Tell that to my stomach."

He let her sit there while ordering the other girls off the truck. She used the moment to take inventory of the surroundings.

Seagulls squawked overhead. A cold wind scented with salt and sand brushed her face.

They were near the water.

The door to a nearby warehouse stood open. A yawning black

244

hole, waiting to snatch and swallow those who dared enter. Or were forced to.

Rachel walked past her without looking, her right hand clasping that of the girl she'd been sitting next to in the van. Chloe took a closer look and realized it was Lindsey. The others filed past and into the warehouse without fuss. Chloe wondered if she'd left enough of a message behind for someone to realize she needed help. Certainly, the fact that she'd remotely let Hank out would be a big red flag. If someone found him.

And before they'd sprayed her, she'd managed to knock everything off the desk, overturn the lamp, kick over the printer, and toss the laptop against the far wall. Then the biggest security guard had tackled her, knocking the breath from her while his partner sprayed her in the face. After that, darkness.

Neal gripped her arm once again and yanked her to her feet. A dozen self-defense moves came to mind, but she waited. "I know you're a cop," he hissed in her ear. "That doesn't matter to me. You're young and you're pretty. You'll bring a good price. Now go." He gave her a hard shove and Chloe stumbled toward the door.

She reached for her weapon, not because she thought it was there, but because it was habit. And, of course, the gun was gone. Probably the first thing they'd taken once she was knocked out.

Neal shoved her into the dark interior of the warehouse. A quick glance at the contents brought a frown. Cars?

A hard hand on her shoulder snapped her head around. "This isn't a tour. Keep walking," Neal said.

Biting her tongue, Chloe did as ordered, taking in as much detail as she could while she walked. "They're looking for me by now, you know."

"Probably."

The absolute unconcern in his voice sent chills skating up her spine.

"They'll find me. They'll find all of us."

"No. They won't." He pointed her to the door and gave her another push.

Chloe wanted to punch him. She flexed her fingers and curled them into a fist. Growing up with three brothers had taught her how to fight. Most importantly, how to fight dirty. And when to make her move.

23

The chopper set down in the designated landing pad. Linc pointed to the waiting vehicle and, after shouting their thanks to the pilot, they raced for it.

Linc slipped into the driver's seat and Blake snapped his seatbelt on. The keys were in the ignition. "How far away are we?"

"Not sure, but we're following those guys." He pointed and Blake spotted the two vehicles.

"The feds in the unmarked cars?"

"Yep. And we've got more meeting us at the port. There's a team scouting the building right now and they're supposed to report in. If the girls and their traffickers are in there, I don't want to go in with sirens blaring and have them panic and start shooting or something."

"Yeah."

Linc pulled in behind the first dark sedan and they raced toward their destination—and hopefully Chloe and Rachel. Within ten minutes, Linc stopped the car. "We're on foot from here."

Together, they made their way down to the side of the warehouse where a SWAT member met them, looking decidedly unconcerned. "So far, there's no activity that we can find."

Blake nodded to the white van parked off to the side. "Who does that belong to?"

"Not sure."

Linc sent a text. "Annie will run the plates. So, there's no one inside?"

"No. The place is empty. We've already cleared it."

"What about the other address?" Blake asked.

"No one there either."

Deflated, Blake walked over to lean against the wall. "I had really high hopes for this place. I don't get it. This was the address in the GPS. If they're not delivering girls here, what are they delivering?"

"Cars?" Linc said. He didn't believe it any more than Blake did.

Blake stepped inside the building and the first thing he noticed was the scent of the ocean. The second thing he took note of were the rows of cars. Row after row. He moved quickly, not completely convinced they weren't in the right place.

Linc followed him. "This address was in that GPS for a reason."

"Yep. I'm not ready to pack it up and go home yet."

"Me either. What do you think it is about this place and not the other one?"

"I did my research while you were driving." He reached the end of the rows of cars and stopped. "And this one has a boat dock."

The water lapped at the sides of the empty area where a very large boat—probably a yacht—could sit. Linc's phone buzzed. He checked it and drew in a breath. "And guess who that boat dock belongs to?"

"Let me see if I can get it in one. All the Wright Exports."

"You win. Belonging to Henry Wright."

"Let me hazard another guess. Uncle to one now deceased Ethan Wright–slash–Carson Langston?"

"Yep."

Blake huffed out a breath and planted his hands on his hips. "Now what?"

"We see if a boat left here recently—what time and who was on it."

Chloe sat at the back of the room on the bench. At least it wasn't a cage.

"A yacht," she whispered. "Of course." It made perfect sense. When she'd first entered the warehouse, she'd thought they'd reached the end of the line, but they'd been herded past the cars to the multimillion-dollar yacht sitting at the dock. "Everyone on board," Neal had called out. "One at a time."

They'd filed on board and been locked in the room. That had been an hour ago. A spread of food had been left on the table. Fruits, cheeses, deli meats, and bread.

And the PDM for Rachel to check her blood sugar and give herself insulin. Chloe rose and went to the closet. She pushed the pocket door to the side and found a wardrobe worthy of a queen. Dresses, short shorts, sequined tops, impossibly high-heeled shoes. No jeans, T-shirts, or anything remotely comfortable—or warm. She grimaced.

No doubt they would be required to pick something out to wear for the auction. She pressed a hand against her churning stomach and turned to walk to the window. Looking out, she could see blue water, other yachts, and a lot of sailboats. No shore. At least on this side. How far out were they?

The door opened and Neal stood there. This time he hadn't bothered with the mask. "Time to eat, ladies. The festivities will begin in a couple of hours. So, let me explain how this works. You will eat, shower, whatever. Then change into the clothing that was chosen for you back at the house. Thelma and Louise will be here to do your makeup and hair. When you're finished, a number will be pinned to your shoulder."

Chloe gave a silent gasp. The number. She was willing to bet the number would match up to one of those paintings at the museum. Somehow there was a code. Each girl was matched to a painting and the buyers perused the "merchandise" in advance. Then bid on the "painting." Checks and balances. An audit would show paintings sold. Not girls.

She tuned back in. ". . . one by one you'll be led to the auction viewing area. The men bidding on you are doing so remotely. Once the bidding is finished, you will be taken to a pickup area where you will meet your new owner."

Chloe seriously thought she was going to hurl. A quick look around said she wasn't the only one. Real fear hit her. What if she couldn't protect them? What if she couldn't protect herself? What if they really weren't found in time? She honestly hadn't given that question consideration, because it never occurred to her that things would get this far. Except they had.

"Now, any questions?" His eyes met the gaze of each girl before locking onto Chloe. "No funny business or I'll just kill you, understand?"

Clenching her teeth, Chloe forced herself to nod.

He frowned, then left.

The girl beside Chloe broke into sobs. "I can't do this," she wailed. "I'm not going to be someone's slave. I'm not going to have an owner. I'm going to college to be a doctor. This isn't happening, tell me this isn't . . ."

Another jumped up and raced to the door, pounding on it with her fists. "Let me out! Let us out! You can't do this!"

Chloe wrapped an arm around the girl next to her and shushed her.

Rachel went to the girl still screaming at the door and dragged her away. "It'll be okay. Stop. We don't want him back in here, okay?"

She calmed immediately, the threat of Neal's return acting better than a sedative. Gulping huge gasps of air, she ran a shaky hand over her hair. "Okay. You're right. I don't want him back in here, but I'm not going to be sold. I'll jump overboard and kill myself first."

"You've made it this far," Chloe said. "Don't give up hope yet. What's your name?"

"Hannah."

"All right, Hannah, save your strength in case you need it." She lowered her voice. "We *are* going to get out of this somehow."

"How?"

All eyes were on Chloe and she sighed. "I don't know, but I'm thinking. Just give me a little time to come up with a plan. But no matter what happens, don't give up. Even if you're passed off to—" she couldn't say the word *owner*—"whoever, don't think that it's over. Hold out hope, okay? Because as long as we're in this area, we've got people searching for us. Promise me."

Hannah swiped the tears from her cheeks, nodded, and returned to the sofa where she curled up and closed her eyes.

Chloe urged her brain to process a plan a little faster. "Okay, girls, listen up. We've got to stop panicking and start thinking." She was going to have to take her own advice. Shoving aside her fear, she waited for the rest of them to look at her.

When she felt sure they were listening, Chloe stood up. "Do any of you see any cameras or monitoring devices in here? Everyone look. And while you're at it, see if there's anything that can be used as a weapon. Anything sharp or heavy."

With them busy, Chloe went to Rachel. "Go eat something. It's been awhile. And you might want to check your sugar."

Rachel glanced at the food. "You have a plan, don't you?" Her soft words were hardly discernable.

"I'm working on one." Sort of.

"Did you see the guards?"

"I saw them."

"What do I need to do?"

Chloe walked over and picked up a slice of bread and slathered mayonnaise on it. She then added meat and cheese and topped it with another piece of bread. "Follow my lead. But you're going to need to eat."

"You think it's safe to?"

"Yes." She popped a piece of cheese into her mouth, chewed and swallowed. When nothing happened over the next few minutes, she breathed a relieved sigh. If they hadn't drugged the girls when they had them earlier, they most likely wouldn't start now.

Rachel fixed herself a plate, checked her sugar and gave herself some insulin, and shot Chloe a thumbs-up. Then she began to eat.

One by one, the girls followed suit. No listening devices or cameras had been found. Chloe had checked light fixtures and every nook and cranny she could reach. She'd even pulled up the edges of the carpet to see if she could spot wires.

But nothing. And nothing that would make a good weapon. Of course not. They would have thought of that before making this the holding room.

She studied the light fixtures. Could she break one of the bulbs and use the sharp edge as a knife? Maybe.

Walking from one end of the room to the other, she ate her sandwich and thought. "Okay, girls, here's what I think we should do."

They looked at her, waiting.

"Just go along with everything. Don't fight them, don't make them mad. Do whatever for now. Even if the auction goes as planned, they still have to deliver us to the men who are doing the buying." Fighting the nausea the words elicited, she rubbed her forehead. "I know I've got people looking for me and I think I've left enough of a trail that they'll be able to follow it." Maybe. "So, don't give up hope and let's just stay alive until rescue happens or I can think of a plan." She was repeating herself, but they needed it. They needed her to give them hope, make them believe they were going to get away and see their families again. Get their lives back. The responsibility sat heavy on her shoulders.

The girls nodded slowly, obviously still scared out of their minds, but glad to have someone on their side take charge.

A plan. She needed a plan. *Think, Chloe, think.*

When the door opened and Thelma and Louise arrived, Chloe was still thinking.

And still coming up empty.

24

"No security footage, no nothing," Blake said. He stood on the dock, hands on his hips, looking out over the expanse of water. Yachts and sailboats and other luxury crafts cluttered the peaceful area. "Where did all these come from?"

"There's some kind of sailboat race going on. Or something. There are a number of good-sized yachts out there as well."

"We need the chopper."

"I've already got it making passes," Linc said. "If they see anything suspicious, they'll call it in."

"So, we just stand here? Wait for the ship to come in?" He wiggled his fingers around the last question. "I'm not liking that plan." He paced. "I want a boat. I want to be out there on the water."

"You want to go search each ship, don't you?"

"I do." He slid a glance at Linc. "You do too, don't you?"

"Of course. We need a search warrant."

"We would. If we were searching." He paused. "What if we just go knocking on doors, so to speak."

Linc raised a brow. "I'm following you."

Probably because he was thinking the same thing. "Good. I've got a picture of Rachel. We'll approach each yacht as two officers looking for a runaway." His frown deepened. "Some of those sailboats—in addition to the yachts—look big enough to hold a lot of people. I don't want to skip them and miss her."

"Let's start with the yachts." He paused. "And if you get weird vibes from anyone?"

"We play it cool and call in reinforcements."

"Will you be able to do that if you think Rachel's being held on one of those vessels?"

Blake rubbed his eyes. "I'll have to, Linc. I'll do whatever it takes to find her—including playing it cool and not attacking anyone I may think is involved."

"Good enough for me."

"Are you going to be able to play it cool if you think Chloe's on one?"

"Guess we'll find out." Linc put in the call while Blake wondered if he believed his own words. If he thought Rachel and Chloe were on one of the yachts, he'd be hard pressed not to act immediately. "We'll have a boat and a captain coming within the next fifteen minutes," Linc said.

That was too long for his peace of mind, but he'd take it. "Fine."

He'd put the wait time to good use. By praying. And calling in more reinforcements.

Chloe finally had a plan. A really bad, risky one, but at least it was a plan. Over the next few minutes, as she had the opportunity, she outlined it to Rachel under the pretext of helping Rachel with her pod. Thelma had turned away. "Leave your PDM hidden under something in the room," Chloe whispered. "Tell them you have to get it before you leave."

"What if you go first?"

Thelma looked at them, and Chloe raised her voice. "You got it, honey?" Thelma turned away once again and Chloe dropped her words back into a whisper. "I don't think we'll have to worry about that. Pretty sure they'll make us go last." She glanced up at Rachel. "We're the outliers."

Rachel nodded.

"You about finished with that?" Thelma asked. "You need to sit down and shut up."

"Almost finished," Chloe said. Back to Rachel, she whispered, "You'll have to tell me where the other girls are, so remember to wait until you find out."

"I will." The teen's fingers shook and Chloe knew she was terrified.

"Shut up, you two," Thelma said. "That's enough. If it's not fixed, it's not fixed."

Chloe closed her lips and patted Rachel on the arm while the girl pulled her shirt over the pod they'd done nothing with.

Louise busied herself with the last girl's makeup. Megan. Chloe met her eyes in the mirror and winked.

Hope flared in Megan's eyes before she lowered her gaze, but Chloe had a feeling she'd stay strong. And that the plan would work. Because she'd only get one chance.

And then it began.

Louise received a call and chose a girl. Over the next two hours, the woman removed each girl one at a time while Thelma stood guard. Louise would walk the girl from the room while the others waited in tense silence. Made up and dressed up, they looked as though they should be waiting for their prom dates.

Not their turn to be sold to the highest bidder.

No one spoke. No one cried. No one fought. Chloe almost wondered if that had been a mistake. A tip-off to their captors that something was up. Every fifteen minutes, the door opened and another girl disappeared. Chloe figured they were taking the ones sold to another location on the yacht.

She slid over to a shaking Megan. "Can you play sick when I nod at you?"

"Easily."

Thelma shot her a look and Chloe walked away, not wanting to get Megan in any trouble.

And then it was just her, Rachel, and Megan in the room. When Louise returned, Chloe nodded.

Megan immediately bent over and retched. Louise shrieked. "Get in the bathroom before you puke on the carpet, you stupid girl!"

Megan bolted.

Chloe looked up and caught Rachel's eye. In spite of being pale and scared, an underlying thread of steel emanated from her.

"I'll help Megan," Chloe said. "Does it matter if the girls go out of turn?"

Louise floundered for a moment. "No, I guess not." She lifted her phone. "I'll let Neal know what's going on." Her eyes hardened. "But get her ready. If she's still puking, she'll just have to go out there anyway."

Chloe nodded and slipped into the bathroom while Rachel let the woman lead her away.

Oh, please, God, let this work.

Megan looked up as Chloe entered. She rinsed her mouth and shot Chloe an apologetic look. "I actually threw up."

"I understand. You did great," she whispered. "Now, we're going to have to go back out there and you're going to look shaky, but holding tight to your composure, okay?"

"Okay. The shaky part won't be hard at all."

"You can do this, Megan."

"You promise you have a plan to get us out of here?"

"I promise I have a plan." Whether it would work or not remained to be seen. *Oh please, God, let this work.*

"Then I can do this."

"Think about what you're going to do when you get home. What do you want to do more than anything?"

"Hug my little sister and tell her I love her. I was so mean to her the day they took me," she whispered. "I don't want those words to be the last thing I say to her." Tears flooded her pretty eyes once more. She whisked them away and straightened her shoulders while she took a deep breath.

"Focus on that."

Megan nodded. "Yeah."

A hard fist knocked on the door. "It's time, Megan. Pull it together and let's get going."

With one last steadying breath, Megan opened the door and stepped back into the room. Louise waited at the exit, door open. Megan walked over to her with a glance back at Chloe, who gave her a slight nod.

The two disappeared and the lock clicked back into place. Chloe browsed the food again, her knotted stomach rebelling at the thought of actually eating, but she was too restless to sit. And Thelma didn't seem to mind her standing next to the food as long as she was putting something in her mouth. So, she chose a square of cheese and a cracker. Then another.

Every once in a while Thelma gave Chloe a sidelong glance. Each time their eyes met, Chloe forced herself to look away, as though afraid of her. And while she was concerned about the weapon in the woman's right hand, she figured she could take it away from her if she had the chance. Which she planned to make happen very shortly.

"You're last, sweetness," Thelma told her.

Chloe stayed silent, working hard to keep her fear and nerves under control.

"You hear me?"

"I heard you."

Thelma raked her eyes over Chloe with a frown. "Get in the chair. I want to pull your hair up. You'll look younger." She pursed her lips. "And the guys do like them young. Although some don't care as long as they're pretty."

Again, Chloe bit her lip and said nothing. She walked to the chair and sat. The woman worked on her for the next few minutes, pulling her hair back in a juvenile ponytail, leaving a few strands curling around her ears. That was fine with Chloe. She usually wore it up anyway—and the style would keep it out of her face. She kicked the heels off and Thelma shot her a glare. "Come on," Chloe said, "I never wear those things. My feet are killing me."

Thelma rolled her eyes. "You better be able to move fast and get them back on before Louise gets here."

"I will." She paused. "So, how did you get into this?" Chloe asked. "Aiding and abetting the traffickers, I mean."

"Same way most of these girls wound up on this yacht. Fell for a cute guy who had nothing on his mind but using me to line his pockets."

"And now you help them."

She shrugged and tried to put on a "don't care" face, but Chloe saw the fear beneath.

"They're still using you," she said softly.

The woman stiffened and her eyes met Chloe's in the mirror. "No. I use them now. They pay me well."

"Louise, too?"

"Yes. We were taken at the same time. Sold to the same guy." She swallowed and looked away as she sprayed Chloe's already stiff hair. "I would have killed myself by now if not for her. She's like my sister."

"Why don't you leave? Both of you? Why don't you escape?"

She shuddered. "Because there's no place to escape to. I have no one now. It's been years. I don't know where my family is."

"I'm a cop. I can find them for you."

A brief hope shone in her eyes. Just for a split second, then it was gone. "It's too late."

"It's not—"

"It's too late! Now shut up!"

Chloe snapped her lips together and waited for Thelma to finish. Before standing, she turned. "Do you mind if I ask you another question?"

Thelma raised her brows and sighed as though weary of the discussion. "What?"

"Did you ever come across a girl named Penny St. John?"

The woman paused. Frowned deeper. "Penny?"

"She was taken six months ago by a guy named Carson Langston—who we now know was Ethan Wright. At least we think he had something to do with it, since he disappeared along with her. At first, we thought he was taken with her, but when no trace of him was found, we figured he set her up and disappeared."

"He's dead now."

"Yes. How did you know?"

"Because Neal killed him. He made sure to show us how much he made the guy suffer. Did you know they were best friends?"

Of course she didn't know that. Chloe bit her lip and shook her head, not wanting to say anything that would close the woman up again.

"Yeah, he killed his best friend. Ethan would have done anything for him. But that's what Neal does. He kills people who cross him, are stupid and attract the attention of the cops, or people he has no use for anymore, so let that be a warning for you."

Chloe met Thelma's gaze. "What happens when he has no use for you anymore?"

Thelma's eyes chilled and her lips curved in a matching smile, all hint of the vulnerable victim from just a few minutes earlier, gone. "That won't happen, not as long as there are pretty and vulnerable teenage girls. As for Penny, I remember her."

Chloe did her best to stay cool. "Will you tell me what happened to her?"

A shrug. "Same thing that's going to happen to you."

"Who bought her?"

260

"I don't know. I don't keep up with the transactions."

Thelma was being awfully chatty. Because she wasn't concerned that Chloe would be able to do anything with the information, no doubt. "Who keeps up with the transactions?" she asked softly.

"Neal."

"On that little laptop I saw him with?"

"Probably."

"Anyone else?"

She laughed. "No, I don't think so. Doesn't matter to you anyway. You're getting ready to be a transaction. Now go sit down and wait your turn."

"It doesn't affect you at all, does it?" Chloe asked. "You have no compassion for the girls, for me?"

Thelma eyed her. "Why should I? No one had any for me." She raised the weapon and aimed it at Chloe. "Now sit."

Chloe sat. Waiting was all she could do at this point anyway. If her timing was right, things were going to get interesting in about seven minutes.

Blake pressed his hands to his eyes. "This is hopeless," he muttered to Linc. "It's been almost two hours and we've turned up nothing." How was he supposed to find Rachel and Chloe when every person they'd talked to had given them a negative answer? "We're wasting time."

Then again, what else was he going to do?

"I know it feels that way," Linc said, "but we're not giving up."

"Of course we're not giving up."

Their boat pulled to the next yacht. Two women, one blonde and one brunette, looking very comfortable in their bathing suits, walked down two flights of stairs and leaned against the rail to greet them. "What's going on, guys?"

With a sigh, Blake pulled Rachel's and Chloe's pictures up side by side on his phone and held it out to the nearest boater. She took it. "We're looking for these two and think they're on one of these yachts out here. Have you seen them?"

"No, sorry." She let her friend look. The friend shook her head and Blake saw nothing in their expressions to indicate they may be lying.

"Thanks."

She returned his phone. "Y'all want to come aboard?" The other woman spoke for the first time. "We've got shrimp and drinks. We can put on some music and have a sunset cruise."

Linc smiled. "Thanks, ladies. Not this time."

"Okay, well, good luck finding your girls. Sorry we couldn't help."

Blake took his seat again and pulled up the pictures of Rachel and Chloe again. Then went to Chloe's. He'd taken it when she wasn't looking, just so he could have a picture of her. She was laughing at something Linc had said the night of their dinner at A Taste of Yesterday. With her head tilted sideways, her eyes glinted at her brother as she teased him about something.

Pretty. And still spunky in spite of being wounded by a jerk. He wanted a chance to show her not all guys were like Jordan Crestwood.

She'd put herself in harm's way for Rachel. The only reason she was at the museum was because she thought she could find something that would help lead them to Rachel.

"What are you thinking?"

Blake shook his head and put the phone away. "That I'm going to punch Jordan Crestwood next time I see him."

"You're going to have to get in line."

"I'm moving to the front."

Linc grunted. "What else?"

A sigh slipped from him. "I don't know. That life is short and we need to grab on to the good times and let the bad ones fade

away. If we can. Is the past really worth holding on to if it keeps
you from living in the present? If it stops your dreams right in their
tracks?" He shrugged. "Sorry. Too much time to think." Yeah, too
much thinking and not enough finding. *Where are you, Chloe?
Rachel?* Panic threatened and he turned to find Linc watching him.

"You're thinking about your dad?"

Blake had confided in Linc long ago. Linc was the one person
who knew just about everything about him. He was ready to let
Chloe inside that tight circle if she was willing. "Yes. And other
people."

"I like that idea," Linc said. "Letting go of the past and grabbing on to the good times, the future, I mean. If one can do it."
He paused. "Chloe's one of those people you want to have in your
future, isn't she?"

Meeting the man's eyes, Blake considered the question. "Yes.
If we weren't so wrapped up in trying to find Rachel, I would
have asked her out by now." He gave a short laugh. "Then again,
if we weren't so wrapped up in finding Rachel, I might not have
run across Chloe again and wouldn't have found out how special
she is."

"She can be a pain."

Blake heard the roughness in the man's voice and knew he was
scared, terrified for his sister. "I'm willing to take that chance."

"Yeah. I'm ready for her to be that pain again. I miss it."

"Then let's find her."

Louise returned with a rattled-looking Rachel four minutes later than Chloe expected her to. "It's in here," Rachel said. "I'm sorry. I forgot about it."

"Get it and shut up. Gotta keep you healthy just a little longer, then you're outta my hair."

"Where are you taking us?" Rachel asked. "Why is everyone in that little boat off the side?"

Louise rolled her eyes. "Get the device and come on!" Her gaze settled on Chloe. "You're next. After I get this one delivered, I'll be back for you." She flicked a glance at Thelma. "Get this place cleaned up and then be at the boat."

"I know how this works. You don't have to tell me every time."

It was the first hint of discord Chloe had seen between the two.

Louise huffed. Rachel found her monitor and tucked it into the pocket of her shorts with a glance at Chloe. Chloe gave her a short nod and Rachel lifted her chin.

Chloe frowned and rubbed her bare arms. If they were going to be riding in an open boat, it was going to be a chilly trip in their skimpy clothes.

The door shut behind Louise and Rachel.

"Get over by the door," Thelma said. "She'll be back as soon as she gets rid of her."

Chloe walked toward the door, then spun and landed a kick on the woman's hand that gripped the weapon. Thelma cried out and backpedaled, trying to get her feet under her, but Chloe moved fast and aimed her heel at Thelma's stomach. A solid hit.

Air whooshed from Thelma and she went to her knees. The weapon clattered to the carpet while Chloe was moving in for yet another punch.

"No! Stop!" Thelma held her hands up in surrender. "Don't hit me anymore."

Chloe grabbed her arm and twisted it behind her back. "Keep quiet or I'll snap your arm. Then your neck. Understand?" A whimper escaped the woman. "I'll take that as a yes. Get in the bathroom."

Her prisoner acquiesced with no fight left in her. The woman could bully teenagers, but when confronted by someone willing to stand up to her, she lost her bravado. Once she had the woman shut in the bathroom, Chloe grabbed a chair and shoved it under the knob. It might hold her for a few minutes, but if Thelma tried hard enough, she'd be out in no time.

Chloe grabbed Thelma's weapon, checked to find it loaded and ready to use. She stepped to the door and opened it slowly, praying she wouldn't find Louise on the other side.

She stuck her head around the corner. Clear. But which way?

Approaching footsteps answered that question. Chloe ducked back into the room and shut the door. She stood off to the side and waited. Seconds later, the knob turned and Louise stepped through. Paused when she saw the empty room.

Just a little farther inside.

"Thelma?" She took another step.

Chloe brought the butt of the weapon down on the woman's head. Hard.

Louise crumpled without a sound. Chloe took the suppressor off the weapon and tossed it aside. If she fired, she wanted it heard. She searched Louise, found the twin to the gun she held, and stuck it in the waistband at the small of her back.

She stepped out of the room, shut the door, and turned the lock. The click gave her great satisfaction. Kicking the stupid heels off, she drew in a breath. Now to find the girls—and the men guarding them. They'd be on alert when she didn't show up for her "turn" to parade in front of the camera for those wanting to bid on her.

She shuddered and slowed, her bare feet cold, the wind whipping around her. Waves lapped the side of the vessel and she crept forward, weapon held ready. With steady steps, she made her way to the lower level. As far as she knew, there were three men. Neal and the two guards who'd snatched her from the museum. And the two women she'd taken out.

Neal was the one she was most worried about. Then again, the two guards had been pretty efficient. Outnumbered and outgunned, she was going to have to divide and conquer.

Low voices caught her attention.

". . . find her. She's on the ship somewhere, so find her now," Neal said. His low, vicious order sent shivers down her spine. "And get rid of Cass and Marie. They're of no use to us anymore."

"What about delivering the girls?"

"They can wait a few minutes. Tell Mike we'll leave shortly. It won't take long to find the cop. I should have known better than to leave her with those two. They can handle a bunch of scared teens, but that cop . . . just find her." He cursed. "He isn't going to like this."

"We'll find her, boss."

"You'd better. Now hurry up." He stomped off and the other man headed for the side. From around the edge, Chloe watched and waited. When Neal disappeared from sight, she breathed in. As soon as she stepped around the side, she'd be in full view of the boat that held the silent girls. They were on the other end. If she'd been able to come from the stern instead of the bow, she could be on him in seconds without him realizing it.

The vessel rocked with the undulations of the ocean. The man guarding the girls had his back to her as he reached for the rope to untie the smaller craft. She had no time to go all the way back around.

A splash from the other side of the small craft pulled her attention briefly from the man. Lindsey gasped. Several girls pointed and whispered.

"What was that?" their captor demanded.

They froze and huddled together.

Chloe scanned the faces and realized Rachel wasn't among them. What had the girl done? And then she broke the surface about five feet away, swimming with long, even strokes as she headed toward shore.

Oh no. She couldn't lose her now. Not when they were so close to being free.

"Hey! Get back here!" He pulled his weapon and aimed it at the swimming girl.

Chloe ran toward him, weapon held in front of her. Her bare feet made no sound as she drew closer to the stern and the bobbing craft next to it.

"Drop it!"

He jerked and spun.

"Drop the weapon!"

He aimed it at her instead.

She fired. Once, twice, three times.

26

Blake turned to Linc. "You hear that?"

"Yeah. Gunshots."

"Where'd they come from?"

"To the left. Go."

The driver gunned the motor and Blake shifted into a position that would enhance his view of the area ahead. Other boat owners who had heard the shots had come from below or were standing at the bow, holding binoculars and gesturing. Still others were moving away from the large yacht, probably afraid more gunshots were coming.

Blake nodded. "Follow where they're pointing while I call it in."

"Hang on."

Chloe lowered the weapon as the man fell into the water. The girls' screams echoed in the humid air. She held a finger to her lips and they snapped their mouths shut, even as hope started to gleam in their eyes.

"Be quiet, there's still more. If anyone shows up, you're not sure what happened, okay?"

They nodded.

"Behind you!" Lindsey cried.

Chloe spun and took a glancing blow to the side of her head. She stumbled, and fell into the boat next to Megan. On her way down, her hand slammed into one of the seats and pain radiated through her wrist and up her arm. Numb fingers lost their grip and the gun tumbled to the floor.

"I'm going to kill you!"

From the corner of her eye, she saw Neal raise the weapon and aim it at her. Three cracks sounded. Surprise flashed across his face before he, too, fell sideways off the vessel and joined his partner in the water.

She stood. And saw the Marine police boat heading for them. Choking back tears of relief, gratitude, and sheer happiness, she snatched the weapon from the bottom of the craft and climbed back onto the yacht. Linc joined her.

"Go get Rachel," she yelled at Blake. And pointed.

He blanched and said something to the driver of the boat. The man turned and headed toward the still swimming girl.

Rachel's arms ached. She might be out of practice, but she was also in her element. In the water, she was powerful and in control. But the farther she swam, the more the fatigue hit her. She knew it was because she wasn't used to swimming in these conditions. Cold and with a strong current that wanted to tug her under. But she wouldn't stop. She had to reach shore and get help. She would do this for Chloe and the other girls. She would prove to her father that he could love her.

Stroke, stroke, breathe. She had the rhythm now. She could make it. When she heard the boat coming up behind her, she put on a burst of speed. They wouldn't catch her. Not again.

But she was tired. So very tired and cold.

"Rachel!"

Her stroke faltered and she stopped, spinning in the water to find her dad looking down at her from the bow of a large speed-boat. "Rachel!"

"Dad!"

"I'm coming to get you." He turned to the driver. "I need a blanket!"

The motor cut and a ladder appeared over the side. In spite of heavy arms and chattering teeth, she swam over to it. And then her father clamped a hard, yet gentle, hand around her wrist and hauled her into his arms.

Linc climbed onto the ship and gripped Chloe by her upper arm. "You okay?"

She shivered and nodded.

Two helicopters buzzed overhead. Other law enforcement, including the Coast Guard and Marine Patrol Officers, surrounded the vessel while others cleared the area around it. The girls were being transferred to another boat, traumatized, but safe.

"I'm okay, but we're not done."

"How many?"

"Two women for sure and another big dude with a big gun."

More law enforcement swarmed the boat.

"Why don't you let us take it from here?"

"Oh no. I'm not missing out on this. And besides, I know where they are."

"Which you could tell me."

"Which I can show you." She explained the plan, the cold forgotten as she talked. "A line going this way, and officers covering the other side. We'll meet at the room I locked the two women in."

Linc shot her a dark look, then spoke into a microphone that she knew was connected to other agent and officer earpieces.

Her fingers gripped the butt of the gun she'd taken from Thelma. "How'd you find me? Hank? Is he okay?"

"Yep. And he's fine. An officer saw him bolt out of the Tahoe and thought there might be trouble. He went in, found the mess you made in the office, and called it in. We put two and two together and headed this way."

"Thank God."

Linc frowned. "You've been through a hard thing, you need to get off this yacht and we'll take it from here."

She shook her head as adrenaline pumped a mixture of fear, anticipation, and determination through her veins. "I'm seeing this through to the end."

With a final scowl and a sigh of resignation, Linc motioned for her to precede him. She led the way around the side of the boat with Linc behind her and more agents following him.

Although she couldn't see them, she knew another line of law enforcement walked parallel to her. They reached the room and she found the door unlocked. "I locked it when I left," she whispered to Linc.

He nodded. "Open it."

She reached for the knob and the gunshot sent her to the deck.

Blake finally forced himself to let go of Rachel, but cupped her face. "Are you okay?"

"Yes." She huddled under the blanket.

"Hold on a sec. Sit here." He led her to the bench seating in the back where she'd be warmer and sheltered from the wind. Turning, he called, "What's happening? Is Chloe okay? The other girls?" They were far enough away that Rachel would be safe should bullets start flying, but close enough for him to see something was going on.

"They're in the process of looking for the other suspects on the ship. All the girls are safe and headed toward shore. We're staying back here out of the way since we've got your daughter on board."

Blake nodded. He got that, he did. But the staying put chafed. He wanted to be there, to make sure Chloe was okay and out of harm's way. But since he couldn't be, he slipped back to sit beside Rachel. He wrapped an arm around her shoulders and pulled her close, surprised she didn't pull away. "What were you doing swimming?"

She shivered and pulled the blanket tighter. "I had to do something. Anything. I th-thought I could swim to shore and get help. I thought if I got h-help and s-saved everyone, you would . . ."

"What? I would what?"

She whispered something and he strained to hear. "What was that?"

Rachel looked up at him. "Love me."

He gaped. "Love you? Rachel, I love you with every fiber of my being!"

"But I'm not yours!" Her cry wrenched his heart. "My own mother didn't want me. Why would you want a child who doesn't share your blood?"

"I'm your father. I was there when you were born. I've loved you since the moment I saw your tiny little red face. And we'll come back to that. But tell me, how did you find out?"

"There was a letter in your desk. I found it. My mom offered you custody six months before she died and it had a lot of details in there, including the fact that she should never have married you and she should have had an abortion." Tears slid down her cheeks.

Blake leaned his head against hers. "Aw, Rachel, I was working undercover when that letter came. Your mom . . ." He hesitated, not wanting to say anything negative about her mother, but feeling like she deserved to know the whole truth.

"Tell me. I can take it."

"Your mom knew I was undercover. I told her if she needed to get in touch with me, she had to go through my supervisor. I gave her his name and contact information. She never sent that through him. I found it when I got home. By then she was dead and you were mine anyway." He shifted to make sure she had a clear view of his eyes. "If I had gotten that letter in time, I would have moved heaven and earth to have signed the papers that were all drawn up and just waiting. After your mom died and I came up for air from the undercover assignment, I went and signed those papers anyway."

"But you didn't have to. You already had me."

"I didn't want there to be any doubt about where you belonged."

"Because of my grandparents?"

He sighed. "Yes. And no." A pause. "Mostly yes."

"But they didn't want me either. I mean, they like visiting and sending me cool gifts, but they don't want a full-time kid cramping their travel plans."

"Well . . ." What could he say? She was right. "Look. Mull on all of this while I try to find out about Chloe."

She nodded. "You really wanted me."

"I really did."

Chloe had waited with the rest of the team, silent and still. After a good sixty seconds with no more shots, she rolled and looked back at Linc. "Where'd that come from? Is everyone okay?"

Linc gave her a thumbs-up. "No one was hit. Sounded kind of muffled."

"I think it came from the room. Ready?" She stood.

"When you are."

She twisted the knob and shoved the door open, staying well covered by the wall. When no shots followed, she signaled to Linc she was going in. He placed a hand on her shoulder and rounded the doorjamb with her.

Louise sat in the chair holding a gun. The man whose name Chloe never learned lay on the floor bleeding from the chest. Weapon aimed at Louise, Chloe crouch-stepped to the side. "Police! Put it down."

The woman stared at the floor.

"Put it down! Now! I'm not kidding! Now!"

The weapon finally landed with a soft thud. Chloe moved in and scooped the gun away. Another officer took the woman to the floor and cuffed her. When he lifted her to her feet, Chloe stepped in front of her. "Cass or Maria?"

"Maria."

"What happened, Maria?"

"He killed Cass. She came out of the bathroom and he just shot her. I knew I was next, so I moved fast and killed him first."

Chloe flicked a glance at Linc. "Check the bathroom." The chair had been moved from the door.

Linc opened the door. "She's here." He knelt and reached in. Chloe figured he was checking a pulse. "Dead," he said.

Chloe's hand started to shake. She stumbled to the nearest chair and slumped onto it. "That's it. That's all of them."

"I'm a Deputy US Marshal. Let me through."

Blake's authoritative order snapped her head up. She stood and walked over to him. He wrapped an arm around her and she leaned against him, almost unable to process that she and the others were safe. "Neal, from the museum, was the ringleader," she mumbled against his chest. "He was in charge. I think. At least on the boat. But I think he was reporting to someone else."

"Who?"

"I don't know. Rachel!" Chloe gasped and jerked back.

His grip tightened. "She's fine. Cold and would probably like some dry clothes, but she's safe. Finally."

"Good. That's good." Chloe swiped a hand over her eyes, trying to ignore the adrenaline crash. Law enforcement had taken over the craft and she noticed they were headed back toward shore. "So, the judge is safe now?"

"Maybe. We'll keep the marshals on him until we get everything sorted out."

She frowned.

"What is it?" he asked.

"Something Neal said. It doesn't add up. He said, 'He's not going to be happy.'"

"Referring to who?"

"I don't know. That's why I think he was working with someone else."

He sighed. "All right. We've definitely got to fit all the pieces together. It's going to be busy over the next few hours getting statements, but when we're done, let's go back to my house so I can start getting Rachel settled back at home."

"You don't need me there. Why don't you take her home and we'll talk later? The chopper will fly you back?"

Blake nodded. "Thank you for understanding that she has to be my priority for now."

"Of course."

"But—" He shifted, his eyes sliding away, then back to hers.

"But?"

"When I know Rachel's okay, could we . . . you know . . . get coffee or a steak or pizza. Or something?"

"Or something?"

"Yeah."

"Yeah," she said. "I'd like that."

27

He threw the glass of bourbon against the wall. Heard the shatter. Watched the glass and ice bounce on the hardwoods. Grief welled, erupting into a howl of rage and pain that vibrated the four walls around him. He fell to his knees, clutching his hair.

He'd failed.

The judge was alive. He'd faked his death and even his children hadn't known.

It was a punch in the gut. A slap in the face.

Completely unacceptable.

His plan to avenge his brother's death had been so well thought out. Nothing could go wrong. He'd planned for months, concocting scenario after scenario until one had finally seemed perfect. Planned to the last detail, with very few unknowns to deal with. He'd started with the threatening letters sent to the judge, detailing the man's death and the suffering he would experience. Those had given him such satisfaction to write.

Knowing the marshals would be brought in and studying each one, discerning who would be the weakest link.

Blake MacCallum had been the chosen one. The fact that the man wouldn't kill, even to save his daughter, had been a definite kink in the plan. And the wreck with the girls, allowing Rachel to escape . . . "Argh!"

He closed his eyes. Idiots. That was the problem. He'd had idiots working for him. Even the backup plan at the courthouse with his hired killer had gone awry.

Unbelievable.

There was something to the saying, "If you want something done right, you must do it yourself."

He stood and walked to the gun cabinet. A quick twist of the key opened the wooden door. He chose his weapon and checked it.

"So, Judge Worthington, I guess I'll just have to take care of you myself."

Sitting around the conference table at headquarters, Chloe and the rest of the task force finished their closing briefs with satisfaction—and questions.

Linc stood front and center. "We recovered a laptop that Annie was able to access."

Hack into was more like it. Chloe shifted and Hank nudged her arm, asking for an ear scratch. She obliged while listening. And she listened while her mind spun.

"On that laptop," Linc was saying, "were messages between Neal Young and Carson Langston, also known as Ethan Wright. The two grew up together and were high school buddies. They were both in the foster system. Neal had a record, but Ethan didn't. Neal was obviously the instigator in convincing Ethan to do his part as Carson Langston."

"His job was to lure the girls in, right?" Chloe asked.

"Right. He was also charged with guarding them—along with another young man named Manuel Garcia who was also friends with Ethan and Neal."

"And who is also dead," Derek said. "What's the connection

between Neal and Alessandro Russo?" He sat next to Jo, who was video conferencing the meeting over a secure line so Blake could be a part of it.

"There isn't one. At least not one that we can find. Once we presented to Stillman everything that happened yesterday, including the fact that his boss, Clyde Harrison, was dead, he started talking. Stillman's connection with Russo was just a fluke. Doesn't look like Russo has anything to do with this particular group of human traffickers. Like we knew before, Stillman was just a low man on the totem pole for Russo, and when he went to prison, he was off Russo's radar. However, Stillman met Garcia in prison, and once they were both out, they kept in touch. When Neal needed muscle with the girls, Stillman didn't hesitate to take Manny up on his offer of easy money. Same with the other guys we rounded up. Just a bunch of ex-cons who don't care what they have to do to make a lot of cash fast."

Chloe leaned in. "I want to know about Penny. Maria mentioned keeping up with the 'transactions.' Is there a way to know where each girl went?"

"Yes. Annie's working on that now," Linc said. "I'm hoping to hear something before the end of the day. Once we find as many girls as we can, we'll form teams and start going after them."

Excitement and hope swirled inside her for the first time in a long time, and Chloe sent up a silent prayer for her cousin.

But something niggled at her. "Neal and Ethan were working together, which means Neal had something to do with Penny's disappearance. I want to see the evidence you gathered from his office and home."

Linc shrugged. "Help yourself."

"So let me get this straight. Neal and Carson and the rest had this human trafficking ring going for at least a year. When the judge came out with this new legislation and his strong stance on the death penalty for traffickers, they decided to get rid of him."

"Sounds like," Blake said. "And they figured out they could use Rachel to persuade me to do the dirty work."

"But what about Alan Garrett?" Chloe said. "Why would Ethan Wright visit him in prison? Why say he was his brother?"

"They were in that foster home a long time. What was the family name? Hopkins? Maybe they called themselves brothers because they had no other family."

Chloe jerked and snapped her head up. "Hopkins?"

Linc frowned. "Yes. Why?"

She snagged her phone and tapped the screen. "Because. I found this when I was searching for the keys in Neal's desk."

Linc took the phone. "What? Neal's desk? As in the guy I shot?"

"Yes."

"Let me take a look," Blake said.

Linc passed him the phone. "Does one of those boys look familiar to you?"

"Alan Garrett?"

"Exactly. But what about the tall kid?"

Blake slowly lifted his eyes. "I think we now have our true motive for wanting the judge dead."

28

He parked his sedan in the driveway and made his way to the front door. His knock was answered by Parker Hunt, one of the marshals he'd done extensive background checking on—as he had done on all the others as well. "Oh, hi, Miles. Come on in. Paula didn't say you were stopping by."

"Thanks, Parker. Paula didn't know." And he hadn't realized Paula would be there. That meant she would have to die too.

Oh well.

Miles pulled his hand from behind his back and shot the man in the chest. Shocked surprise flickered briefly in his eyes before he went down and didn't move.

His partner, Justin, rounded the corner, weapon in front of him. He spotted the gun in Miles's hand, his partner on the floor.

He fired and missed.

Miles didn't.

He swept the weapon aside and stepped over the man clutching his bleeding abdomen and shot him once more in the head.

A scream brought his gaze up to meet Paula's. She broke off and stared. "Miles? What are you doing? What—"

"Where is he?"

She blinked. "Who?"

"Your father. The murderer."

"He's not here." Tears slid down her pale face. "What is this all about?" she whispered. "I don't understand."

"Alan and Neal are dead because of him."

"Who are Alan and Neal?"

"My brothers."

She raked a hand through the hair she'd left down. Just as he liked it. They were supposed to meet later, so he knew she'd done it to please him. That very fact made him hesitate a fraction of a second.

"Police! Freeze!"

Miles dove for Paula, grabbed her and wrapped an arm around her neck. She let out another scream and twisted away from him, but he grabbed a hunk of that hair he'd been admiring and yanked. A squeal of pain erupted from her, and he jerked her back against him with his left hand and raised his weapon with his right to hold it against her right ear.

He recognized the FBI agent holding his weapon on him. "Linc St. John. You killed my brother." His gaze swept to the man beside him. "And you. Blake MacCallum. If you had just done as you were told to do, we wouldn't be in this situation."

"Kill the judge for you? Not a chance."

"Just goes to show you, research can be faulty."

"So, you set all this up, just to kill Judge Worthington."

"I did. I knew Neal was involved in the human trafficking business. It was easy to convince him I wanted in. And besides, he wanted revenge for our brother's death as well."

"Which one of you killed the woman who testified against Alan?"

"That was me. The witch. Alan begged Judge Worthington to allow his attorney more time to gather evidence, but he was denied it. As a result, Alan died. And he was innocent!"

"So, you kidnapped Rachel," Linc said. "Stuck her in with the other girls and waited for Blake to do your dirty work."

"But he wouldn't do it!"

"No," Blake said. "It wasn't that I *wouldn't* do it. I *couldn't* do it."

Chloe had snuck in behind the guys and, with a heavy heart, checked the two marshals on the floor. Justin was dead. Parker was hanging on. Barely. She did her best to stem the bleeding, but didn't hold out much hope for him. She'd also put a call in for backup and now she and Hank headed down the hall looking for a way to come up behind Miles and his hostage.

At the end of the runner, she stopped and knelt. A pat to her shoulder brought Hank up on her back. She didn't want his nails clicking on the hardwoods she had to cross in order to get to the sunroom. Once in the sunroom, she lowered Hank to the floor and whispered for him to stay. He sat and watched her, eyes tracking her every move.

She slipped to the second door and glanced around the edge. Linc and Blake were holding Miles at gunpoint. Miles had his automatic pistol to his fiancée's temple.

". . . let us walk out of here and you'll never hear from me again. I don't want to die, but I will before I set foot in prison."

"Suicide by cop?" Blake asked. He moved a little closer, and while Miles eyed him, he didn't change position or loosen his grip on the weapon.

From her vantage point, Chloe could see Paula shaking in the arms of the man who'd betrayed her. Chloe lifted her weapon and aimed it at the back of his head. Unfortunately, if she was even a fraction off, she might hit Paula.

"Let her go, Miles!"

He jerked, spun, bringing Paula with him. Paula jerked and tripped. Her movement took her captor by surprise and he must have loosened his grip. She landed on the floor.

Two weapons fired three shots each.

Chloe dove for Paula and yanked her out of reach. She tossed the woman to the side like a rag doll and rolled. "Hank, *apport*!"

In a blur, Hank passed Chloe and latched on to the man now writhing on the floor, still gripping his weapon.

Miles screamed when Hank's teeth sank into his arm. Chloe scrambled to her feet, took three steps, and soccer-kicked the weapon from his hand. "He's down!"

Backup rushed in as Linc and Blake raced to her side. Linc flipped the bleeding man and Chloe dug a knee into his back as she cuffed him. He choked and she rolled him to his side while he blinked, clinging to a life that was quickly fading. "He was my brother." Blood dripped from the corner of his mouth. "They were my brothers."

"Neal and Alan," Chloe said.

"Yes," he wheezed. "Half brothers. I was supposed to watch out for them."

"Why kill Ethan?"

A gasping cough rattled from him. "A . . . weak . . . link. Couldn't let him get . . . caught."

"You set this all up!" Paula threw herself at her former fiancé and landed a good punch to his shoulder before Linc hauled her off. "You did this! You used me!"

The wounded man coughed up blood. "And now my brothers . . . and I . . . will finally be together ag—"

Chloe knew the moment life left him. His eyes took on that look that only dead people had.

Ben Worthington stepped into the den, gun in hand.

"Drop the weapon! Drop the gun! Now!" Officers' voices blended as one.

"It's okay!" Blake crossed to the man's side and took it from him.

"I couldn't get a shot," the judge said. "I heard the shots and went to get my weapon. When I came back, Miles had the gun on her. And then you were here and I . . . didn't know what to do. So . . . I waited."

"Good decision," Linc said.

Paula rushed to his side and he held her to him. She sobbed into his shoulder and tears dripped down the judge's chin. "I heard you tell Miles I wasn't here."

"I couldn't let him hurt you." She hiccupped and swiped a hand across her face. "I knew you'd come running. And I just couldn't let him kill you."

Chloe placed a hand on the woman's back. "It's over."

29

A WEEK LATER

Chloe leaned back and crossed her arms while she surveyed the dining table. Her family. Albeit, they were all a bit crazy—that came with the occupation. Even Ruthie could have a weird sense of humor.

Her father, who sat next to her, tapped her shoulder. "Earth to Chloe."

She blinked. "Oh. Sorry."

He held up the flat, square box. "Pizza?"

Even though she was full, she took another slice and bit into it. Pizza night at home. One of her favorite times to get together. "You guys did a good job, Dad."

"What do you mean?"

"Balancing family and high-profile, stressful careers. You and Mom managed to stay together and build a family. Granted, we're a bunch of weirdos and have our issues, but at least we're all on the right side of the law."

A light smack on the side of her head made her jump. "Who are you calling a weirdo, weirdo?" Brady asked.

"Derek."

"Oh, sorry." He hung his head for a moment, then rubbed the

285

spot he'd smacked even though he hadn't hurt her one bit. "Okay. You called that one right. You owe me a head smack."

She grinned. They both knew she'd collect. Her father snorted and shook cheese onto the two pieces of pizza he looked eager to devour.

Her mother's phone rang and she stood to answer. Izzy fed her pizza to Ryan Marshall, her husband, and Ruthie rolled her eyes at Chloe as though disgusted by the sappy display. Derek stole the half slice left on their mother's plate and ate it in two bites. Blake sat to her right, with Rachel next to him. The noise level in the room rivaled that of a sonic boom. She loved it. Most of the time.

Blake gave her knee a nudge under the table and tilted his head toward the den. She stood. "Excuse me a minute."

"And me," Blake said.

Rachel's eyes narrowed, but Chloe thought she saw a flash of happiness there before she lowered her gaze back to her pizza. Derek let out a low whistle and Brady raised a brow as he watched them leave.

She wondered if Blake placed his hand on the small of her back on purpose or just out of habit. He held the door open and Hank shot through it into the fenced yard. Chloe took a seat on the porch swing and grabbed the blanket draped over the back.

"Want me to light the firepit?" he asked.

"Sure."

Once he had a nice flame flickering, he grabbed the ever-present marshmallows and roasting sticks. "I haven't done this in a long time."

She smiled, nerves dancing in her belly. Before they'd found Rachel, he'd hinted at his interest in going out with her. "Is this our coffee date?"

He settled beside her and she offered him part of the blanket. "Hmm. No, we'll save that one for later in the week, if that's all right with you."

"Of course." She fell silent, then turned to lean against him. He slid an arm around her shoulders and she gave a sigh of contentment. Hank bounded back over and dropped his rope on the floor.

Blake picked it up and threw it.

"Hank will love you forever," she said.

He gave a low chuckle.

"How's Rachel doing?" she asked softly. This was the first time she'd seen him since rescuing the girls.

"She's okay. Not great, but I think she'll get there with the help of the counselor we've lined up." He brushed a strand of hair from her eyes, and his touch set off the butterflies.

She cleared her throat. "Good. I'm glad."

"How are your dreams?"

"Scary sometimes."

Blake hugged her. "I'm sorry."

"They'll pass."

Her mother knocked on the door leading to the porch, then stepped outside. Tears streaked her cheeks.

Chloe pushed away from Blake and stood. "What is it?"

"They found Penny," she whispered. "She's coming home."

While the family celebrated, Blake glanced at his phone when it buzzed a third time in ten minutes.

Frank.

It's now or maybe never, Blake.

He sighed.

"What is it?" Chloe asked. She'd slipped up to his side while he wasn't looking.

"Nothing."

"Right." She turned away and he caught her hand.

"It's my brother. Our father is dying and he wants me to come to the hospital to say my goodbyes."

"So, why are you still here?"

"Because I hate my father and I don't have anything to say to him. Not even goodbye."

"I'll go with you."

"So will I, Dad," Rachel said softly behind him. "You need to do this."

Blake turned and blew out a breath while he pinched the bridge of his nose. And he knew he had to do it. *I can't forgive him, God. I know I'm supposed to, but I can't do it.* No, Blake couldn't do it on his own. Maybe God would make it possible, though. "All right, we'll go whenever you're ready. I don't want to take you away from this time of celebration, though."

"It's fine. I'm thrilled Penny's coming home. She's going to need a lot of help and care in the coming months. Probably years, but at least she'll be here."

"Agreed."

Chloe took his hand and a lump formed in his throat.

"Come on, Dad," Rachel said, "you can do this."

He nodded. "In a few minutes."

Linc slipped up beside them. "The cops found evidence in Miles's house. Penny was definitely there. They found her phone slid up under a cabinet in the half bath. It also looks like she pulled out some strands of hair. DNA came back a match to her." He shook his head.

"That's what you get for being a part of a cop family," Chloe said. "Anyone else in the house involved?"

"He lived alone, and while he had people working for him, they claim they had no idea the girls were being brought there for his approval. I'm leaning toward believing them. Miles was slick and covered his tracks well."

"He just picked the wrong girl to take," Rachel said. Fire flashed in her eyes and pride made Blake reach out and squeeze her fingers.

"Absolutely," Linc said. "You're the real hero in this whole thing, Rachel. Don't ever forget it."

"Thanks," she whispered. Then cleared her throat. "So, are you coming to my swim meet in a couple of weeks?"

Linc grinned. "Wouldn't miss it." Turning serious, he eyed Blake. "How's your dad?"

"Getting ready to go find out."

The silent ride to the hospital didn't take long. Blake appreciated that neither Chloe nor Rachel tried to make small talk. Instead, they let him think while he drove. Once they were on his father's hall, Rachel hugged him and Chloe placed a light kiss on his lips. He swallowed and vowed to take her up on that hint of more to come.

Blake stepped into his father's room and found Frank sitting in the chair next to the bed.

His brother looked up and let out a low breath. "You came."

"Yes. For you."

Frank nodded. "He wakes every once in a while, but less and less. The doctors think it's a matter of days."

"Is he in pain?"

"No. They don't think so anyway." Frank paused. "Why? Do you want him to be?"

Blake jerked. "No. Of course not." He paused. "You really think I could wish that?"

"I don't know. I did for a while. Then I came to realize that he doesn't need me—or some disease—to punish him. He did that to himself his whole life."

"What do you mean?"

Frank narrowed his eyes. "Do you ever remember him smiling? Did you ever once see him happy?"

"No."

"I think it's because he wouldn't let himself be. Because he didn't think he deserved it."

"He didn't."

His brother ran a hand through his hair. "He's talked a lot these past few weeks. I understand him better."

"And that's enabled you to feel compassion for him?"

"Yes."

"What do you understand better?"

"Things from his childhood that he could never get past. Things like his father beating him and Uncle Greg until he feared for their lives. So much that he went to the cops, made sure Greg was safe, then left to live on his own. Things like his fear of the dark stemming from living in a storm drain and digging in trash cans for food from the time he was twelve until he was finally picked up at fourteen by a cop who got him help—and into a foster home." He shook his head. "But the damage was done."

Blake let the words sink in with a bitter heart. "We didn't turn out like him. Neither did Uncle Greg. How did his brother wind up his complete opposite?"

"Greg has a different personality—not to mention he was adopted when he was six."

Blake pressed his fingers to his eyelids. "I guess."

"He's suffered, Blake," Frank said as he leaned forward and took their father's hand in his. "I don't want him to suffer anymore. I want him to be free of the pain of this life and to have joy and happiness in the next. I want that for him—and us. So that when we're finally all reunited in heaven, we can have that relationship we were never able to have here on this earth."

For some reason, Blake's throat grew tight and his eyes burned. He pictured his dad as a little boy being beaten by his father. It wasn't hard to bring the images to mind—or the fear and anger that went with them. He knew. He'd lived it.

"You think that'll happen?" he asked Frank.

"I've talked to him about eternity and God and forgiveness. And I've prayed with him. I hope he understood. That he was praying along."

"He doesn't deserve heaven or happiness." His words were cold, but his heart wasn't in them.

"Who does?"

"Ouch." The truth hurt sometimes. Blake rocked back on his heels, then walked to the window to stare out into the bleary day. He'd been angry at his dad for a very long time. "How do I let go, Frank?"

"Tell him you forgive him."

"Even if I don't mean it?"

"Even if. Because you will one day."

Blake walked back to the bed and watched his father breathe. Heavy, labored drags of air that were painful to see and hear. He cleared his throat and opened his mouth.

But couldn't force the words out. He shook his head. "You know me, Frank. I can't say something I don't mean."

Frank's eyes flashed a sadness that pierced him. "I get it," Frank said. "Maybe one day."

"Maybe," Blake said and took another look at his father. "Aw, man," he whispered. He thought about his conversation with Linc while they didn't know if Rachel and Chloe were dead or alive. *I forgive you, Dad.*

The words were there. He could almost say them. "I . . . don't want you to suffer anymore, Dad. I hope you find peace." There. That was about as close as he was going to get right now.

With one last look at his dying father and a wave to his brother, he slipped out of the room.

Chloe and Rachel waited in the hallway and he wrapped an arm around each of them. Chloe leaned into his side while Hank popped to his feet. "You okay?" she asked.

He kissed the top of her head, then did the same to Rachel's. "I'll be all right. I think I'll be able to forgive him one day."

"That's progress."

He smiled. "Yeah, it's progress. Now, who's hungry?"

"Kinda full of pizza right now," Rachel said.

Chloe nodded. "Ditto. But I can always eat ice cream." She glanced at Hank. "I'm sure he could use a treat as well."

At the word "treat," Hank woofed. Rachel laughed and scratched his ears. "Burger Barn?" she asked.

Blake grimaced. "You mean Grease Pit?"

"Come on. They have an amazing ice cream bar."

"I'm in," Chloe said. They headed for the exit, arms wrapped around each other. A unit.

Family.

Gratitude caused his eyes to fill, his throat to clog.

"You okay, Dad? What's wrong?"

"Nothing." He cleared his throat. "Not a thing."

In fact, everything was just about as close to perfect as he could hope for.

———

Chloe's heart stuttered as she caught a glimpse of the emotion going on in Blake. She'd grown to like this man entirely too much. And *like* was really too tame of a word. She more than liked him. When the silent admission didn't send panic racing through her and heading for the nearest exit, she smiled.

And she smiled all the way to Burger Barn, through ordering her ice cream and savoring the first bite while Hank settled under the table at her feet with his cup of vanilla topped with a doggie treat.

"Why are you smiling?" Blake asked when Rachel excused herself to talk to two girls sitting in the corner, giggling.

Within seconds, Rachel was back to get her ice cream. "Is it okay if I bail on you two?"

Blake heaved a dramatic sigh. "I guess."

Rachel rolled her eyes, then leaned over to kiss him on the head. "Thanks, Dad."

He blinked and his eyes watered even as he looked away. "Sure, babe."

Once Rachel was settled with her friends, Chloe cleared her throat. "Because I like you."

He raised a brow. "What's to like so much?" he asked and took a bite of his caramel chocolate crunch.

"All the things that don't get on my nerves."

He choked. Sputtered. And laughed as he wiped his mouth. "Wow. Not even a hint of hesitation there."

She grinned. "I like that I can do that to you."

"What?"

"Make you laugh."

"Yeah," he said softly. "So do I. I like a lot of things about you too."

"Like what? Besides the things that don't get on your nerves."

"I like your wit. Your compassionate heart. Your bravery. I like that you don't give up when things get tough. I like that you like my daughter enough to risk your life for her."

"You do like a lot."

"I like that you like me," he said with a wink. His eyes turned serious. "Would you go out with me?"

Butterflies kicked in. "I am out with you."

"I mean us."

"On one condition."

"Name it."

"You have to feed me steak."

He laughed again, looking younger and more carefree than she'd seen him since he'd arrived at the hospital to find Rachel missing. "Steak it is."

"And chocolate."

"Definitely chocolate."

"Hey, what's going on here?"

293

Chloe looked up to see Brady, Linc, Ruthie, Derek, Izzy, and Penny heading toward their table. "What are you guys doing here?"

"A little bird told us you'd be here. We wanted to get ice cream too."

"Mom's a little bird?"

"She said you texted that you'd call her after you were finished getting ice cream. And we all know where the best ice cream is."

Chloe stood and went to hug her cousin. "Hey, Penny." Penny shot her a tight smile and her eyes slid to the girls in the corner. "Want me to introduce you?"

A shrug.

"I think you'll like Rachel. She was taken by the same guys who took you."

And just like that Penny relaxed. "Finally," she whispered.

"No one wants to bring it up?"

"No."

"And it's awkward for you to do so?"

"Yes." She met Chloe's eyes, gratitude shining.

"Come on."

Penny walked with her and Chloe introduced the girls. Rachel stood and hugged her fellow survivor. Tears gathered at the back of Chloe's eyes and she drew in a breath. "Well, I'll just leave you to it. What kind of ice cream do you want?"

"Red velvet." Penny sat next to Rachel, and the four girls started chattering.

"Red velvet it is then." She turned to find the others staring at her. "What?"

"How'd you know? How'd you . . . she hasn't said two words since we picked her up."

"Because I . . ." She paused. "I don't know. I just did. Now go get the girls some red velvet and let me get back to my conversation."

"About?"

"Where Blake's going to take me to get some steak."

"Ooh . . ." Their voices blended as Chloe sat.

She rolled her eyes, but smiled.

"You're smiling again."

"Yeah. I have a feeling it might become a habit."

He clasped her fingers. "Walk with me?"

"What? Now?"

"Yeah. I don't want to kiss you in front of them."

She stood and led the way out the door, Hank at her side. Once out of sight of her nosey siblings, he pulled her close and slanted his lips across hers. His kiss left her feeling breathless, cherished, and eager for more. When he lifted his head, she found her smile still there. "I think we can add kissing you to the list of things I like about you."

He laughed and pulled her close for a hug. "Me, too, Chloe. Me, too."

Chloe looked around his shoulder to see Rachel and the rest of her family standing in the window laughing. Rachel sent her a thumbs-up and Chloe's smile stretched into a grin.

Read on for a Sneak Peek from
THE NEXT BLUE JUSTICE **NOVEL:**

CODE OF VALOR

Available Everywhere
SPRING 2019

1

Brady St. John sat on the porch of the cabin he'd rented for the next two weeks and let his mind drift behind closed eyes. Unfortunately, the current took it to places he'd rather not revisit, so he lifted his lids and let his gaze settle on the lake.

Peaceful. Gentle. A great place to solo dive or fish for a large bass and catfish. He'd had the catfish for dinner tonight. Remnants of that meal now lay pushed to the side, along with two ears of corn, a side of baked beans, and an apple pie his sister, Chloe, had made and insisted he take with him.

On his vacation.

Because he'd needed a break before he snapped like a toothpick. Only now the October evening air had gone from brisk to downright freezing, sending goose bumps to pebble his skin under the long-sleeved sweatshirt. But he wasn't ready to go inside just yet.

He finished cleaning the Glock and wiped it down. Setting it on the table next to his empty plate, he shook his head as his sister's voice echoed in his mind.

"Go somewhere peaceful, someplace quiet," Chloe'd said.

"Where you can go diving or just sit. And be. Like the Drummonds' cabin on Lake Henley. They rent it out on a regular basis, I think."

"Yeah, during the summer. Lake Henley's closed up for the winter."

"So sweet-talk them into letting you stay there. They probably wouldn't mind making a little extra money on it."

"Maybe."

"You need to, Brady, you've been through a lot. Don't think, just go. And just . . . be. And take your Bible with you."

He'd realized she was right. He probably did need a break. Especially after the latest case where a mother had driven her two children, ages four and six months, into the river, drowning all three of them. On purpose. Not to mention the fact that Krystal had managed to make a complete fool out of him. What had he seen in her anyway? She'd been smart. He'd liked that. And beautiful. That hadn't hurt either. And mercenary.

But he wasn't going to think about that. He was going to sit.

And be.

So here he sat.

Just . . . being.

And he was bored out of his skull. He sighed and leaned back to stare at the porch ceiling. No, not bored. There just weren't any distractions, which meant too much time to think about things he'd rather not think about. *That* was the real problem. He should have asked one of his brothers to come with him.

With a groan, he rose and raked a hand through his hair. Fine. He'd go inside and make a fire, warm up—and pack. So he could go home and do what he did best.

Which was to throw himself into work until he was so exhausted he fell into bed and slept without nightmares.

A scream ripped through the air and he froze for a split second before reaching for his weapon.

With the sun setting in the next several minutes, light was quickly diminishing.

Another scream.

Brady shot outside, off the porch, and into the yard, trying to discern the direction of the cry. There. On the water.

A speedboat was motoring out to the middle of the inlet, aimed toward the open water, and the silhouettes of two people came into view. One sitting behind the wheel. The other sat in front, hands tied to the rail that ran along the side of the boat. She struggled, yanking and twisting against her bonds.

"Hey! Let her go!"

The driver jerked a head in Brady's direction. Then lifted his weapon and fired. Brady dove to the ground and rolled. The bullet missed, but was a little closer than he was comfortable with. He lifted his head to see the man taking aim at his captive. She stilled, head ducked, shoulders heaving with her sobs. Brady fired while running toward the water. The man jerked and swung his weapon back in Brady's direction.

And then the woman was loose. She launched herself over the side and into the water. The man's curses reached Brady even as he settled back into the driver's seat and spun the wheel. The boat sped away.

Brady caught sight of the woman's head just above the surface, but her arms flailed, slapping the water.

She went under.

Brady ran to the edge of the dock, stopped long enough to shuck his sweatshirt and loafers, and dove in. The icy water nearly stole the breath he held, but it wasn't the first time he'd swum in freezing water. He reached her in ten long strokes.

Just as she was going back down, he got behind her and slid his forearms beneath her armpits, lifting her head up once again. Her back pressed against his chest. She gasped and coughed. Started to struggle.

"Hey, hey, it's okay, relax. I'm here to help you. Rest your head back on my shoulder and just breathe, okay?"

She gave one last hacking cough, then went limp. Hoping she hadn't passed out, Brady kicked toward the shore. The dock would get them out of the water faster, but if the guy decided to start shooting again, he could pick them off.

"Are you conscious?" he asked. Then kicked, wishing he'd had the time to get rid of the heavy jeans, but he ignored the weight and aimed them for land.

"Yes."

"What's your name?"

"Emily," she gasped. "Chastain."

"I'm Brady. Are you hurt?"

"I d-don't t-think so."

But she was cold. "Can you swim?"

"No. I mean yes, but . . . no strength."

"All right. Just be still and don't fight me, and I'll have us on shore in a couple of minutes."

She trembled against him. A combination of fear and cold. Finally, his feet found the sandy bottom of the lake and he hefted her into his arms.

She gasped, coughed, then wiggled. "I can walk. I'm too heavy to c-carry. P-put me down."

He wanted to laugh. "Be still. I bench-press more than you weigh. A lot more."

She stilled and he set her next to the dock, out of sight of the lake, protected by the wood. "Stay here for just a second."

Shuddering, she nodded. At least he thought it was a nod. Keeping low, hunched against the wind that sent shudders whipping through him, he made it to the end of the dock, all the while feeling like he had a target on his back.

But no one fired. He shoved his feet into his shoes and grabbed the sweatshirt. He hurried back to find Emily curled into a ball, back against the dock post, tremors wracking her frame.

Without asking for permission, he tugged the sweatshirt over her long-sleeved T-shirt and swept her into his arms once more. She didn't protest, simply turned her face into the side of his neck and clutched his shoulders.

Emily used the towel to clear the steam off the mirror and tried to calm her shaking. The hot shower had chased away the bone-deep cold, but the horror of what she'd just lived through wouldn't loosen its hold. She'd thought she was going to die.

Tears dripped down her cheeks as the images flashed in her mind.

A knock on the door made her jump and she pulled the plush white robe tighter, then swiped the tears from her cheeks. "Yes?"

"You okay? I've got some sweats and a dry sweatshirt you can put on while your clothes and shoes dry if you want."

She opened the door and looked up into the kindest blue eyes she'd ever seen. The gentleness she found there eased her pounding pulse. "Thank you." She took the clothes from him.

"There's a hair dryer under the sink too. If you want to use it."

"I do. Thanks."

"Anything else you need?"

"No. I'll be out in just a moment."

He nodded and she shut the door.

After drying her chin-length, chocolate-colored hair, she changed into the clothes, for once doing so without studying herself in the mirror and judging. She had to roll the waistband to shorten the length, then roll a thick cuff around her ankles. The sweatshirt hung to midthigh. Once she had on the wool socks, she took a deep breath.

She was alive and finally warm.

Only now she had to go explain to the man who'd just saved her life why someone wanted her dead and that he was now in danger as well if they managed to figure out who her attacker was. If not, then Brady would probably be all right. Which meant she should leave quickly.

Gathering her nerves, she stepped out into the hall and followed it into the spacious den area. Her rescuer sat in one of the wing-back chairs facing the warm flames produced by the gas logs. He'd showered and changed into jeans, warm socks, and a red-and-blue flannel shirt. His right hand worked a cloth over the weapon held in his left hand. Probably the gun he'd fired at her captor.

"Excuse me while I take care of this," he said. "It went into the lake with me and I need to get it dried out just in case we need it."

"In case they find me here, you mean?"

"I would think that whoever was in the boat would be long gone, but you never know about people—or how desperate they are."

His hands stilled and his eyes locked on hers for a moment.

"He seemed pretty desperate," she said. She stepped up next to him and held her hands out to the fire. "This is lovely."

He gestured to one of the chairs to his right. "Have a seat. Your clothes and shoes are in the dryer."

"Thanks." She lowered herself into the chair and curled her legs under her. "I should probably leave as soon as my clothes are dry. I don't want to put you in danger."

He went back to cleaning. "I'm not worried about it."

"But I am."

He glanced up again. "Don't. I can take care of myself. And you."

"But—"

"Seriously. Okay?"

She sighed. "Okay. For now." She took in her surroundings for the first time. "This is a nice cabin. Big, but still cozy."

"I think so. It's got three bedrooms and three baths." He shot her a smile. "Too much room for one guy, but the people who own it are friends and gave me a deal I couldn't refuse."

"Good friends if they let you undo all their winterizing."

He laughed. "Yeah, they are. And I promised to leave it like I found it." He studied her.

With a deep sigh, she shook her head. "Thank you for saving me. I probably would have drowned if you hadn't jumped in." She paused. "Actually, I might not have made it to the drowning part. He was going to shoot me."

His hands stilled. Those blue eyes met hers. "You want to tell me what that was all about?"

She shrugged. "It's complicated."

"I've done complicated before."

"That's cryptic."

His lips curved, but the slightly haunted expression that slipped into his eyes said he'd seen things better left alone.

"I'm a financial crimes investigator for a bank," she said.

His hands paused in their cleaning and he looked up. "I've worked with a couple of those before. Cool job if you like numbers."

"It can be. Apparently, it can also be quite dangerous," she muttered.

"After your late-night swim adventure, I'm inclined to agree." He set the cloth aside and put the parts of the weapon back together, then wiped it down once more. "So, you think your job had something to do with all this?"

"Pretty sure."

"Why's that?"

"I think someone didn't like what I was investigating, decided to grab me as I was walking out of work, throw me in the back of a trunk, and bring me here to kill me."

Finished with the weapon, he set it aside and turned his full attention on her. "I know that was scary for you."

"A bit of an understatement, but yes. It was definitely scary. And they would have gotten away with it, too, if not for you."

"Did the guy on the boat say anything? Give you any clue about why he wanted you dead?"

"No. That was the weird thing. He never said a word. Even

when I was begging him to tell me why." She shuddered and looked away, the fear washing over her once again.

"You said they grabbed you as you were leaving work. How did they do that?"

"They drugged me."

"How many of them were there?"

"Two of them, I think. Could have been three."

"So they got you after work. Did you yell? Try to grab someone's attention?'

"I never had a chance. And even if I had, it was late and there wasn't anyone around." She rubbed her eyes. "It all happened so fast. They stuck me with a needle and whatever was in it made me feel weird and lethargic. I remember being in the trunk, but I must have passed out, so I have no idea how long they drove or what happened up until I woke up in a shed tied to a boat ramp."

"What time did you leave work?"

"I don't know, around midnight?" She shook her head. "I'm a night owl. I don't have anything to rush home to." She grimaced. "That sounds pathetic, but as long as I'm doing my job, my boss, the bank manager, Calvin Swift, lets me flex my hours so they're convenient for me." She paused and stared at the flames. "I fought them, but—" Goose bumps pebbled her arms, even though she wasn't cold. "What lake are we on anyway?"

"Lake Henley."

"I've heard of it but don't know much about it."

"It's private. Mostly second homes people rent out. I think there are about five year-round residents, which means during the winter, it's a ghost town." He shrugged. "That suited my purposes."

An interesting comment she'd like to follow up on, but had a feeling he wouldn't say anything more. "And probably why my kidnapper thought it would a good place to dump a body," she muttered then sighed. "So, what day is it? Is it still Wednesday night? Early Thursday morning?"

"It's Thursday night." He glanced at his watch. "A little past nine."

Her shoulders slumped. "So I lost a day?"

"Looks like it. Anyone you need to call and let them know you're okay?"

"I probably should call Heather. She's got to be wondering where I am."

"Who's Heather?"

"My best friend."

He handed her his cell phone and she dialed the number. It went straight to voicemail. "Heather, call me when you get this. Only call me on this number as I don't have a phone right now. I was kidnapped and almost killed and I need to talk you ASAP." She paused. "And no, this isn't a bad joke." She hung up and rubbed her forehead.

"Are you okay?" he asked. "Or is that a stupid question?"

"Not stupid at all. I'm just a little worried. Heather always answers her phone and the fact that she didn't . . ." She shrugged. She fell silent, then shook her head. "Heather will call me back when she can. I guess I need to go to the police and report this."

"I called it in while you were warming up. They're sending one officer to take your statement, but unfortunately, there was a big wreck nearby with fatalities and this is a small town. The majority of officers will be responding to that first until help from other counties arrives. I told them you were safe for now and the guy in the boat was probably long gone. Which means they'll get to you when they can."

She blinked. "Oh. Okay."

"Who was he? The one in the boat?"

She shook her head. "I've never seen him before."

"How'd you get loose from the railing?"

"Dumb luck? The grace of God? I was struggling pretty hard and he'd been in a hurry when he tied me to it." She pulled her sleeves back just far enough to reveal the rope burns. Blood had flowed from them before her dip into the lake, but had washed away during her impromptu swim. They stung like fire, but it was better than the alternative.

"If I have to choose between the two, I'll go with the dumb luck," Brady said.

"Hmm." She paused. "What is it you do exactly?"

"I'm a detective with the Columbia Police Department. Occasionally, I work with the dive team when they're shorthanded, but my main job is criminal investigation."

She gaped, then snapped her mouth shut. "Wow. Okay, then. You might not be very happy with God right now, but I'm thrilled with him for sending you my way."

He barked a short laugh and rose to grab his pack by the door. He rummaged through it and she watched, curious. He returned to kneel in front of her. "Let me see those wrists."

"They're fine."

He took her right hand in his anyway. The feel of his warm fingers wrapped around hers chased some of the horror away.

"You don't believe in God?" she asked, sliding her hand out of his grasp and pulling her sleeve down over the wound.

"I believe in him." He nodded to her wrists. "And they're not fine. Let's wrap them for now. Give them a chance to heal and keep the germs out. You don't want them to get infected."

With no energy to argue—and feeling uncharacteristically compliant—she let him bandage her wrists. When her sleeve rose a little too high to reveal a multitude of white scars crisscrossing the inside of her forearm, she said nothing, just adjusted the sleeve to hide them. He glanced up and caught her gaze, a question in his eyes she had no intention of addressing.

"Why are you mad at him, then?" she asked.

He blinked. "Who says I'm mad at him?"

"A number of little clues you've dropped."

"Like?"

"Like choosing dumb luck over divine intervention. Body language when I mentioned God. Changing the subject to my wrists." Should she push him on that or leave it alone? It really wasn't fair to expect him to answer deep personal questions if she wasn't willing to respond in kind, was it?

Then again, she knew first hand that life wasn't fair.

He raised a brow, then focused on her wrists. When he was finished, he replaced his supplies and returned to his chair.

So, he wasn't going to answer. Alrighty then. "You always carry bandages and antibiotic ointment?" she asked.

"I do when I'm going to be fishing."

"Ah, smart."

"I try."

A pause. "So, are you going to tell me why you're mad at God?" she asked.

"No."

"Okay. Then what are you doing out here all by yourself?"

He tilted his head as though surprised she didn't keep pushing. "I'm on vacation. Where are you from?" he asked.

"Sicily. The city in South Carolina, not Italy, much to my regret."

"Is that where you were kidnapped from?"

"Yes."

"I know that city well. It's about fifteen minutes from where I live. I have some good friends who work out of the Midtown Region police department."

She offered him a small smile. "I don't even know why they had to make it a separate city. It might as well be Columbia."

"True, but the family who founded it missed Sicily—the other one back in Italy."

"You know your history."

"Yeah. I do."

She smiled. "The Italian influence is one of the things that I love

309

about Sicily. One of the reasons I fell in love with it and decided to move there." She yawned. "Apparently, the low crime rate report was a big old lie, though."

They fell silent and her eyes lowered to half mast. She was warm. She was safe. She was sleepy. She let her eyes shut all the way and stay there, close to dropping off, but vaguely aware of Brady moving in the background.

The window behind her shattered. She dove out of the chair to the floor. Brady's body covered hers. He had a weapon in his hand before she could blink. Flames spurted from the floor in front of the fireplace and the sharp sting of gasoline burned her nose.

"What's going on?" she cried.

He yanked her to her feet and grabbed his pack. "We've got to get out of here."

Smoke curled around her. "How?"

"The back door. Through the kitchen. Laundry room first. We need to grab your shoes from the dryer on the way out."

Another explosion shook the cabin as Brady led her to the kitchen's laundry room. The heat intensified. Moving fast, he grabbed her shoes and stuffed them into his pack. A quick look at the kitchen door said they weren't going out that way.

"Stay here." He ran to the front door and caught sight of two figures darting behind his truck. The front door was out. They'd be picked off as soon as they set foot outside. He bolted back to Emily and pulled her into the laundry room.

"What are we going to do?" she gasped.

He grabbed the rope connected to the attic stairs and yanked. Once he had the steps down, he pulled her in front of him. "Climb!"

Acknowledgments

As always, I have to give many thanks to FBI Special Agents Dru Wells (Retired) and Wayne Smith (Retired). Without their input, I would be floundering in a sea of law enforcement mistakes. Their information is always spot-on. If anything is deemed inaccurate, please chalk it up to author license.

Thank you to my critique buddies who help me brainstorm and create.

Thank you to my awesome agent and friend, Tamela Hancock Murray. It's been ten terrific years. Thank you for traveling this journey with me.

Thank you to my amazing editors, Andrea Doering and Barb Barnes. The books would never be as good without your magic touch.

Thanks to my amazing and wonderful family, Jack, Lauryn, and Will. You're the best and I love you all the most!

A huge thanks to the fans who purchase the books. You all are so special and I'm so grateful to each and every one of you!

Thank you, Jesus, for letting me do what I do. May your presence be felt on each page, touching readers' lives long after you've taken me home to be with you.

Lynette Eason is the bestselling author of the Women of Justice series, the Deadly Reunions series, and the Hidden Identity series, as well as *Always Watching*, *Without Warning*, *Moving Target*, and *Chasing Secrets* in the Elite Guardians series. She is the winner of two ACFW Carol Awards, the Selah Award, and the Inspirational Readers' Choice Award. She has a master's degree in education from Converse College and lives in South Carolina. Learn more at www.lynetteeason.com.

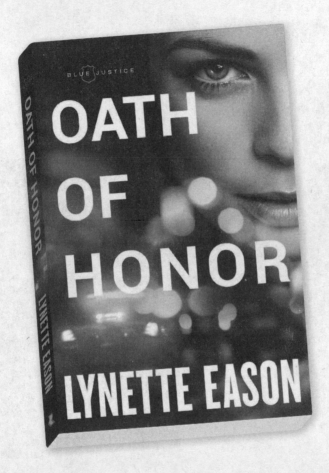

Join Eason, Pettrey, and Henderson for
MORE HEART-POUNDING ROMANTIC SUSPENSE

Three bestselling Christian romantic suspense authors team up to bring these intense novella collections where costs are high and the past doesn't always stay the past . . .

BETHANY HOUSE
a division of Baker Publishing Group
www.BethanyHouse.com

Available wherever books and ebooks are sold.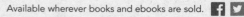

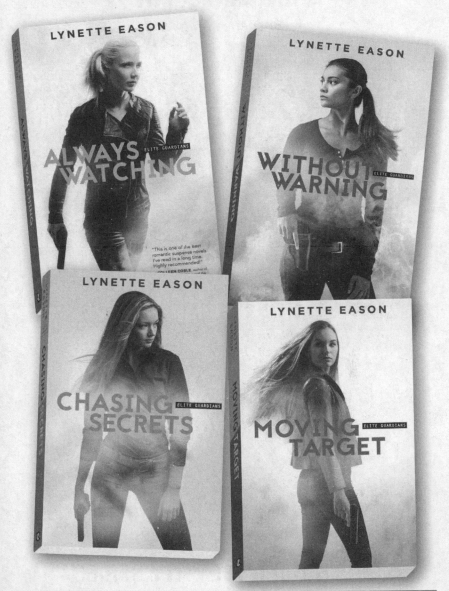

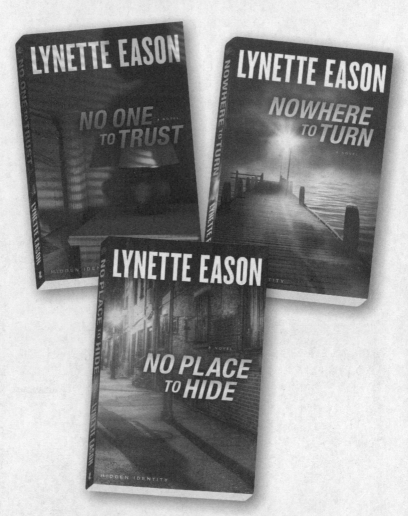

Meet
LYNETTE

LYNETTEEASON.COM

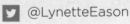 Lynette Eason | 🐦 @LynetteEason